Boggart
and Fen

The Knights of Liöfwende

Look out for . . .

Attica

Boggart and Fen

Book Three of The Knights of Liöfwende

Garry Kilworth

www.atombooks.co.uk

A paperback original from Atom Books

First published in Great Britain by Atom 2004

Copyright © 2004 by Garry Kilworth

The moral right of the author has been asserted.

A CIP catalogue record for this book
is available from the British Library.

ISBN 1 904233 11 2

Typeset in Cochin by M Rules
Printed and bound in Great Britain
by Bookmarque Ltd, Croydon, Surrey

Atom
An imprint of
Time Warner Book Group UK
Brettenham House
Lancaster Place
London WC2E 7EN

This book is dedicated to

Julie Kilworth

CONTENTS

PART ONE

Mallmoc on the March

ONE

The goblin pedlar was trying to sell Jack a pair of shoes.

'See, mortal, these are made of the finest woven reed grass. You could do worse, you know. Special price, just for you, being as I like you. *Like* you? I love you like a brother. I would trust you with the hunch on my back. If you asked me, I would give you my last three remaining teeth, rotten though they may be. Two crooked sixpences, that's all I'm askin' *you*. The others over there, it'd cost *them* a lot more, but this is between you and me. I'm letting them go at a cost to myself. I shan't even be making a bent penny. Just for the sake of a sale. Can't say fairer than that, can I?'

The goblin's breath smelled worse than marsh gas. Jack was reminded of the stereotyped used-car salesman. It was true that his shoes had holes. But *grass* shoes as replacements? He couldn't see them lasting five minutes. He wasn't a youth who was easy on shoes. He liked to kick things. Stones, twigs, clods of earth. His shoes went through hell, really, and it wasn't surprising they didn't last long.

'No, sorry – they're – they're much too small. They're made for faerie. I take size nines.'

The goblin, who was quite ugly to start with, screwed his face into a hideous mask. He was big for a faerie, coming up to Jack's shoulder. There was a lot of lumpy muscle on him too. Perhaps he had some boggart in him somewhere? Anyway, he looked menacing. A shock of dark hair bristled from his large head, falling as stiff as straw around his shoulders. He stared at Jack, still with the ugly expression, his eyes like wet flints.

'We could soon fix that, mortal,' he grated. 'I could cut your feet to fit. Only need a couple of centimetres off the front.'

'I'd lose my toes!' gasped Jack.

'What do you need toes for?'

Jack didn't feel this deserved an answer. He left the goblin on the edge of the wood and joined the others quickly. The goblin shouted a name after him, but Jack chose not to hear it. Why get into a fight with a goblin pedlar, the most bad-tempered of the forest faerie? Gnomes were fine. Lovely creatures, really. Even pixies and elves were not too bad, providing you didn't mind the odd prank. Marketplace goblins weren't all that bad, once they got to know you. But goblin pedlars were the Rottweilers of the faerie world, when it came to dealing with mortals.

Jack went over to Spiggot, his boggart friend, who was busy polishing his armour. Kling, the water rat, was eating as usual: some fancy-looking dish he had cooked himself out of watercress and mushrooms.

Rosamund, the maiden from medieval England, was talking with Jack's latest rival for her affections, Solomon. Solomon was a young monk, from her own time, who had followed her into Liöfwende. The pair seemed animated. Rosamund's face was shining. Part of the reason for this, Jack knew, was that she had someone who understood her medieval language. Not simply the language in itself, but all the little nuances of speech which often went over Jack's head. She was able to communicate with someone who knew *exactly* what she was talking about, without having to ask the meaning of words like 'candle-waster', 'fardels' and 'hempseed'.

'Ah,' cried Solomon, when he saw Jack coming. 'The candle-waster cometh, bearing more fardels than a hempseed.'

Rosamund giggled.

'You watch it, baldy!' retorted Jack, determined to give as good as he got.

'Baldy?' cried Solomon. 'Dost thou refer to my holy tonsure in such fashion?' He touched the shaven circle on his head. 'Fie, youth!'

'Twit!' muttered Jack. He went to sit with Kling, who was wiping round his tin plate with a piece of bread. 'What's he on about, anyway?' Jack asked the water rat, who was a walking encyclopaedia. 'What did he say to me?'

'He called you a bookworm – someone who wastes candles reading at night. It's not true of course, you have no books in this place, but you did call yourself a student . . .'

'I would've thought Rosy would approve of that. Anyway, he's the bookworm. He's the scholar, isn't he? That's all monks do, mess around with books. Illuminating letters and stuff.'

'True, they are artists with the stylus and vellum. But Rosamund likes warriors. The monk is a warrior-priest as well as a scholar.'

'Oh, is he? What about the fardels and the hempseed bit?'

Kling licked his whiskers to get off the last of the gravy.

'A fardel is a burden and a hempseed is a small boy destined for the gallows.'

'I'll give him fardels,' muttered Jack. 'We'll see who the warrior is around here.'

Kling put a ratty forelimb around Jack's shoulders. This being Faerieland, or Liöfwende, to use the faerie name, the talking rodent was a giant amongst his kind and he was almost as big as Jack himself.

'Take it from one who knows,' said Kling, picking his fangs with one of his claws. 'She'll come round again, if you don't make an ass of yourself in the meantime. Give the monk some rope. Let him drivel on, Jack. Slow and steady wins the race. Of course, some women like a bit of dash about a man, a rake in shining armour, but Rosamund is not one of those. Not really. Just play for time, son. Play for time.'

Since Jack had been in Liöfwende he had grown in spiritual stature. He was no longer the callow youth who had been shot through the invisible walls between the real world and Faerieland by a motorcycle accident. Several incidents and adventures in this place had carved character in the raw material that not long ago had been the would-be student engineer on his way to a college interview. He was a deeper human being now, able to rationalise, able to use a little wisdom. But then again, he was in love with Rosamund, and besotted young men act in stupid ways. It was touch and go whether Jack would heed the rat's wise advice, or simply allow his chafed feelings to get the better of him.

'Gather round everyone,' called Spiggot, the boggart leader of the group. 'Time to form our battle plans.'

The boggart son of an ironsmith, Spiggot had been chosen as the unlikely leader of an army of fairies, in the battle against the sorcerer, Mallmoc. Nutbrown in complexion, stocky in stature, simple and pleasant-looking, Spiggot took his calling seriously. He had to. The whole of Faerieland life as they knew it was at stake, not to mention the real world beyond the wall which divided the faerielands of Liöfwende, Thristlac and Eri-innis from Mortaland, the world of mortals.

Spiggot's parents did not approve of what he was doing. Nor did his beloved Fen, a female boggart. But then they would not have approved of *any* boggart who was upstart enough to believe he was as good as a fairy. Boggarts were made to bash iron and that's what they believed Spiggot should be doing. Not gallivanting over the countryside like a high-born fairy knight with a special task set by the fairy King of Northumberland.

They gathered round at the base of a blighted oak, a tree that had been torn to pieces at the root by the dreaded tree-eating thrum.

'Here's what's going to happen,' began Spiggot. 'Word

has it that Mallmoc's castle is on the move. We have to get our army together . . .'

'It's called *mobilising*,' interrupted Jack. 'You mobilise an army.'

'Quite,' said Spiggot, flicking a look at Jack. 'I knew that. Please do not interrupt in future, Jack. I'm trying to think here, which is not what this head was born to do.' He scratched a sticky-out ear with a grubby, chipped fingernail. 'If you keep butting in, I'll get confused. I've got it all worked out, see. First we mobilise the army of fairies. We then attack the ulcugga, defeat them, and go on to destroy Mallmoc's castle. We get rid of the sorcerer — I'm not sure how to do that bit yet — then we find the locking-stone to the magical cairn. We drive the thrum back underground, put the locking-stone in place, and Robert is your nephew.'

'You mean, Bob's your uncle.'

'If you say so, Jack.'

Jack said, 'Sounds like we've got our work cut out for us.'

'Let's make an account of our assets,' said Solomon, taking a piece of vellum, a stylus, and finally a scraper to erase any mistakes he might make on the animal-skin paper, from the folds of his habit. 'What do we have in the way of weapons and artefacts with which we might vanquish our foe?'

Rosamand said, 'There's Jack's magic crossbow, the bolt of which changes to a hawk when in flight, then back to a bronze bolt again before it strikes.'

Solomon scribbled. 'Good, I mark it then, the magic crossbow.'

'Then there is Jack's shirt of bumblebees,' she

continued, 'which is not so much a weapon, as a thing to keep one warm on cold nights.'

'Still, an asset,' replied the young monk generously. He wrote, 'Jyack's bummbel-shirte'. 'And more?'

'And Jack is expert at sleight-of-hand.'

Solomon looked up with a frown. He was getting a little tired of hearing 'Jack's'. 'Does no one else have a thing they own?'

'My weapons and armour,' answered Spiggot. 'My sword, shield and helmet and stuff.'

'I mark them down,' cried a grateful Solomon, glad they had got off the subject of Jack. 'The boggart's "stuffe".'

'Then there is Jack's bottle,' continued Rosamund, relentlessly, 'full of strange snakey things.'

'Bottle,' muttered Solomon, through gritted teeth. He made a mistake with Jack's name, forgetting the essential 'y', and automatically reached for his scraper. Then his hand fell away, as he wickedly decided to let the error stand, so that future readers would find the name offensive. 'Thus the strange bottle is marked, along with the name of its owner.'

'And I have the eagle's eyes,' continued Rosamund. 'These grey eyes that were given me by the faerie, in place of mine own blue ones.'

'Ahhh,' sighed the young monk, looking at her, 'and how I miss those sky-blue orbs.'

Jack snorted, 'I think she looks fine with *any* set of eyes.'

'Thank you, kind sir,' she said, smiling at him.

'For mine own part,' said Solomon, darkly, 'I should never have allowed the faerie to steal a lady's eyes, but then I was not there to prevent such a dastardly deed taking place.'

Rosamund intervened with, 'Then there is Jack's slitter, awarded him by the Irish fairy king.'

'Jack's slitter,' snarled Solomon, 'is thereby marked down.'

'And Jack's pair of silver shoes, those that crush the wearer's feet.'

'Jack's this, Jack's that,' spat Solomon. 'Marked and marked again.'

'And finally, Spiggot's quivvel, for finding locking-stones.'

'Not *Jack's* quivvel,' cried a now incensed Solomon. 'Surely my lady, it must be *Jack* who owns this device? Jack owns *everything*.' He began to get reckless. He babbled, 'Jack surely professes ownership of the whole world. And who would do such a thing, but an agent of the Devil, to be sure. I challenge thee, Jack-of-all-things, to deny thou art a lover of Satan's hordes. Heretic! Thou shalt be pressed by stones, drawn on the rack, hung and quartered, thy innards trailed out of thy abdomen . . .'

'Here, here, steady on,' said Kling, 'there'll be none of that inquisition stuff here, human. You'll be calling Kling a familiar next. Just you settle down, chum.'

Solomon looked wildly about him and realised that his fiery rhetoric had carried no one with him. Even Rosamund was looking at him with distaste in those eagle's eyes of hers. He immediately humbled himself and begged pardon, for his 'tongue had become temporarily unhinged'. The assets all duly recorded and set down for future reference, should the need arise, the group then decided to bed down for the night. Three of them slept under the stars, but Rosamund had a tent, made for her by Spiggot's ex-fiancée, Fen, who thought that no young lady should sleep in the open. The night humours, Fen had said, would cause coughs and colds. Thus was the maid protected from the dew the next morning, while the others were soaked.

TWO

Arriving with the dew was one of Spiggot's intelligence agents, the indomitable Puck or Robin Goodfellow. Puck was able to fly about the world at night, a facility given him by the old fairy king, Oberon. He was also able to make himself invisible, to sneak around and listen to conversations, or view things without others knowing he was there. Puck had some important news to impart to Spiggot.

'Mallmoc's castle is now an ironclad on the move.'

Spiggot, like many other faerie, was secretly in awe of the great Puck, who stood amongst the dew which sparkled from the tips of grass blades like crushed crystals. The energetic Puck glowed with energy. He was breathtakingly charismatic and it took all Spiggot's willpower not to bow to his spy whenever the latter appeared in his presence.

'The castle is sailing across the meadows?'

'Cruising on the high landscape, ploughing a furrow from north to south. Its front is shaped like the bladed bows of a ship. Its turrets are now decks from which to view the way ahead. Soil sprays like spume about its plimsoll line. It's a mighty vessel carving its way through valley and over hill, parting the turf and sending flints flying in its wake.'

'Do we know where Mallmoc's going?' asked Jack. 'Does he have a destination in mind?'

Puck folded his arms. He was dressed in his usual livery: Lincoln green, with a long jaybird's feather sweeping from his Robin Hood hat. An imposing figure, he turned his penetrating eyes on the mortal. Jack felt a tingle go down his spine as the creature studied him from head to toe. Finally Puck seemed satisfied with his assessment of the youth and answered him.

'It's my guess that Mallmoc's heading towards Sutton Hoo. There are certain weak points in the fabric of the invisible walls between Mortaland and Liöfwende, which might be breached by such a machine. Sutton Hoo is an ancient burial site, with several time layers laid one on the other. It's a special place to man and faerie alike. There, like at other places such as Glastonbury Tor and Stonehenge, mortals and faerie are closer than is normally the case. They're ghosts to each other, still, yet they drift by and sense the presence of an otherworld.'

'Mallmoc's going to smash through at Sutton Hoo?' cried Jack. 'He'll emerge from one of the boat burial mounds! This vessel of his, the iron castle, will stave a hole between the two worlds.'

'Which will widen and widen, until there is no

division,' added Rosamund. 'The two worlds will merge, with Mallmoc as the undisputed ruler of both.'

Puck smiled. 'The young ones understand.'

'And his hordes of ulcugga fairies?' questioned Spiggot, gravely. 'Where are they?'

'They are protecting the flanks, the front and the rear, of the cruising castle. The inriders are on horses, but the outriders are mounted on fire-tongued purple dragons, which they hatched from stolen eggs. Any attack on the castle must be preceded by a charge to breach the ranks of the ulcugga, who I have to say look very formidable, boggart. You have your work cut out for you. They are present in their thousands, being the most numerous of the fairies. You will need all the help you can get.'

'Using bogles on owls and nightjars, I have sent messages out to the four points of the compass, calling on the armies of the Thristlac seelie court and unseelie court, the Northumberland fairies born of the pipes, the ferocious mamau, the tylwyth teg who ride black rats and enjoy mimicking, the coblynau and gwragedd fairies from Snowdonia, the tuatha dé of Eri-innis, and others. They should all soon be on the march south, to meet with us near Madwoman's Stones on the moor which is the plateau of Kinder Scout in the Peak District.'

All this left Spiggot short of breath. The boggart was inclined to be very formal with the overwhelming Puck.

'Then they will not be in time. You must find some way of slowing Mallmoc's castle down, before it reaches Sutton Hoo. Now I must away, for there are sights to be seen and words to be heard. I shall be vigilant in the cause, for it grieves me sorely to see the thrum eating away at the roots of our dear old oaks, and other trees, and we must drive them back where they came from, into the stomach of the Earth, where they belong.'

With that, Puck vanished.

Spiggot and his crew turned and gaped at each other.

'How are we going to delay Mallmoc?' wailed the boggart. 'We are but one faerie, three mortals and a mere water rat.'

'Less of the "mere", if you don't mind,' grumbled Kling, 'unless you mean a lake or pond, in which case it's all right.'

Jack said, 'Could we build defences? Around Sutton Hoo?'

'We couldn't stop the iron castle-ship with bricks and mortar, or even boulders. It will cut through them without a pause. It would have to be something harder than iron and where would we find that?'

'Diamonds are harder than iron,' said Solomon.

Jack said, 'And so is steel.'

'Stele?' asked the monk. 'What is a stele?'

'It doesn't matter,' sighed Spiggot, 'we have neither.'

Kling said, 'Do we need to stop it? Couldn't we send it in another direction?'

'That's silly,' said Rosamund. 'How will we turn such a metal monster from its course?'

'No, wait,' cried Jack, thoughtfully, 'he may have something there, Rosy. Spiggot, how will Mallmoc navigate his landship? Will he know the way to Sutton Hoo by instinct or prior knowledge? There are no roads or landmarks such as we have in the mortal world. If there are, I haven't seen 'em. How will he find his way through woods and fields which all look much alike? There are no townships. Just the odd boggart village or gnome hamlet. Nothing in the way of towers or big buildings.'

'Good point, Jack,' said Spiggot, rubbing his brown hands together. 'Why, I suppose he will navigate by the stars, using such magic as he can muster for such a purpose. To my knowledge he hasn't been south of Rutland before. Nor have the ulcugga, who are a midland clan of fairies. They are in unknown territory. The stars. It must be by the stars.'

'Not a very reliable guide, to such a precise spot,' said Jack.

'No indeed, but as I said, he will have certain help from his sorcery – though in truth, magic does not work well on a science. Is navigating a science, Jack, or an art?'

'It uses maths and stuff. I guess it's a science.'

'I thought so. Well done, Jack, for your idea.'

'Hey!' cried the water rat. 'It was Kling who thought of it.'

'Now now, rat, you always try to claim credit.'

'But it *was* Kling. Oh, forget it.' Kling walked off in a huff. 'When you want another idea Kling will be down by the stream.'

'Now, how do we use this knowledge?' asked Rosamund. 'Can we alter the positions of the stars, change their courses?'

They all looked up, but it was day of course, and they could see no twinkling diamonds in the sky.

'We've hit the flaw in Jack's plan,' Spiggot groaned. 'We can do nothing to change the heavens.'

'We don't need to,' Jack said, triumphantly. 'All we need to alter is Mallmoc's perspective of the heavens. The way in which he views them. Or knobble his astro-labe or whatever he uses to calculate with. Or call on cloud cover, so the sky is hidden from sight. Something of that nature.'

'Brilliant!' cried Spiggot. Then, in a quieter tone, 'How do we do that?'

'It will take some thought,' the youth replied. 'Solomon, have you any ideas?'

'Can we stop the beating of the sun's heart, as it travels around the Earth? Can we halt the swimming of the stars, as they circle our world? I think not.'

Jack shook his head. He was not going to point out to this medieval monk that it was the Earth that moved around the sun. It would be useless anyway. A mindset from the monk's era would not be able to comprehend such a change in its thinking. It would reject the notion outright.

'Kling?' cried Rosamund. 'We need thee, now.'

The rat came back, his whiskers dripping with fresh water from the stream where he had been drinking.

'Kling knew it,' he said. 'Well, then, listen and learn. Kling has heard of a magical tune that will draw forth the spirits of earth and stone, and have them dancing in the moonlight. Such a cluster of spirits – translucent forms – will act like a warped lens when peered through. Mallmoc is an old wizard, a *very* old wizard, whose eyes are not what they were in his youth. If you could create a wall of such spirits, one which escaped Mallmoc's attention, you could alter his perception of the map in the sky, as Jack suggested.'

'Brilliant!' cried Spiggot. Then in that quiet aftertone, 'How do we find this magical tune?'

'We ask around,' replied the rat. 'Kling suggests we start with Gulnar Peck, the half-giant who lives in an old iron mine near here. He plays a mean penny whistle. He might know the tune.'

'Let us go forth,' cried Spiggot, extending a hairy arm dramatically to point in a westerly direction. 'To Gulnar Peck, the half-giant.'

Kling was hitched to the cart which contained their goods and supplies and off they went. After encounters with roaming spriggans and their spiky parasites, by evening they were approaching hills turning purple in the mellow light of the falling sun. Thistles were bowing their heads ready to bear the heavy darkness which was encroaching on the land. In the gloaming rabbits were emerging, testing the evening air with their noses, eyes watchful for foxes who even in Faerieland were hunters and killers. The birdsongs floated over lea and bottom land, sweet and tuneful as ever.

'You know what I miss here?' said Jack to Spiggot, 'Sheep and cows. You don't see any sheep and cows in Liöfwende. The meadows are empty, except for rabbits and hares. Don't you yearn to see a gambolling lamb in the spring? Or a newly-born calf staggering after its mother?'

'No, Jack. We don't eat pork chops here.'

'Pork comes from pigs.'

'We don't eat pigs, either.'

'Well, anyway, I miss 'em.'

'I'll buy you some for your birthday,' grunted Kling, pulling the cart. 'Maybe we can persuade one of them to help me drag this thing.'

They crested a rise at this point and ahead of them was a huge quarry cut into a hillside. Jack was surprised to see such an eyesore, for the faerie did not like interfering

with natural landscapes. He guessed it was a mine for
metal ores, since metal was one of the elements required
by faerie for armour and weapons. However, when he
asked Spiggot he was told it was a mine for semi-
precious stones, used in faerie craft work.

'You wouldn't get all of those from one place in the
ground.'

'You do in Liöfwende – this is Faerieland, don't forget.'

Jack was impressed. 'And who uses these stones?'

'The pixies make small boxes out of marble and inlay
them with the semi-precious stones,' explained Spiggot.
'Minerals such as cornelian, garnet, agate chalcedony,
malachite, lapis lazuli and jasper. Ivory they can get from
the tooth fairy. There's nothing so unblemished as milk
teeth. You can often see the tooth fairy in the early dawn,
going home with a sack of children's toothy-pegs on his
back, his night's work done.'

'What about mother-of-pearl and coral?'

Spiggot looked suitably shocked, as Jack knew he
would do.

'Those are living creatures, Jack – we would never
take things from living creatures.'

'Quite right, too,' grinned Jack. 'Just testing. And the
boxes are used for what?'

'To keep things in, of course. Sometimes, Jack, you
are a bit dense.'

As they approached the quarry, in which there was a
large cave which went into the cliff, it began to sparkle
with millions of pinpricks of light. These lights were all
of different colours: blue, orange, green, white, gold, red.
This was the effect of the moonlight on the exposed semi-
precious minerals. Now Jack knew why they had left the

quarry looking so raw and open. It was not the beauty of
the landscape during the day which had interested the
faerie, but this coruscation at night. It was like a vast
show of multi-coloured stars, whose twinkling could be
seen for miles. Breathtakingly beautiful, this scene had
Rosamund gasping. She was a little girl again, allowed to
see inside her mother's jewel box.

'Oh, wow,' said Jack. 'Cool.'

As they continued into the quarry, someone lit a fire
outside the cave, and it flared into life. This provided the
light for the party to see by. In the fire's glow they could
discern a bulky shape: a muscled form, squarish and
chunky. As they approached, this form rose and stood
above the flames. The figure was about three metres high,
not massive and towering like the Irish giants Jack had
previously encountered, but big just the same. This, he
guessed, was the half-giant of whom Kling had spoken.

What was amazing about the creature was not his size,
nor even the contained power of his body, but his
burnished-bronze hair and beard. It spread about his face
like a child's picture of a sun. It was like a lion's mane,
rather than that which decorated the head of a human. In
the middle of this wild-looking fuzz was a benign face,
gentle and unthreatening, with soft lustrous eyes. The
mane itself was huge and rambling: a briar patch out of
control. Jack could see small creatures within the tangle
of hair: tiny birds, butterflies, moths and crickets. They
seemed quite comfortable there, as if well at home.

'Good evening, Gulnar Peck,' said Spiggot with deference in his tone. 'Greetings from the son of Gnomon
and Quagmarish, the boggart Spiggot. You may have
heard of me? They call me the Faerie Knight.'

'Good evening, boggart.'

The half-giant sounded wary. These were dangerous times, with rogue wizards sailing the landscape in iron ships. Already the impetuous pixies and elves had gone to war and had been defeated, routed by the forces of Mallmoc. Their artefacts and weapons were scattered amongst the shrubs and bushes of battlefields all over the countryside. The news of the Gilscipe thrum, devouring all the trees in the kingdom, had travelled far and wide too. Even powerful half-giants needed to be vigilant, when four or five unknown and unexpected beings approached him out of the twilight.

'May I ask the reason for this visit?' said Gulnar Peck. 'If you have come to steal the stones I guard, you will have a great deal of trouble.'

'No, no. Nothing like that,' replied Spiggot, hastily. 'We seek your help on another matter. May we share your fire?'

'Certainly, the hospitality of a half-giant is not to be scorned. Seat yourselves. Are they mortals you have there?'

Kling threw off the traces of the cart. 'Right first time, giant. Would you like one to eat? Kling recommends the monk. He's got the makings of some juicy crackling, that one.'

Solomon gulped, but Gulnar Peck merely laughed. 'A water rat. Always thinking of their stomachs, water rats. I suppose you want some food, rodent?'

'Funny you should ask that. You wouldn't have any lemon soufflé handy, would you? Or a pashwari naan? Anything like that?'

'There's some stale cheese at the back of the cave.'

'Par for the course,' sighed Kling. 'Well, if you'll excuse a hungry rodent, Kling will sniff it out, though that shouldn't be too difficult.'

Kling vanished into the recesses of the cave.

'Sit down,' Gulnar Peck said to the other four. 'So, mortals, eh? How is the world of human beings?'

'Oh, you know,' replied Jack, 'war, pestilence, famine, all that sort of thing.'

'Three horses of the Apocalypse,' cried Kling from the depths of the cave, his mouth full of cheese. 'No one can ever remember the fourth.'

The companions sat at the fire and immediately the half-giant found some wooden bowls and began ladling soup into them. He handed them round, accompanied by chunks of softly-baked bread. Goblets of fresh stream water were also passed to them with the same polite gravity. The travellers accepted them gratefully. They were hungry and thirsty after tramping over the countryside. For the moment there was nothing but the sound of masticating jaws and grateful burps. Jack thought this show was disgusting. Clearly none of the others did, even Rosamund.

'Where's your table manners?' cried Jack.

'What table?' asked Solomon, reasonably.

Once the meal was over, Spiggot told the half-giant why they were visiting him.

'We need your help. You must be aware that Mallmoc is cruising through the turf, ploughing a furrow right down the middle of Liöfwende? We must divert him from his course. He's heading for Sutton Hoo and if he gets there, death and destruction of all we hold dear will follow.'

'I know it,' came the reply. 'But what can a poor half-giant do?'

'When you lived in the real world, you were shepherds and goatherds, weren't you? In ancient Greece and Persia. Then the age of myth ended and you had to come here, where we took you in and gave you a home.'

'And I am grateful for the generosity of the faerie, boggart – but still, I have not the strength to stop Mallmoc's castle.'

'No, not that. But listen to me. As herdsmen you had to entertain yourselves, it being a very lonely occupation. And since you cannot sing and have no feeling for poetry, you taught yourselves to play the penny whistle. Isn't that so?'

The half-giant nodded. 'It is now part of our instinctive nature, to play the flute. We are expert.'

'That's what I mean,' cried Spiggot, eagerly. 'And you know the tune which draws forth the spirits of the Earth?'

Gulnar Peck's head went back. He looked very grave. Clearly this question had disturbed him to very core of his being.

'Such secrets,' he said, 'must remain in the flute. I do know this terrible tune of which you speak, but am bound by the laws of my clan to reveal it to no other ears but our own.'

Jack said, quickly, 'You will have no clan if Mallmoc isn't stopped.'

'Still, I cannot. You ask too much of me. Whatever the reason, I will be ostracised from my kind. No one will speak to me. I will be shunned. Do you know the shun? It is horrible. I could not bear it. To have other half-giants turn their backs on me as I approach? It is a lonely enough life, a solitary enough existence, as it is, without being rejected.'

The half-giant hung his head in the firelight. Solomon looked at Rosamund and shrugged. Spiggot looked at Jack and shook his head. Kling belched loudly from the back of the cave. For a moment no one said anything. They were absorbed in their thoughts. Then Kling came out of the cave, licking his paws.

'Kling found a custard pie in there too — hope you don't mind.'

The half-giant did not even reply. He was still too upset by having to say no to his guests' request. It was not that he did not want to help. All his instincts were bent in that direction. Half-giants were philanthropic, generous, gregarious creatures, who loved to assist those in trouble. The laws of hospitality demanded it of him. But Spiggot was asking too much. Gulnar Peck could not break the code. He was bound in honour never to use that tune in anger. Only on special occasions, under strict controls, could the melody that roused the spirits of the Earth be played.

'You do understand?' he pleaded, breaking the silence. 'It is impossible for me.'

'Oh, well, as to that,' replied Spiggot, not prepared to smooth the half-giant's feelings, 'you must do what you feel is right. But I hope when Faerieland is barren and bare of trees, and faerie are wandering the landscape out of their heads with madness, that you remember you could have prevented the world from coming to an end.' He sighed and stood up. 'There it is, then. Come on mortals, we must be on our way. We have to find someone who *is* prepared to help us. Clearly we are not wanted here. This is a place of *secrets*.' He spoke the word scathingly. 'Ugly little secrets, like those whispered in the shadows by men wearing black cloaks and wide-brimmed hats. Secrets, hiding the truth . . .'

Gulnar Peck put his face in his large hands.

'Please . . .' he said.

Jack could see the half-giant's nails, square-cut at the ends and chipped. They were the hands of a creature who knew honest toil. They were a farmer's hands, a cowherd's hands, a ploughboy's hands. He felt sorry for the big fellow, who after all was a simple creature with a strong desire to please. The myriad small creatures in the half-giant's hair and beard had gone all of a twitter. Little balls of feather fluffed their wings and chirruped. Crickets clicked like mad, hopping from one side of the head to the other. Mice left their nests and ran to a neighbour's property. Spiders scuttled beneath follicle arches to an imagined safer place. These residents all sensed that their home-carrier was in an agony of spirit, caught between a terrible duty to keep a secret and a desperate desire to please.

'. . . please. If I could help, I would. I am not permitted. I am not allowed. I am forbidden.'

'I think we get the message,' replied Jack.

'It's not my fault,' cried Gulnar Peck, his face lifting out of his hands, streaked with dirty tears. 'I don't make the laws of the half-giants.'

'You could bend one little law,' suggested Rosamund, 'to save mankind and faeriekind.'

'It would not be *bending*, it would be *breaking*.'

Spiggot sensed a weakening in the half-giant's tone.

He sat down again, quickly. 'Ah well,' he said, picking up a stick and stirring the fire with it, 'there's nowhere we can go tonight. I suppose you would not object to us sleeping round your fire, Gulnar Peck? *That* wouldn't be breaking any rules, would it? That would not breach the code of the half-giants I take it? Or would you like to turn us out into the night?'

'No, no, please stay. Here, have some more soup and bread. I have plenty,' said the half-giant, anxious to make amends. 'If not I can soon make some more. Please, fill your plates.'

'The food would taste like ashes in our mouths,' answered Spiggot, laying back, his head on a log. '*Wet* ashes,' he added as an afterthought. Jack thought Spiggot was overdoing it a bit, but the poor half-giant groaned. His soul was in an agony of torment. They all remained motionless, as if locked in their own thoughts, for over an hour.

The fire died, its soul floating up to heaven. Shadows darkened. The moon found some clouds to hide behind. Out in the night foxes barked coldly and badgers answered. It was a time for reflecting, for listening to inner voices, for wondering and making hard decisions.

THREE

It was Jack who broke the uncomfortable silence.

'When is a secret not a secret?' he asked.

Spiggot asked, 'What's that Jack?' He stirred the embers in the stone grate and a redness turned to flames. Firelight flickered and shadows danced again.

'I was pondering on the nature of secrets.'

'That sounds very deep, Jack.'

'Let me ask you, Gulnar Peck,' continued Jack, turning to the half-giant, 'how many people know of the tune to draw out the spirits of earth and stone? How many?'

Gulnar Peck looked a bit confused. 'I don't know how many. All the half-giants in Liöfwende. Some others.'

'Which others? Which of the faerie?'

'Well, the Cornish piskies know it of course, along with the tune for the Floral Dance.' He laughed. 'Those are the only two melodies they know.'

'But there's only one or two piskies,' said Jack, slyly.

'Oh no, there are *hundreds*.'

'And any others?'

'No – not unless you count the creatures of nature.'

'The creatures of nature?'

Gulnar Peck nodded. 'Yes, you know, birds, bees, all the singers amongst the animal world. They know it by instinct. We had to learn it.'

'They why aren't the birds singing it all the time?'

'There is no call for them to do so. They have to be *asked*, Jack. They aren't real people like us. They need someone to lead them – a sort of orchestral conductor, if you like.'

'And I suppose the wind knows the tune?'

'Of course, and the sea. The wind and the sea know all the tunes that ever were or ever will be. That's in their nature, Jack.'

'Sounds to me like it isn't a secret.'

Gulnar Peck said quickly, 'Oh yes, it's a secret all right.'

Jack murmured, 'A secret is only a secret if one or two people *only* are privy to it. If hundreds of piskies, all the half-giants in the land, all the birds and bees, even the sea and the wind . . . the *wind*, mind you, which blows *every-where* – if they all know it, it can't be a secret. It's just something half the world knows about and half the world will eventually find out about.'

'You're trying to trick me with words,' cried Gulnar Peck, leaping to his feet. 'You think because I'm a simple-headed half-giant . . .'

Rosamund said, 'Jack doesn't think you're simple-headed.'

'No?' cried the half-giant, uncertainly.

'No, of course not, because thou art bright and articulate, art thou not?'

'Yes, I am.'

'There you are, then.'

'But,' continued Gulnar Peck, miserably, 'he's trying to wheedle the secret out of me.'

'No he's not,' continued Rosamund gently, 'because, as he explained, it isn't a secret at all. It's something most beings know and a few don't.'

Gulnar Peck's eyes widened. '*You* know the tune.'

'Yes,' said Rosamund, 'I didn't want to interrupt Jack, because he was in full flow, but I do know the tune. It goes like this,' and she began to hum a sweet melody.

'No it doesn't!' shouted Gulnar Peck. 'It's not that at all.'

'Art thou accusing a maid of lying?' snapped Rosamund, jumping to her feet. 'Think thee the only creature who knows what's to do?'

'Thou – I mean – you didn't do it right.'

Hotly now. 'Yes, I did.'

'No, you didn't!'

'Prove it!'

'It goes like this,' and Gulnar Peck began to sing a weird and marvellous song.

A chill went trickling down Jack's spine and Solomon looked worried and crossed himself. As the notes came out, like the strains of some unearthly music created by pagans in an England far back in time, Jack had an inkling he had heard the sound before. Yes, definitely. It was when his aunt had taken him to the Morris dancing festival at Thaxted in Essex, where dancers from all over

the world gathered. At midnight, the culmination of the
festival, one set of dancers gave a strange and terrible
performance, coming out of the shadows of the church-
yard on the hill. They wore antlers on their heads. They
cavorted in a sinister way, making sinuous and serpen-
tine movements, down the cobbled street. One of the
male dancers was dressed as a woman, and wielded an
inflated pig's bladder on a stick, while the fiddler who
produced the chilling music wore the mock clothing of a
priest. Even at the time – Jack had been about seven
years of age – he realised he was witnessing something
ancient and forbidden.

Gulnar Peck stopped singing suddenly. He went a
deathly white.

'You tricked me,' he groaned. 'Now the shunning will
start.'

'Abbot's Bromley Horn Dance!' cried Jack, triumphantly, the name coming to him suddenly. 'That's
what it is!'

Gulnar Peck blinked. '*You* know it?'

'I have heard it once or twice before.'

'You know the name, then,' said a relieved half-giant.
'I did not tell you the secret. You knew it already.'

'Correct!' said Jack. 'Have no fear, Gulnar Peck, they
can't shun you for telling me what I already know.'

'No, they can't, can they?' cried the half-giant, joyfully.
'They can't shun Gulnar Peck, now.'

With that, the half-giant took out his penny whistle,
fashioned from a Norfolk reed, and began to play. The
haunting tune made the hairs on the necks of the listeners stand on end. Jack could see Solomon quivering, as
if he was witnessing devil-worship in his own back

yard. Rosamund's eyes were round with fear. Jack
himself experienced a tightness round the chest which
made it difficult for him to breathe. It was a preternatu-
ral sound, far worse than the singing of the same eerie
tune. The reed flute caught the tone exactly. Thin strains
like the songs of snakes, if snakes could sing, wove
thread-like into the fantastical evening air. This was like
no other music. It was not a threatening sound: more of
a macabre, blood-curdling melody which might wither
flowers, freeze running hares in their tracks or bring a
severed head to cry vengeance at the axeman.

'Now the spirits dance,' whispered Spiggot into Jack's
ear. 'See, out in the twilight.'

There were indeed shadowy shapes coming from the
earth. They rose like the heatwaves that shimmer from
hot sands. Their dance was peculiar, as if the ghosts of
snakes were standing on their tails and wriggling to the
rhythm of a minor key. There was nothing substantial
about them. Jack could see no definite shapes. Nor actually could he see the spirits themselves. What he saw was
the movement of air, the rippling of shadows, nothing
more. It filled his heart with dread to see such a sight. It
was as if he were a visual witness to graves opening up
on Salvation Day and the dead rising and cavorting joyfully upon consecrated ground.

After it was all over, Jack spoke to Solomon, the
shared experience breaking down the barriers between
them.

'Did you ever see such a sight? Did you ever *feel*
such?'

'Not I,' shivered the monk, ''twas demons manifest, of
that I am certain sure. Mine own father was but a maker

of shoes, and my mother a sewer of dresses. My grandfather, indeed, was also a shoemaker, who made some
shoes for the baron. The baron thus finding the shoes
pleasing, asked the old man if he had any sons. My
grandfather pushed me forward, for I was at that time
playing knock-me-downs in the corner, and the baron
took me and gave me to a learned man and thus I became
a noviciate priest . . .'

Jack listened with glazed eyes, as he got the whole of
Solomon's life story in great and small detail. He guessed
that in the monk's time there was very little in the form of
entertainment and what one did was regale the listener
with a lengthy recounting of one's life experiences. The
monk had a dull voice though, which was enough to send
charging steed to sleep. It droned on and on, until Jack
could have screamed with boredom. He did not scream,
because it was the first time that Solomon had opened up
to him, and in order to defeat your enemy, you have to get
to know him. Jack was hoping to hear something which
would give him a hold over the meddlesome priest. Yet,
Solomon, it seemed had led a chaste and blameless life,
except for his passion for Rosamund.

'Surely,' said Jack, 'you will go to the devil for your
sin of coveting a young lady?'

'Not so,' answered Solomon piously, 'for it is love.
Who can be damned for loving a lady, if indeed she be a
maiden? Were she betrothed to another, then *that* would
be a sin. No, my Lady Rosamund is free to love where
she chooses, and I too am not bound to another. Once I
was too lowly for such a lady, but no more. I am now of
a different class.'

'But you're a priest,' Jack pointed out, 'and supposed

to be wedded to the Church. Aren't you monks supposed to be celibate or something? What about your immortal soul and all that?'

'I would renounce my vows tomorrow, if it meant that I would gain the love of my lady.'

Now before Solomon had come along, Jack had believed Rosamund was in love with *him*. And indeed she had all but professed as much. But the monk was full of flattery and praise, saying there was nothing too good for the Lady Rosamund, that all men were vile slugs beside her enthralling beauty. Solomon was making Rosy so conceited she was becoming unbearable. Jack couldn't go along with this sycophantic stuff. If Rosy had a smut on her nose he told her so. If she was being bad-tempered, he told her to snap out of it. If she said something he didn't agree with, he argued with her, and didn't automatically acknowledge that she was right. Jack was an ordinary boy of the twenty-first Century, and liked his girls plain.

In response to this, Rosamund began to put on airs, and tell Jack he was not giving her the respect and deference due to one of her status.

'What you want me to do, Rosy, is kiss your feet. Well, you might get that from Solly over there, but not me. I'm – I'm very fond of you, but I'm not your slave, any more than you're mine. We're just two friends, equal partners, not one better than the other.'

This put Rosamund in a huff. Well, it would. She was having her head turned by an ingratiating monk. It was all very unsatisfactory and unfair from Jack's point of view and he was doing his best to see a way round it.

For the moment he had to put his own problems aside.

Spiggot was calling a conference. Now they had the tune
they had to find a way to use it. They couldn't simply
stand in Mallmoc's way and sing it themselves. They
needed an orchestra, or choir, to do it for them.
Preferably a hidden one. Solomon suggested birds.

'No good,' Kling pointed out. 'Birds do not sing at
night.'

'The wind, then,' cried Rosamund. 'The wind has a
voice.'

Spiggot replied, 'It doesn't always blow loud enough.'

'Streams, becks, rushy waters,' suggested Gulnar
Peck. 'These always have a voice.'

'But not always in the right places,' Kling said. 'They
are bound by their beds and courses.'

As he listened to the noises of the night around him,
Jack suddenly had the answer.

'Crickets!' he cried. 'Let them be the singers.'

Spiggot stared at Jack with respect. 'Oh, yes – the
crickets. They sing at night, definitely – and they are
everywhere.'

'Trouble is,' pointed out Kling, who was quickly
attaining a reputation for dampening spirits, 'crickets are
percussion kings, but they don't have any melody. They
can tap out a beat, but they can't trill a high note. In
other words, they've got the drums but not the fifes.'

Jack, who had seen the dawning of admiration in
Rosamund's eyes, glowered at the rodent.

'So what do you suggest?' he growled. 'Haven't you
got any suggestions?'

'Now don't look at Kling like that, Jack. Yours was
the best idea. And it has given Kling an even better one.
Master's son,' he said, addressing Spiggot, 'what about

the whirligigs? On their own they make annoying individual sounds, but if they were to form an orchestra . . .?'

'The whirligigs!' cried Spiggot, who had not the best
brain for rooting out new ideas, but knew a good one
when he saw it. 'Why, that's the best notion, Kling. We
shall use the whirligigs.'

The three mortals looked mystified.

Jack said, 'Whirligigs?'

'Surely, 'tis some form of festival fair,' cried
Rosamund. 'One in which maidens are twirled by their
swains on wooden seats.'

'I like not the sound of this werlygeg,' Solomon said.
'To my ears the word sounds like a pagan ritual, mayhap
a parliament of incubi.'

'No, no,' explained Spiggot, 'whirligigs – well,
they're – they're whirligigs.'

Kling became impatient. 'What the master's son means
is that they are a hybrid lifeform, half animal, half plant.
They come in many shapes and with different properties.
A thistle-whizzer, for example, is a kind of spinning disc
with hairy edges. It flies out of thistle patches at a
hundred miles an hour. A gorse-springer like a curled,
well, *spring*. They shoot out of gorse patches, a dozen at
a time, their tails making a screeching sound . . .'

'And a privet-skimmer is a dart-like creature – something like an ear of corn – which zings from privet
hedges like an arrow.' Spiggot was determined to regain
control of the conversation before Kling stole all of his
glory. 'There are many whirligigs, all of them as different
as seashells or butterflies are to one another. They fly out
of their various host plants at night, spinning, zinging,
whistling into the darkness.'

'Why do we never find them in the morning?' asked Jack, reasonably.

'Because they only live a few hours, then they become hard and crisp, like the seeds of weeds. Indeed, that's what they get mistaken for in the morning. Seeds. You don't have whirligigs in Mortaland, Jack, that's why you don't know about them. They're particular to Liöfwende.'

'And you say they're half animal, half plant?'

'Kling said that, not me. I suppose he's right. A bit like coral polyps or pitcher plants that eat insects. No one quite knows where to put them, in the animal kingdom, or the world of growing things. *I* think they're insects, but I know Kling will disagree . . .' Kling nodded to confirm this. 'Others believe them to be wholly vegetable. A lot of the birds think that, because they like to eat them, and they don't want to feel guilty about it. You know what birds are like. Well then, let's get to it! The whirligigs!'

That night, Kling and Spiggot set about teaching whirligigs the ancient tune for raising the spirits of earth and stone. They learned quickly. It was true those that had been taught the song died before the morning sun rose in the sky. However, they still had time to pass the message on to their offspring. It only took three nights before the music was bred into future generations of whirligigs, so that they were born with the knowledge.

Jack was fascinated by it all. Each of the whirligigs had their own note. Not like the crickets, who all spake with the same back leg. The whirligigs used the air rushing through holes and gaps in their bodies to produce the strange melodies. They flew into the face of the wind and their twistings, spinning, whirling bodies cried out, each with their own particular note. A thistle-whizzer, for instance, made a constant wavering siren-like sound. A gorse-springer made a *boing-boing-boing* sound, but one that trailed away at the ends, so *booooünnng* would probably be more accurate.

When all the different notes of several species of whirligig were put together they made a reedy tune and could copy even the most complicated melodies. Jack was surprised he had never heard them before, but Kling said he hadn't been listening. This was true, Jack realised. It wasn't before you concentrated and actually paused to listen, that you heard things. Take the dawn chorus, for example. It's there every day of the year, sometimes louder than others, but who wakes up to the sound of the birds? Spiggot was actually relying on this attitude of the human mind to ignore everyday noises. He hoped Mallmoc, the sorcerer, would not recognise what he heard.

'Look at them go!' he cried, like a five-year-old watching a fireworks display. 'Look at them whiz and wail!'

The basil-rockets were his particular favourite, flying like torpedoes with a particular twisting motion, through the night air. Basil-rockets sounded a bit like a washing machine whose bearings have gone — a sort of high-pitched grating noise. Within the orchestra of its fellow whirligigs, though, it was music which came from the gills of the basil-rockets.

In order to watch for Mallmoc's castle, the companions built a ship's crow's-nest at the top of a tall pine.

Jack, who had done some sailing, fixed up a bo's'n's chair with which they could winch each other to the top. There they took turns to sit and view the skyline, waiting for the dreaded ironclad castle to come into view.

It was during Jack's watch that it first appeared.

It was dawn. The red rays of the rising sun were just piercing the sky, when Jack saw a huge black shape appear on the horizon. Around the shape were thousands of fairies, many on horseback, others on foot. They swarmed the countryside before and after, and on the flanks, of the mighty object. Thick black smoke belched from chimneys on the roof of the oncoming ironclad, filling the sky with ugly clouds. Smaller dots flew at the sides of the castle, and fell to Earth. Jack knew these were birds who were for some reason attracted to the sorcerer's home, but on striking the sides they killed themselves, and dropped to the ground stone-dead.

Jack had been inside that terrible iron castle, had stoked its furnaces with black coke, and sweated blood on to its iron decks. He shivered in the early coolness of the day as he watched it ploughing through the fields, leaving a mighty brown gash through the green, a deep horrible scar, in its wake. As Puck had foretold, it was actually *sailing* through dirt as if the landscape were an ocean. And there, up on the bridge, the fearsome captain of the craft, was the bent and crooked spectre of Mallmoc.

'He's enjoying himself!' cried Jack, looking through a handmade spyglass that Spiggot had fashioned from a bamboo tube and crystal lenses. 'He's loving it! See the way he's leering at the thick ugly trench he's leaving behind. What an evil sod he is, churning up the turf just for fun. He's a damned hooligan. He ought to be behind bars.'

Jack was aware that right at this moment he sounded like his own father, but he was more than indignant, he was seething. That someone should enjoy the spectacle of a torn and scarred landscape made his blood boil. Faerieland, for all its faults, was a beautiful place, the sort of virgin Britain only imagined in dreams. There were cloud-like woods and tall, ancient forests, vast green rounded meadows covered in wild flowers, silvery-clear streams that tumbled over smooth stones, purple moorland, and wild hedgerows. It was the sort of place many Brits hoped heaven would be, when the end came along. Mammals and birds, fish and insects, were all part of the scenery, filling Faerieland with life and movement. To think that someone would actually enjoy destroying this wonder of the natural and unnatural world was quite shocking.

A rook flew into the branches of the tree and sat on a bow near Jack as he continued to watch the oncoming vessel.

'Ugly son-of-a-cuckoo, ain't he?' said the rook.

Jack lowered the spyglass. 'Oh, you're one of those birds that talk.' Jack knew that Kling was not the only animal in Liöfwende who had a brain and could speak. Even certain rocks and trees had the power.

'That's me,' said the rook. 'One of those.'

A chill suddenly swept through Jack.

'You're – you're not one of Mallmoc's spies, by any chance? An ulcugga in disguise?'

'Would I tell you if I was?'

'Probably not.'

'Well I ain't, so rest your beak. I wouldn't work for that goatsucker if he had been hatched from the egg of an eagle. If he was a slug I wouldn't bother to eat him. Don'tchu worry about that, hen.'

'Good. I'm relieved to find I believe you. Look, will you fly down there and warn that boggart on the ground that Mallmoc's castle is bearing down on us. I'd be very grateful.'

'Happy to oblige!' cried the rook, sweeping off the branch and spiralling to the Earth below.

Jack looked down and saw Spiggot speaking with the black bird. Then the boggart went to the bo's'n's chair and Kling winched him up alongside Jack. The mortal youth pointed to the horizon. Spiggot stared, his brown face wrinkling in dismay.

'Look what he's doing to my fields!'

Jack said, quietly, 'I know.'

'He's a fiend, that's what he is. Oh, Jack, I've just thought, what if he gets here before the night comes, and passes through during daylight. The whirligigs we've taught the tune to are in this district. The melody won't spread far and wide quickly enough to divert the wizard from his course.'

They watched and wondered, trying to estimate the speed of the castle-ship. It was not going at any great rate. This they gauged after about an hour. In fact Mallmoc could not have judged it better if he knew he was supposed to rendezvous with them at the witching hour. It was indeed about midnight when the great vessel heaved into the spinney where the companions had been ensconced. It crashed through young trees like a relentless war tank, uprooting them, snapping their trunks, forcing them aside. Mallmoc was not going to alter course in order to preserve a thicket. Not him. Grim-faced and determined, he stood on the bridge, charting by stars the most direct course to Sutton Hoo, unconcerned by any beauty in his path.

The underground homes of badgers, foxes and moles – even faerie such as subterranean gnomes – were left gutted in his wake. Dead bodies littered the ground. Ulcugga fairies, with their long beautiful hair and hand-some silvery complexions, rode over the corpses with nary a glance at their master's nasty handiwork. Some, those on foot, might have paused to kick a carcass out of the way, but beyond that they might have been witness-ing the deaths of common houseflies. The lovely fairies swarmed about the castle, ever vigilant in their protec-tion of its walls, sending pixies and elves, goblins and trolls, running for the hills. The ulcugga were fierce fighters, their knights feared by most other faerie races, and they were ruthless in their methods of maintaining power and control.

'Oh what a sight to behold!' groaned Spiggot, from their hiding place in the spiky gorse. 'Who would glory in such wanton ruin?'

The companions, in their gorse fortress, safe from the mounted ulcugga who never went into such brakes for fear they would scar their beautiful steeds, watched as Mallmoc suddenly brought the castle to a halt on the crest of a rise. The choir of whirligigs was in full flow. From the earth shadowy shapes, hard to define in the growing darkness, were rising like mirages to warp the night sky. Mallmoc frowned and consulted the heavens. He studied the star path he had been following the previous night and found his course had altered during the day. This was not unusual, since during light hours he only had the sun to guide him, and it was such a large and unreliable orb it was difficult to chart an accurate direction by it.

However, the change was greater than normal and he stood a long time on the bridge, looking up at Ursa Major and Ursa Minor, Orion's belt, the seven sisters, and other sparkling constellations embedded in the map of the sky. Finally, to the relief of Spiggot and his companions, Mallmoc shrugged. The sorcerer had accepted the deviation. He ordered a change of course which took him in a wide curving arc towards another distant hill. Although he did not realise it, Mallmoc was now heading in the general direction of Hampshire. The star patterns, warped by the shimmering forms of the spirits of earth and stone, drew the sorcerer off in the wrong direction.

All night long the great ironclad's prow, incongruously matched with a castle's turrets and towers, carved a ditch directly south. The ulcugga followed obediently, confident in their master's navigational skills. At a greater and safer distance the companions also trailed behind, wondering what would happen once the morning came, and Mallmoc stopped to take stock with the rising sun.

PART TWO

A Traitor in the Camp

ONE

Indeed, when morning duly arrived, Mallmoc was furious. He stared at the direction in which the sun was rising and shook his head in disbelief. Sending for Prince Rincortle, the leader of the ulcugga, he consulted the formidable fairy on the state of things.

'I'm certain I followed the right star path last night, yet here we seem to have ended up a good way off our course. I really don't understand what's happened.'

Rincortle narrowed his fairy eyes. 'Could it be,' he said, his hand on the hilt of his sword, 'that there's a rival sorcerer? Perhaps that boggart Spiggot has found another wizard who's using his magic to thwart your intentions?'

Mallmoc's eyes opened wide. 'Of course. That must be it. But who? Who hates me enough to assist my enemies? Merlin hasn't stirred from his ice caves for over a thousand years. Once King Arthur had died he said he had no use for the world. Gandalf? I thought he'd left for other, more celestial regions. It could be Craggenfen, of course, that charlatan from the Orkneys. I once imprisoned him in a peat hag for a hundred years. It's possible he may be nursing a certain resentment. Yes, yes, Craggenfen. It must be.'

'If he's a charlatan,' said Rincortle, 'then surely his magic must be false and he wouldn't have the power?'

'Oh, that's just my way of insulting him. His magic's quite strong. Just not as good as mine.'

Rincortle knew that wizards enjoyed flattery and was not slow in giving it. 'But then no one's as clever as you, sire.'

'True. True.' Mallmoc stroked his wizened face with his scrawny hands. 'Now what're we going to do about Craggenfen?'

'Shall I send our bogles out on their owls and night-jars, to seek for signs of the Orkney sorcerer?'

'Will the bogles return? We're holding them against their will, after all.'

'No,' agreed Rincortle. 'Probably not.'

'Then we'll have to use familiars. Bring me a cage of rats from the dungeons. Three dozen should be enough. I'll instruct them and we'll send them out once the darkness falls. We'll soon locate this meddlesome wizard. Once I know where he is he'll wish he never interfered. In the meantime we'll rest here and stoke up the furnaces.'

'As always, sire, you have things under control.'

Rincortle went off to do his master's bidding, while Mallmoc took down a book from his library shelf and pored over it. It was entitled *Spells to Avenge a Wrongdoing, where the Wrongdoer be a Fellow Sorcerer.*

❖

The companions were all standing on the crest of a hill, using the spyglass in turn to study the bridge of the ship-castle. They were gratified to see that the vessel had come to a halt and did not seem in a hurry to start again. Any delay was in their favour, allowing the bogles to get the messages to the allied fairy clans, and the clans themselves to march.

'What's he doing now?' asked Jack of Spiggot, who had the glass to his eye.

'Just standing, staring, looking out over the . . . oh, I forgot about those. Hide, quickly!'

Everyone scattered to some boulders, where they found themselves hiding places. A few moments later, two ulcugga knights glided over the hill riding on purple dragons. The shadows of giant, stretched wings topped by those of their dragon-riders, swept across the ground. Then they were gone, over the downs, out towards a distant river.

The companions emerged again.

'That was a close shave,' said Spiggot, who had never shaved in his life, since boggarts did not grow hair on their chins. 'Wasn't it, Jack?'

'Let me have use of the glass now,' said Solomon. 'I have not yet employed the instrument.'

Spiggot gave the spyglass to the monk, who did as he had seen done, and put the small end of the tube to his eye. He immediately jerked it away and stared at it in horror.

''Tis the work of the Devil!' he cried in alarm. ''Tis an instrument for the transmogrification of monsters!'

'No, no,' Jack explained. 'It's simply a set of spaced lenses in a tube. Let me explain. If you take a disk of convex glass, and look through it, objects will seem larger. They're not really, of course. It's an illusion. Here, see? Spiggot used two crystals for lenses and made a telescope. Well, it's not exactly a telescope because it doesn't expand and retract, but that's what we call it in the modern era. A spyglass to the likes of you.'

Rosamund snatched the glass and put it to her eye. She was much more worldly, much more flexible than the monk. She shrugged.

'Bigger,' she said, simply. 'It makes things nearer and bigger.'

'*Seem* nearer and bigger,' Jack said, rather pedantically. 'They're not actually.'

Solomon tentatively put the glass back to his eye. He remained motionless as he fought to control his baser instincts. What his soul screamed out for him to do was fling the Devil's device as far away from himself as possible. His conscience cried out in fear. Surely the use of such engines was a mortal sin? But another feeling took over. That of curiosity, which is stronger than most others, and often wins. Gradually he became interested rather than frightened by what he saw. Then suddenly he focused on the figure on the bridge of the castle-ship. Mallmoc. He let out a cry of recognition.

'Mal du Morc of Aquitaine!' he yelled.

'Quiet,' shushed Spiggot, 'there may be dragon-riders around.'

Solomon was excited. 'But my Lady Rosamund, 'tis Mal du Morc. The royal magician from the court of the Queen of Aquitaine. I saw him once when his monarch journeyed to the court of our most gracious king. Thy father, the baron, was his appointed guardian for the period of his visit. He is from our time, my lady, and no doubt has the secret of passage. Mal du Morc could assist us in returning us to your father. We could escape this faerie hell and be home.'

'Hast thou forgot my father will burn thee at the stake?'

'Not again, surely?' said Solomon. 'Once he sees that it didn't work the first time, he'll surely let me live.'

'He'll accuse thee of witchcraft and have thee drowned on the ducking stool.'

Solomon thought for a moment, then said, 'I'm willing to take the risk, my lady, if it means I'll win thy hand.'

Rosamund recoiled as if Solomon had suddenly changed into a lizard.

'*My* hand? I think not, sir. My hand is spoken for.' She looked shyly in Jack's direction. 'Another, I think, desires and deserves it.'

Jack was startled. He decided he would never understand women. For the past week or so, Rosamund's attention had been solely on the monk, as if she preferred his company to that of any other. When Jack had tried to speak with her, she had all but snubbed him. Yet here she was, telling his rival that the medieval youth didn't stand a chance. Her heart belonged to Jack. It was all very mystifying, but also quite gratifying. Jack was in with a chance. More than a chance. Rosamund had made her choice. He smiled at her and she smiled back, turning bright pink.

Solomon glowered, first at Jack, then at Rosamund.

'We'll see what thy father has to say about *that*,' he said.

Spiggot stepped in here. 'Solomon,' he said, 'I don't

think you realise what an evil man Mallmoc is. He won't help you. He'd rather shrivel your heart to a walnut kernel and watch you die in agony, writhing on the ground at his feet. I understand that you miss your homeland. I'd miss Liöfwende, if I were locked in Mortaland. But Mallmoc isn't the one to ask, believe me. Once all this is over, I'll ask the King of the Northumberland fairies to find someone to send you back. How's that?'

Jack did not like the crafty expression on Solomon's face, when he answered Spiggot with, 'Oh, as to that, yes – I think that'd be a good solution, boggart. I thank thee.'

'Think nothing of it,' replied Spiggot.

Later, Jack, in an aside to Spiggot, asked, 'Do you think we can trust the monk?'

'Why, Jack, he's a man of religion. His word is sacred.'

'There're good men of religion, the vast majority of them, but there are also a few rotten apples, Spiggot.'

'Oh, Solomon isn't rotten, Jack. You can see it in his face. He's angelic. Look at his wonderful halo of hair. No one with such a halo could be mistrusted, could they? You must still be feeling jealous of him. For shame, Jack. For shame.'

So Jack left it at that. It was no good arguing with the boggart when he had an idea in his head. They all spent the rest of the day in idle contemplation, occasionally looking through the spyglass at Mallmoc's castle, but even that palled once it was certain there was to be no activity. Jack and Rosamund played five-stones, that being the only pastime available to them. Kling went rooting around in a nearby wood for truffles. Solomon spent the time brooding, staring moodily at the skyline. Spiggot sewed up a hole in his jacket, using a thorn as a needle and spider's thread for the cotton. He admitted to himself when inspecting his work afterwards, that his mother Quagmarish would have made a neater job of it.

Evening came around at last and Mallmoc's castle-ship began to move again.

The companions, or most of them, were happy to see that the sorcerer had learned nothing during the day. The whirligigs were out, raising the spirits from the Earth beneath, and the roof of the world was once more twisted by their invisible shapes into presenting a false picture. Mallmoc, who had spent all day spelling the wizard Craggenfen, felt confident he had destroyed his enemy from a distance and that now his navigation skills would have returned to him. He charted a course from the star paths and fully expected that the following morning would see him well on his way towards Sutton Hoo, that ancient and enchanted burial ground.

TWO

'Jack,' said Rosamund, holding her nose, 'thou art becoming much like a sewer in thy fragrance.'

Jack was taken aback. He knew he was not entirely wholesome: none of them was. You couldn't be out in the field, on the march, and not pick up a bit of dirt. That was inevitable. But for Rosy to accuse him of stinking! Why, it was true she washed more than most, but still she was not without her smudges and smuts. Jack sniffed his armpit. Well, it was a *bit* high. But that was because they had been trudging all day long under the hot sun. A man was entitled to sweat a bit.

'All right, Rosy,' he said. 'I'll go and clean up.'

Jack followed a path in the moonlight down to a pool which was filled by a clear stream. The water was sparkling and clean, much like all the rivers, streams and lakes in Liöfwende. Kneeling down at the edge, he stared into the water. He remained wary. You couldn't trust pools in Faerieland, even if they did look innocent. Not so long ago he had been changed into a fish by a creature which lurked in such a place. He studied the willows, dipping their green fingers into the water. Yellow flags decorated the far bank. It looked peaceful enough. Then he stared down into the water and got a shock. There, looking up at him, was a monstrous face framed by long, wild, lank, unkempt hair. The face was covered in a wispy beard. The teeth in the creature's mouth appeared yellow and unsavoury.

'Uggghh!' cried Jack, revolted. 'Is that me?'

It was indeed the reflection of his own face. The strong moonlight clearly picked out his unruly state. He looked at his fingernails. They were long and dirty. Now Jack, in his former life in the real world, had been quite fussy about his appearance. An engineer needs to be, since he is always messing around with oil and grease. Yet, here he was, looking like something out of the rag bag. A tramp. A hobo. He felt as if he should have a card around his neck, reading 'Unclean'.

'Got to do something about that,' he muttered, appalled. 'No wonder Rosy turned up her nose. I look ghastly.'

He went back to the camp and sought out Kling. The rat was resting in the roots of a blasted oak. Jack roused him.

'Kling,' he whispered. 'I need your help.'

'Well, just ask,' grumbled the giant rodent, sarcastically, 'Kling is on call night and day.'

Nevertheless he followed Jack out of the camp until they were far enough away to talk in normal voices.

'You carry scissors in that cart?' asked Jack.

'Of course,' replied the rat, 'I have to cut my claws occasionally, otherwise they get too long and sharp.'

'Good. Can you get 'em? I want to trim my nails and I want you to give me a haircut.'

'Oh, really?'

'Come on, Kling. Look at me. I'm a mess.'

Kling studied him. 'Not a pretty sight, Kling has to admit. First off, go and bathe, thoroughly. Here,' the rat went to a plant and took some leaves. 'This is soapwort. Use it to scrub yourself. Then Kling suggests you get a birch twig, mash the end, and use it to brush your teeth. It works, look at mine.' He flashed Jack some gleaming white fangs. 'I'll go and get the scissors and meet you on the edge of the pond.'

They parted, Jack going back to the pool again. He stripped off and dived naked into the water. The shock of the coldness took his breath away for a moment, but he soon got used to it. There was an anxious moment when he thought of giant pike, but he soon dismissed this from his mind. This was no time to be cowardly. Jack swam to the bank, took the soapwort leaves, and scrubbed himself thoroughly all over. By the time Kling arrived he was as clean and shining as his grandmother's front stoop.

Jack left the water, dried himself on his shirt, then put on his slacks and sat on an old stump. 'Number four, please.'

'Eh?' muttered Kling. 'You'll get a pudding basin cut, and like it.'

Kling combed Jack's hair down around his face and the back of his head, cut about six inches off the bottom. He trimmed Jack's fringe at the front. By the time he was finished Jack looked like a page boy from the court of a king. Next, Kling went to work on his fingernails and toenails. Once Jack's ablutions had been taken care of, there were still more matters of personal hygiene. Socks and shirt, underclothes, all were washed with the soapwort leaves. Kling then used strips of bark to patch Jack's old old worn shoes and polished them with grass.

By the time Jack was ready to walk back to camp, he felt brand new.

'That's better. Thanks, Kling.'

'Don't mention it. Or if you do, follow it up with a chocolate bar.'

'The very first one I get will be yours.'

At that moment, something stirred in the grasses. Jack was conscious of two red eyes, peering wickedly from the ground. Then they were gone. A chill went through him. They were the eyes of an evil fiend.

'What was that?' whispered Jack. 'Did you see it?'

'No, but Kling smelt it,' muttered Kling. 'Kling knows his own kind. That was a rat. A *common* rat, if Kling isn't mistaken.'

'Is that unusual, for hereabouts?'

Kling said, 'It was a rat – yet not a rat, if you get my meaning.'

'No, frankly, I don't. Is there some other rodent here that resembles a rat, yet isn't? I know *you're* not really a giant rat. Water rat's just the nickname people use, isn't it? You're a water *vole*, really.'

'Correct, Jack. But what Kling is talking about, is *familiars*. That rat was a demon in disguise. There're more of them about. Kling can smell them. They're seeking something.'

'Us, perhaps?'

'Perhaps. Yet — no. This is most unusual. The odour . . . let's go back to camp, Jack, and wake the master's son.'

Spiggot was duly roused. He sat up and rubbed his bleary eyes. Rosamund woke too, though Solomon remained fast asleep, snoring loudly.

'What's to do?' asked Spiggot. 'Are we under attack?'

'Perhaps,' replied Kling, and he explained about the rats.

'It could be that they are Mallmoc's familiars? He must have sent them out to spy on us.'

'On us,' repeated Jack, 'or *someone*. Perhaps he doesn't know who or what he's looking for? What are we going to do about them? The rats, I mean. We can't hunt them in the night. We'd never find them.'

Rosamund said, 'We need rat hunters to help us.'

Jack looked at her admiringly. 'What a good idea, Rosy. You mean, like the ratters they used to use in the nineteenth century? Terriers.'

Spiggot came in here. 'Not dogs — but natural killers of rats,' he explained. 'Foxes or badgers . . .'

'Or wolves,' added Kling.

'Wolves!' agreed Spiggot, emphatically.

'How do we get wolves?' asked Jack. 'Even supposing there are some out there.'

'Oh, they're out there all right,' the boggart confirmed. 'We howl them in, Jack. We call them from the timberlands and with the hunting howl of the wolf. It's easy. It goes like this . . .' and Spiggot lifted his face to the moon, his lips went into the shape of an 'o', and he let out a most spine-chilling howl that carried over the woodlands. He let go another couple in the same vein.

'There, Jack. Do you think you could get the hang of it?'

Rosamund immediately threw her head back and bared her teeth, mimicking Spiggot's cry exactly. Jack, not to be outdone by a girl, also had a go, but he lacked the depth and mellowness of tone. However, he persisted. Rosamund was well into it by now. Spiggot continued with his mooning notes. Jack fell in behind them, the howling from his throat becoming more authentic by the minute.

Solomon woke, startled. His eyes were round with fear. There were wolves all around him, baying for blood. He leapt to his feet and ran, crashing through the bushes, into the night. Rosamund and Jack called after him, but their shouts were drowned by the answering howls from the hills around the camp. The real wolves had heard. They left their lairs and ran helter-skelter in the gorse and bracken, seeking the rats the howls had told them were there for the taking.

Solomon found himself surrounded by foul creatures of the darkness. He witnessed grey-cowled wolves devouring red-eyed rats, breaking their backs and crunching on their muscled flesh and brittle bones. The screams of the rats were like human screams, shrill and penetrating. He believed he himself was being hunted. Fear was caught in his throat like a live bird. Running full pelt into the darkness, his habit catching on thorns and prickles, he was soon lost to his companions. He finally fell, sobbing, in a natural ditch, where he cowered for the rest of the night.

In the morning, Kling announced that the rats were gone.

'Can't smell tail or hair of one,' he said, satisfied. 'They've all become wolf suppers, Kling is certain.'

'But where's Solomon?' asked Rosamund. 'Where's the monk?'

'He'll find his way back, Rosy,' assured Jack. He hadn't liked the monk, but he wished him no real harm. 'He can't have gone far.'

But the morning passed and Solomon was nowhere to be found. They went out and called his name, as loudly as they dared, bearing in mind that the outriders of the ulcugga were about. Pixies answered from rabbit holes, mocking them. 'Down here! Down here!' Elves called, 'No, no, over here, in the wild flowers,' from the safety of daffodil patches. But Solomon himself never appeared again. They could only hope he had survived the night and had found something to eat.

All was not well in the sorcerer's castle.

'Again!' cried Mallmoc. 'Why have we left our course again? We've gone miles out of our way. Our destination's as far from us as it ever was.'

Prince Rincortle entered Mallmoc's chambers and threw a small flour sack on the desk of spells.

'What's that?' asked Mallmoc.

'The remains of the wizard Craggenfen,' replied his fairy general. 'You wanted him destroyed?'

Mallmoc picked up the small bag. It was very light. 'In here?'

'Just ashes and dust. There's not much left of a wizard once he is exposed to a blast from your magic. Some of him blew away on the wind. We brought this back, just to show you he is no more.'

'Then who,' raved Mallmoc, clenching his claw-like hands, 'is thwarting our passage to Sutton Hoo?'

'Who would benefit, sire, but the brown boggart?'

'Ha! True. True. It must be they. But how are they managing it? They have no real magic to speak of. Have they help from someone powerful? I can't think it.'

'Puck is giving them assistance.'

'But Puck isn't Oberon, nor anyone like. Puck has certain skills, certain talents, but they don't include high magic. I don't understand how they're doing it. My own navigational efforts . . .'

'Are faultless, sire, I am certain.'

'Yet still we deviate.'

The sorcerer went quiet for a while as he contemplated his problems. When he spoke, it was to voice them. 'We've been delayed. This isn't drastic in itself, but it gives the fairy clans time to rally. What if we were overtaken and attacked? Surely the ulcugga will defeat all who come against them? The ulcugga are fairy warriors through and through. The situation then, isn't disastrous. Yet, we need to discover the whereabouts of our enemies. They need to be put down, like sick animals.'

At that moment, there was a commotion outside the chamber. Rincortle went out to see what it was all about. He returned a moment later, smiling. He had a creature by the hood and was hauling him inside. It was a monk. A noviciate monk. It was Solomon.

'We have one of them here,' said Rincortle, 'and will soon know the answers to our questions.'

Solomon wrenched himself away from the fairy general's grasp. He dusted himself down and said, indignantly, 'I came of my own accord. I wasn't captured. I brought myself here.'

'Is this true?' asked Mallmoc of Rincortle. It was always better to have a willing informant, rather than drag the information out with torture. 'Did he find us — or we him?'

'The mortal hailed one of our dragonriders,' conceded Rincortle.

Mallmoc turned and gave Solomon a greasy smile. Then his expression changed slightly. 'Do I know you?' he asked. 'Have we met in another life, perhaps?'

'Yes, sire,' explained Solomon, eagerly. 'I saw you at the castle of Baron Guillaume de Arundel, on the occasion of his third marriage to the Lady Faulette, when his second wife met the same fate as the first, and he was widowed yet again.'

Mallmoc stroked his chin. 'Yessss. I remember you. Weren't you the tutor to his daughter? I never saw her, but I recall him pointing you out to me at the banquet. I think he mentioned he was going to have your head taken from your shoulders for daring to aspire to marriage with the maiden. Is that what happened? Is that how you came here?'

'I was burned at the stake,' replied Solomon, mournfully. 'That's how I came here.'

'You shouldn't go chasing after young maids, should you?' said the sorcerer, smirking. 'Especially the daughter of Arundel. Didn't you know the baron is a wild beast on two legs? He would sooner squash a man's head like a coconut than give him wayfarer's cake and ale. And the maid wasn't in your league, friar. I'm told she's quite beautiful.'

'But she's *here*,' spluttered the monk. 'And I found favour with her. She did look on me,' his expression changed and he balled his fist, 'for a while. Now she minces and curtsies before that oaf Jack-o'-lantern. Would that I broke his nose for him, before departing his company.'

'Fie! A friar talking violence. But, you say she's *here*?' Rincortle's brow furrowed. 'The maid we captured. The one you had here in your hands. *She* is the daughter of Arundel.'

'I came to ask if you would send us both back to our own time. Can you do that, sir? I would give you certain informations for that favour.'

Mallmoc's eyes glittered. 'She is here! I should've seen the resemblance! Yet, she looks nothing like her father. She must take all her looks from her mother, a Scottish princess from the Isle of Skye. Well, well. It would be fortunate indeed to get Arundel's daughter in my dungeon. So we'll get her again. We might need allies when the walls come down between Faerieland and Mortaland.'

'And I shall help you capture the rebels,' Solomon said. 'I'm now the agent of Mal du Morc.'

Rincortle sneered. 'You change sides quickly, mortal. Treachery must run in your blood.'

'I only betray those who betray me,' snarled the monk. 'I've been wronged and seek revenge for those wrongs.'

'Can you lead us to my enemies?'

Solomon looked crestfallen. 'Alas, sire, I know not where I am in relation to them. I simply followed the boggart where he led. If I could take you to them, I would.'

'Methinks you are somewhat of a fool.'

'I am only a monk, sire, new to this world of faerie. I know not the paths and hidden ways. Everywhere looks the same to a mortal such as I. Simply hills, valleys and flatlands. I am lost in Liöfwende.'

'Well, well. We'll see what use we can make of you, friar,' Mallmoc said, granting that the pathetic youth did not know one end of the valley from the other. 'If you prove a worthy aide, I may let you live. I may even grant your request to be returned to Arundel's castle. Otherwise you'll fuel my furnaces with your teeth and bones. In the meantime, you can copy some spells I've scribbled down on scrap paper into my Great Book. I take it you're good at illuminated letters? Some illustrations in the margin would be nice too. A few green dragons and yellow demons spitting brimstone. One or two horrors of hell, perhaps, along with a friar burning like a tallow candle? Off you go then. And while you're working you can hatch a scheme for catching those pests who continue to irritate me.'

Solomon opened his mouth to tell Mallmoc the reason why his craft had gone off course. But then he closed it again, saying nothing. It was his only trump card and he did not want to reveal it too early. Better to wait, he thought, until the right time came to flick it out.

'Now why haven't those rats returned,' growled Mallmoc, looking out of a porthole. 'Where are they?'

'Ah, now,' said Solomon, 'I can help my lord with that.'

'Sutton Hoo,' explained Jack to Rosamund, 'is in Suffolk. You know — I told you there's a boat burial there, of some king or other.'

'Raedwald,' muttered Spiggot. 'Anglo-Saxon.'

'Yes, I think you're right, Spiggot. I remember the name. There are lots of other burial mounds there too. Raedwald was from quite early on . . .'

'Seventh century Mortaland,' Spiggot said.

'That's about right,' continued Jack. 'Those others were from time before and time after this Raedwald. There's a visitor's centre there now and they have some treasures from Raedwald's mob. His nobles.'

'They're called thanes,' added Spiggot.

Jack asked, 'Who are?'

'Raedwald's mob. His nobles.'

'Oh, well there you are then, Rosy. The jewelled buckles and torcs of thanes. And by *now*, I mean, the twenty-first century. That's where I come from. It's got all sorts of things you haven't got in your time, Rosy – like cars, mobile phones, computers, TV, DVD – masses of stuff. You won't know what I'm talking about. But people are much the same, at any time, aren't they? I mean, look at you and me, we get on like a house on fire.'

Rosamund blinked. 'Which house is on fire?'

'No, that's just a saying . . .'

'Do you mind stopping your chatter now, Jack?' asked Spiggot. 'We've got to get our heads together again. You know those whirligigs won't fool Mallmoc for much longer. He'll discover how we're warping the map of the heavens soon. We need some new plans.'

'All right,' replied Jack, 'no need to get peeved. I'll sit and think for a bit. As an engineer – or at least *student* engineer, I ought to come up with something.'

'I was thinking more of Rosamund. She's been through sieges and things like that, haven't you Rosamund? You know about engines of war. Giant catapults and battering rams? What happened when your father's castle was last besieged? How did they get in? Or how did you keep the enemy out?'

'We were never under siege for long. My father would ride out with a great horde of savage knights and slaughter the foe. He is a big man, broad and tall, fearless and ruthless. He and his knights would drink all night long, then mount their steeds, lift the drawbridge and with curses most foul and not fit for a maiden's ears they would charge those who would lay siege to us, hack them down with battleaxes, spill their brains with maces, chop their livers with broadswords . . .'

'I think we get the picture,' murmured Jack.

Rosamund continued. 'There have been many heads on spikes, decorating the gates to our castle. Some of them belonged to foreign kings. I never saw what happened to the arms, legs and torsos, but we had large bonfires to keep us warm in the winter.'

'So,' said Spiggot, his eyes beginning to glaze over, 'your father always broke the siege early.'

'Always. Yet he was successful with his own wars. Oft he would lay siege to a neighbour, just for the merriment. He and his knights captured many a rival baron that way, razed his castle to the ground, and stole his lands. Would you like me to tell thee how he triumphed?'

'If you like,' Spiggot said, thinking they were going to get more gory details.

'Why, then my father would first attempt a direct assault on the castle, battering at the doors and scaling the walls. If that failed he would fill the moat with rubble, then build an earth ramp to the battlements. His soldiers would charge up the ramp and enter the castle that way. Once, I remember, his enemy was as clever as he. This neighbouring baron fashioned a hole in his own castle wall, right where the ramp was rising, on the inside. When the stones had been removed he ordered his men to tunnel inside the ramp until it collapsed, thus thwarting my father's schemes. But my father soon put a stop to that, by filling baskets with bricks and using them as a base for the ramp. These were packed inside and could not be removed.'

Rosamund finished her explanation. Clearly her father was a monster of a man, yet she was proud of his achievements. Jack found this hard to understand. He could only think that people in medieval times had a different way of looking at these things. For all the emotion Rosamund displayed she could have been describing a cricket match rather than an attack on a castle in which many men must have died. However, something she had said had sparked an idea in him and he blurted it out immediately.

'A bear trap!' he cried, triumphantly.

THREE

Spiggot said, 'What's that, Jack? What kind of trap?'
'They're pits with sharpened wooden stakes at the
bottom, to kill the wild animal when it falls inside. Of
course . . .' He was about to say the stakes would not be
needed but the principle was what he was advocating,
when he saw Spiggot purse his lips in horror.

The boggart cried, 'For shame, Jack! Why would you
want to kill a poor innocent bear? And in such sneaky
way? I'm sorry, I thought better of you, Jack. A murderer of dumb creatures! For shame.'

Kling said, mildly, 'Who are you calling "dumb"?'

'No, you misunderstand me,' Jack explained. 'Rosy
here was talking about tunnelling. It made me think of
bear traps – well, they just call them that, we don't *do* it
any longer. What I mean is at one time hunters used to
trap wild animals in pits, by digging the hole and cover-
ing it with branches and grass. The unsuspecting beast

would crash through the cover and impale itself on the wooden spikes. We could do the same with Mallmoc's castle-ship. Dig a pit, disguise the opening, and — there you go!'

Spiggot's eyes opened wide. 'I see what you mean now, Jack. So long as you don't kill bears any more . . .'

'I never did,' replied an exasperated Jack, 'I'm just using it to illustrate my plan.'

'Good. So, let us think this scheme through.'

The water rat came into the conversation again.

'Kling can improve on that. No need to dig a pit. Why not burrow under a field, make it hollow beneath the turf. What better way to disguise the trap? You could use gnomes. They're good miners. They're always digging for things under the ground. Get some gnomes, is my advice, and carve out a nice big hole underneath an innocent-looking meadow.'

The other three looked at each other and nodded.

'This might work,' said Spiggot, excitedly. 'We could stop Mallmoc in his tracks, couldn't we? Gnomes. We need to call on some gnomes.'

'Are there any to be found in this province?' asked Rosamund.

Spiggot said, 'There're gnomes *everywhere*.'

'Especially in gardens,' Jack joked.

That day they spent walking the downs and listening for the *chink chink* of a pickaxe or shovel beneath the ground. It was an area of chalk and flint and Spiggot felt sure they would find some gnomes mining for flints. These they would fashion into prehistoric-looking tools — axe heads, scrapers, knives — and then enter Mortaland at night to scatter them in archaeological digs. The flint tools they made were beautiful artefacts, worthy of an artist in stone. It gave the gnomes great pleasure when they thought of humans finding these objects and attributing them to their own ancestors.

When Jack was told of this he shook his head in disbelief.

'Why would gnomes go to all that hard work, just so that mortals who found them would think they had been made by cavemen? What kind of mischief is that?'

'No, no, it's not mischief, Jack. Gnomes love to make things and nothing gives them greater pleasure than seeing their very own works displayed in glass cases, at which mortals peer and exclaim in wonder. It doesn't matter to a gnome that a piece of card says "Neolithic flint knife, probably used for skinning antelopes, found by Professor JJ Jubbly on Wickenstone Farm, Norfolk." The fact is, their work of art, their creation, is on display in a museum and is viewed as something marvellous. Of course they'd like to carve things in semi-precious minerals – they're the guardians of such earthly treasures, you know – but they're aware that your cavemen wouldn't find enough jasper, cornelian or agate to make all those tools, so they content themselves with working in flint.'

'And that makes gnomes feel good?'

'Of course, we all like our creations to be admired, Jack. If you go into any museum at night, which people never do, of course, you'll find dozens of gnomes looking with pride into the display cases. You must have seen their tiny handprints on the glass, when you've been yourself? The clay from their boots on the marble floors? You mortals are so unobservant sometimes. I wonder you get through life without accidents.'

'Well, actually we don't, but you can't blame us. I mean, who goes looking for the residue of gnomes in museums? How are we supposed to know the telltale traces of the lumpy little fellows? It's not something we think about – ever.'

This conversation had taken place while the companions were roaming the meadows. At noon they came to a rather gentle rise in the landscape. Here there were distinct sounds of metal hitting stone beneath their feet. Spiggot immediately cupped his horny hands around his mouth and hollered at the turf. The chinking noise stopped for a moment. Spiggot yelled again. A faint annoyed bellow asked what 'in all the minerals of the Earth, precious and semi-precious' Spiggot wanted. The boggart told the speaker who he was and that he wanted to talk to the gnome in charge of the mine. A short while later the metal horn of a pick thrust its way through the turf. A hole gradually appeared. Finally a disgruntled-looking elderly gnome emerged. He was a third of Jack's height.

FOUR

The fellow that stood before them was a keg-chested individual with a beard down to his shoes. On his head he wore a tall, pointed, yellow cap and on his large feet were long, pointed, yellow shoes, both of which were filthy with dirt. His shoulders were muscled beneath a thick green doublet, but below his waist his legs were as thin as twigs. All his strength seemed to be in his upper body. Huge hands added to the strangeness of his figure. Yet you would never dare to laugh at such a creature. There was a fierceness of eye, a brow that spoke of hard-headedness, which made you pause to think before you might say anything untoward. Red-veined cheeks, behind the bulbous nose, quivered with indignation at being summoned from supervising his mining below the surface. Here was an angry gnome.

'What dost thou want?' cried the gnome. 'Speak, before I brain thee with my pick!'

Rosamund was delighted. Here was a talker of the old tongue. Her face shone and she clapped her hands.

Spiggot nevertheless took a step back and, keeping a wary eye on the implement in the gnome's hands, said, 'Bear with me, friend gnome. I seek your assistance in a matters so grave it concerns the fate of Liöfwende and all the other faerielands hereabouts.'

'Nice speech,' murmured Jack, approvingly.

'What care I of things that happen on top of the world,' growled the gnome. 'We gnomes live underground and have no truck with surface matters.'

'Unfortunately for you,' Jack said, 'when things happen up here, they affect you lot down below. There's a sorcerer over yonder—' Jack thought this word a nice touch, since it smacked of olde worlde speech— 'who would smash through the walls that separate Liöfwende from Mortaland. This same wizard also let the thrum out of Gilscipe. You know they eat oak roots?'

'Dost thou take me for an idiot, stripling? Of course I know what are the thrum. What is the name of this sorcerer? Is it Mallmoc?'

Spiggot said, 'The very same.'

The gnome stroked his beard as Spiggot told what would be required of the gnomes. The one in front of them, who gave his name as Jinty Mustardbath, did not interrupt Spiggot through the whole of his explanation.

When the boggart had finished, the gnome said, 'And art thou the faerie knight of whom the whole kingdom is speaking?'

'I am he,' Spiggot replied, puffing out his chest.

'Don't let his looks fool you,' interjected Kling, 'there's a good bit of knight under that boggart skin.'

'Quiet, rat,' snapped Jinty, 'I'm thinking. Who was it who ploughed a great trough over the land, destroying a great many of our mines? Was that Mallmoc?'

He was assured it was the sorcerer in question.

'In that settlement, we are with thee, boggart. Whether thou be knight or no, I cannot say, but those who cause collapse in the mines of the gnomes of Grudril, must be prevented from causing further destruction.' He whipped off his hat revealing a flaky hairless scalp, which he scratched with obvious satisfaction. 'Come, all of you, and follow me down.'

Jinty leapt through the hole. The others followed with more caution, not knowing what lay beneath. They need not have worried. At Jinty's shout a spiral wooden chute was put in place below. First Jack slid down it, shooting round its polished corners. Then came Spiggot and Rosamund, and finally Kling, who looked as nervous as Jack had ever seen him. Clearly the rodent was not used to slides of any kind. All four companions ended in a heap at the bottom, the experienced Jinty having leapt out of the way with alacrity once his feet touched the floor of the chamber.

When they had sorted themselves out and were standing on their feet, they all peered into the dimly lit recesses of the gnome flint mine. It was lit by glow-worms in jam jars, just as Jack expected it would be. In the gloomy atmosphere they could see several rows of gnomes similar to Jinty (but with shorter hats) making peculiar sinuous movements with their bodies and limbs. These were as co-ordinated and disciplined as any military group could organise. Jack watched, fascinated, as he realised what was going on. None of his companions had a clue.

'Is this some ritualistic dance?' asked Spiggot of his host. 'They look so intent.'

'*Tai chi*,' replied the gnome. 'Once work stops we always do warming down exercises.'

'Tie what?' asked the boggart, puzzled.

'We learned it from a mortal who fell beneath the rubber wheels of a chariot. He was very good. Very good indeed. Did thou knowest this *tai chi* is practised in the parks of many eastern mortals every morning that the sun rises? This mortal's father brought the art from his homeland, which is far from England, and taught it to his offspring. The son then went and stepped in front of a number twenty-seven omnibus, the destination of which he told us was East Ham. Finding himself in Liöfwende, the mortal thought to employ his time here usefully. Thus he taught us *tai chi*.'

'What does it do for you?' enquired the polite Spiggot, who was bemused by the exercises. 'Is it magic that comes out?'

Jinty shook his head. 'Not magic, but a fine relaxed frame of mind, a well-toned body, leading to a healthy lifestyle. Such is needed by miners, who toil from dawn to dusk, chipping away at the centre earth. They need to stretch their limbs and torso, gently working the neck and the rest of the spine, getting good rich oxygen into the blood. Thee should try it. It has really changed the lives of the gnomes who live down here. We would oft rise from our beds with aching limbs and buzzing heads. Now we are up with the moles, ready – nay – *eager* to start our work.'

'I don't know, it looks a bit sinister to me,' muttered Spiggot. 'Are you sure it's not for conjuring spotted snakes?'

'Such creatures have no need of *tai chi*, they being supple creatures with languid movements.'

'And what are you all chewing?'

'*Ginseng*. Now, we must discuss this fiend Mallmoc and his foul plans. A hollow field, thou sayest?' He stroked his long beard again. 'Methinks a *honeycombed* field might be better, for how are we to prevent the turf from collapsing on our heads, if not otherwise supported? If we honeycomb the field with tunnels and chambers, it will hold the turf, but not any heavy machine which crosses it. What sayest thou, boggart?'

Jack nodded at Spiggot. 'It makes good engineering sense,' Jack said.

'Honeycombed it is, then.'

Jinty added, 'We shall make it as a wormery and hie this Mallmoc hence to his doom, for once we have him trapped, we shall batter him with shovels and picks until he begs for mercy.'

'I think it best we just capture him,' Spiggot advised. 'Battering with shovels sounds a little too violent for gnomes.'

'Thou art right, friend mortal, but it is a great shame we are so gentle. Now, what dost thou say to a repast? Work cannot start until tomorrow and we must feast before then. Wilt thou all join us in a banquet?'

Jack was extremely hungry and he had an idea that the gnomes would not be as fussy as boggarts. Spiggot rarely had meat on the table. Occasionally he had allowed Jack to have rabbit, but only once had eaten it himself. Spiggot had professed to be very ill afterwards. In the main, boggarts ate only mushrooms, chestnuts, crab apples and other field fare. The words 'vegan' and 'vegetarian' were not used, but most boggarts, brownies and bogles ate only things that grew in the earth. Fairies, especially ulcugga, hunted deer in the snow and ate venison. When Jack had been in Xuagguaqac – Standing Stone City – he had eaten his fill of meat, but since on the march he had only had the occasional haunch of rabbit.

'Be happy to join you,' said Jack, quickly, before Spiggot could refuse. 'I'm sure Kling would like something to eat.'

'Kling would be delighted,' said the rodent, 'though I doubt we shall be served gourmet food here. Do you use spices? Probably not. Doubtless you have only herbs. Well then, no matter, when Kling lived in Mortaland we were so poor my mother used to give us water sandwiches to eat . . .'

Kling rambled on, as he often did, about food he would like to consume, food he had once digested and food he was about to tuck into. Rats only had one deity and that was the God of Food. It was, Jack supposed, because in Kling's normal environment, in the world of mortals, rats were often starving. They scratched and scraped around and fought over crumbs. Only here, in the kingdom of faerie, did rodents walk about with a full belly, boasting about cordon bleu cooking.

'And Rosy too. She looks a bit peely-wally, don't you think, Spiggot?'

'I'm famished,' growled Rosamund, needing no encouragement. 'Dost thou eat meat, Jinty? I would sell my grandmother into slavery for a game pie or a leg of smoked ham.'

'Of course we eat meat,' cried Jinty. 'Meat is our speciality. Ha, see how pale the boggart goes. He is a rare one, that Spiggot. If thou dost but mention red meat he goes green at the gills. Never mind, boggart, we shall find thee some dandelion stalks to chew on or some boiled beet with stinging nettle gravy. For myself I like cooked and tender flesh, to add red corpuscles to my blood. What say you, mortals?'

'Oh, we agree,' said Jack, eagerly. 'Don't we, Rosy?'

Rosy did.

So at seven o'clock in the evening (though who could tell in subterranean regions?) they gathered in the Great Earth Hall. It was a huge square, cut out of red clay, the walls decorated with ground ivy. Flaming torches hung in iron cages on the walls to give them light. There were large terracotta tureens on the wooden tables, with ladle handles poking between lid and rim. On platters (or trenchers, as Spiggot called them) were hunks of acorn-flour bread. Benches had been laid out for them to sit on, but quite honestly Jack was so hungry he would have sat in a box of nails.

The gnomes themselves were scrubbed clean and had rolled up the sleeves of their doublets in order not to let them dip in the gravy. Jack was amazed to see that their arms were covered in tattoos. It was not something he expected of faerie. They also had large hooped earrings in their lobes and one female gnome even had a nose stud. All the tattoos were of flowers and/or firearms. Jack shook his head in wonderment and said to Jinty, who sat next to him, 'What's with the tattoos?'

'These?' Jinty glanced at his arm. 'I wish we'd never had them done, but a mortal fell down a rabbit hole one day and said they were art. Likewise with these.' He tugged on his single earring. 'He persuaded us to have them and once they were done we couldn't get them off.'

'He did? But why only flowers and firearms?'

'Guns 'n' Roses,' explained the gnome. 'It's something to do with music in Mortaland.'

Jack knew the heavy metal group, of course – and liked their music himself. These gnomes were a strange mixture of ancient and modern. Their speech was archaic, yet they seemed to embrace everything new that came their way. It was a refreshing change from traditional and conservative boggarts who disliked any change that did not go at snail's pace. Jack was loath to call Spiggot rigid in his views, but the accusation would not have been unjustified.

'Well, I never would have guessed it.' He rubbed his hands and nudged Rosamund. 'Here we go then – good red meat. What is it, Jinty? Let's have a look.'

'Grace first,' said Jinty, with a stern look.

The gnomes clasped their hands together and then said a prayer, thanking the Creator for all things that lived under the earth and requesting politely that he curse all things that lived on the surface. Then the lids came off the pots. Jack glanced eagerly into the one in front of him. He was a little disappointed. 'Spaghetti in tomato sauce?' he queried.

'Worms,' replied Jinty, in a satisfied voice. 'Roasted round worms. I told thee thou would be well fed down here, with good red meat. There are fried grey slugs, if the worms do not take thy fancy. Or crunchy snails. We even have crispy dragonflies, done in butter. For the side dishes there are coachman beetles in black sauce. Much has been said about our coachman beetles. Here, try some earwig casserole. Tuck in, mortal, tuck in.'

Jack glanced across at Spiggot, who gave him a smug grin.

'I've got walnut cake,' said the boggart, 'being a non-meat eater.'

The feast was not a good one for the mortals. They did not want to upset the gnomes by refusing the worms and grubs, yet their stomachs revolted each time they took a mouthful. Rosamund, Jack admitted, was better at holding it down than him. Jack had to keep excusing himself, saying he needed the toilet, in order to throw up in private. Somehow they got through the evening, but it was a long and unhappy one for the humans.

Kling, on the other paw, tucked in with great relish. No fastidiousness about slimy things and crawly things for him. He would have eaten them live and kicking, raw as nature in the wild, if that was how they had been dished up. Jack could not believe how gross his water rat friend was when it came to filling his belly. Earwig stew seemed to be his favourite and since the gnomes had ensured plenty of this local delicacy was available he could pig out to his heart's content. While Jack winced at every mouthful, Kling sent spoonful after spoonful of earwig sludge down his ratty throat.

Spiggot simply ate his cake, bread and vegetables, and smiled sweetly at Jack, nodding gravely whenever the mortal excused himself and left the hall for the pit in the loo chamber along the tunnels.

'Mealtimes will never be the same again,' Jack later confessed to Spiggot. 'In future I'm going veggie like you.'

Spiggot knew that Jack would not keep to this promise, but he sympathised with him and said he was sorry he did not warn him.

'You seemed so intent on getting your red meat – well, to the gnomes there's nothing so red as a roasted worm.'

'Don't remind me,' groaned Jack.

There was some comfort to be had. They slept that night on soft beds of newly-mown hay. The hay smelled wonderful and was a great inducement to sleep. Jack dreamed of past summers chasing butterflies by the village pond and helping with the harvest out on the farm. There is something about the scent of hay that brings a golden warmth into one's mind and helps to recall only good and happy days, while the long days of rain and boredom are tucked safely away somewhere at the back, out of reach.

Dreams. Of trout in clear streams, live oaks in full leaf, a long dusty lane and no urgency to reach the end, sticklebacks in jam jars, frog spawn, hacking thistles with a stick, a shy weasel slipping into a ditch, watching rabbits gambol out in the stubble, making bows and arrows in the wood, scrumping apples from Rankin's orchard, wandering down by the broad river to see the boats, a thousand thousand summers rolled into one day, and bed with soft white sheets as a perfect end to it all.

'Wake up, Jack, we are to work today.'

'What?' Jack opened his eyes to see Rosamund towering over him. He sat up. 'I don't feel like breakfast,' he said.

'Thou hast not been offered such. Thou hast slept through the breaking of the fast. 'Tis time to take a shovel and dig.'

Jack rose, drank from a barrel of water, and splashed some on his face, before joining the ranks of the shovel-bearers. Today (though who could tell underground) they were going to honeycomb a field into which they would lure the sorcerer's craft. Off they marched, down a tunnel which would lead them to the place where they were to begin digging. As they went along, the tunnel became smaller and lower. Jack, Spiggot and Rosamund had to stoop and bend, until they were actually crawling on their hands and knees, while the gnomes remained upright. It seemed to Jack that the gnomes shrank in height as they went into lower regions. He mentioned this to Spiggot, who of course had the answer.

'You're quite right, Jack – they are able to fold down into themselves, like a concertina.'

'How?'

'It's the worms they eat. You know, worms can make themselves long or short – they can squash down or stretch up. You are what you eat, they say, and gnomes have learned the trick from the worms they swallow.'

Thus the flattened gnomes were able to walk upright and chatter away to their fellow miners, though their voices underwent a strange change. They got deeper and more guttural as they wrinkled down into themselves. Finally, they were so flattened Jack could not understand a word they were saying. He and his companions were almost on their bellies now and the earwigs and ants were taking revenge on them for eating their friends and relations.

Happily, they eventually reached the appointed place and there the hard work began. The gnomes set up a chain of earth buckets, for dumping the soil removed from under the field. Some of this they threw into old mole and badger chambers, but for the most part it had to be ferried right back along the tunnel, taken to the surface, and spread over agricultural land farmed by goblins growing their produce for market. It was a long and laborious process, but the gnomes were used to it. They worked like – well, like gnomes – their muscled bodies entirely suited to manual labour. Spiggot, too, was not unused to hard physical work. Jack and Rosamund suffered. They had aching backs and arms before the morning was out and were finally put on field kitchen duties, which suited them better.

'Bake some cockchafer pasties,' ordered Jinty, 'and try to keep the shells crisp. Gnomes hate soft-shelled cockchafers. Oh, and thou wilt find some dragonfly larvae in the canvas buckets. Use them as a garnish.' He ended with, 'And no picking! It'll spoil thy lunch.'

'Definitely no picking,' said Jack through gritted teeth. 'You can be sure of that, Jinty.'

Thus the gnomes and the boggart toiled, while the two mortals were left with an earth oven to make the pasties. Kling was not with them. He maintained his claws were no good for holding a shovel, though he seemed to manage to grip his dinner trencher quite well. The water rat had stayed in bed. His snores had followed them down the dark tunnel. Jack had no doubt Kling would turn up at lunch time. This was indeed the case. The moment a metal ladle clinked against a metal pot, there was Kling, trencher in paw, ready to help with getting through the repast.

'Hmmm, pasties,' he said. And then to Spiggot, 'Oh, you've got a visitor, master's son. Someone from the old village.'

'My father?' asked Spiggot, going pale. 'Has he come to order me home?'

'No, not the master. The mistress.'

'My mother?' wailed Spiggot. 'What's she doing here?'

'Not her, neither, dimwit. It's your old sweetheart.' Kling went all coy. 'You know – *her*. She's come looking for her swain.'

And there, emerging from the tunnel, was a female boggart.

'Fen,' whispered Spiggot, clearly overcome. 'My little Fen.'

'I'm not your little anything, boggart,' said the new-comer. 'I'm nobody's fool now that Boskywod is a toadstool.'

Fen had been Spiggot's beloved, until he left the iron-smith village to become a faerie knight. But she had tired of waiting for him to return, as young females often do whose loved ones have gone to war. In fairness to Fen, Spiggot had never actually walked her through the dog daisies, so she was not sure how things stood when he left. In his absence, Boskywod-the-ratcatcher, Spiggot's best friend, had courted Fen. His persistence wore down her resistance and when he made her a fairy swing in the old oak, she allowed him to walk her through the dog daisies. After that, Spiggot was out of the frame, and Boskywod squarely in it. However, Spiggot's return to the village had churned up old feelings, and the outcome was that Boskywod had taken his own life, and become a toadstool.

'Well, what have you come for, then?' said Spiggot, clearly out of sorts. 'Just to taunt me?'

'Why should everything be about you?' cried the snubnosed female boggart, tilting her chubby little chin.

'I've come to help with getting rid of Mallmoc. The dreaded thrum are advancing in the south, killing all the oaks and elms and hornbeams. I saw it was time to do something.'

'Fine. You can do as you wish. You're free to do anything you want.'

'Yes, I am.'

'Fine.'

'Yes.'

Rosamund saw it was time to intervene, before either of the boggarts said something they would regret for ever. She took Fen aside and asked her to help with feeding the hungry gnomes, who had been watching this exchange with some impatience, their tummies rumbling. Fen gladly turned to Rosamund to assist, speaking brightly now of her journey to gnome country, telling Rosamund and Jack how she had found them.

'I met this goblin who said he had tried to sell a mortal a pair of grass shoes. He said this mortal tried to cheat him . . .'

'I never did,' gasped Jack.

'Yes, we all know what goblin pedlars are like, Jack, so I didn't believe him. But he put me on your trail. And from there I simply asked those I met in the woods and out in the fields – elves, pixies, brownies.'

Jack said, 'But if you found us that easily, why aren't the ulcugga on our tails?'

'Because the other faerie would not betray you, Jack. Mallmoc is feared by all. They can see what he is doing to Liöfwende. Faerie are usually quite selfish creatures, and only interested in what is happening in their own back yards, but the sorcerer's plans threaten us all.'

'Well, I hope you're right, Fen – but I wonder about traitors amongst the other faerie.'

'You're more likely to find traitors amongst mortals,' Fen added, significantly, 'for I've heard of one who's now with Mallmoc. His name is Solomon and he has a pate like a mushroom.'

Rosamund gave a little cry. 'Not Solomon? He wouldn't betray me.'

Jack said, 'I don't think it's you he believes he's betraying, Rosy. He's done this to get at me. He knows how I feel about you and he's jealous.' Generously, Jack added, 'I'd be the same in his shoes. I think he's daft, because he surely can't expect you to be happy with him, but us blokes in love don't think very straight, do we? Anyway, what can he do to us? I can't see what use he is to Mallmoc, except another mouth to feed.'

'He's a renegade priest, Jack. He can help with magic.'

'Oh, I think that's stretching it a bit, Rosy. He's just a lad with a grudge. No, I don't think you need to worry about old Solly. His temper's worse than his bite . . .'

'What have you for me, friar? Now that you've had time to study the books? Come, you turncoat monk, earn your keep.'

Mallmoc had the tonsured youth before him, in his chamber of magic, and Solomon seemed pleased with himself.

'Why, sire, I've fashioned a device for seeing others, though they be at a far distance from ourselves. See.'

He produced a copper plate, highly burnished, which seemed to have the properties of a mirror. Yet when one

looked into it and spoke the names of those one wished
to see, their images appeared. Solomon murmured the
names of his former companions – Jack, Spiggot,
Rosamund, Kling – and showed Mallmoc the smoky but
unmistakable figures of the four. Mallmoc stared into the
dish. It was not clear where his enemies were. The place
was dimly lit, that much was certain, possibly in a dark
forest? Yet no trees could be discerned in the gloom.
Then another creature came into view.

'This looks like a gnome,' he growled. 'Are they underground? What would they want amongst the gnomes?'

'Ha!' cried the monk. 'They're hiding from us. What
better place than dark secret chambers beneath the
earth? Yet they've reckoned without the genius of
Solomon! I'll keep them under observation, expose them
to our view, keep a watchful eye on their movements.'

Mallmoc frowned and paced the floor, his scrawny
hands clasped behind his back.

'You'll do more than that. It could be a simple case of
hiding themselves until their fairy allies arrive.
However, I don't trust that boggart. He's a deviant
thinker. Perhaps there's more to it than simply hiding
from the ulcugga? I can't send my fairies after them.
Guerrilla warfare under the earth is not to the liking of
the ulcugga. They're not urban fighters who can battle
in the unfamiliar confines of gnome tunnels and passageways. The gnomes would slaughter them, turning
pick and shovel tools into weapons, using their knowledge of their underground system to good advantage. I
know them of old. We must resort to guile. You must
seek the boggart out and discover if you're right, then
report back to me.'

Solomon went pale. 'I – how can I spy on them? They will know me for a traitor now. Please, sire, do not send me to my death.'

Mallmoc was unmoved. 'You will go,' he said.

PART THREE

Solomon's story

ONE

Solomon set forth not knowing where to go but also in the knowledge that he would be in deep trouble once he got there. Thus he wandered aimlessly and miserably through the woodland where the ulcugga had left him. It was clear he had to come upon some local faerie of whom he could ask the whereabouts of the gnomes. However, by noon he had come across no one. The world seemed empty except for squirrels and starlings. When he had been with Spiggot's group they had been forever pestered by goblins, elves and pixies, yet none of these creatures seemed to be about now. Leaving the woodland he found himself in a kind of wilderness, which even the birds had forsaken. At least in the woodland there had been wild creatures. Out here on the wastes, there was nothing.

'That Mal du Morc,' he grumbled, close to tears, 'might have given me a guide. How am I, a complete stranger to this world of nymphs and dryads, expected to know the paths?'

Suddenly Solomon stopped and whirled round. Staring back at where he had been, he could see nothing. Yet, at that moment he could have sworn that someone was dogging his footsteps.

'Nothing,' he murmured, staring over a landscape bare of anything living except some patches of reeds. Yet it was a dark brooding place, with a malevolent feel to it. The shadows of the boulders and ragged tree stumps seemed cold and hostile. He was resented in this place where the wilderness silence settled like fine dust around him. Menacing spirits of the ground chilled his soul with their invisible presence. 'Nothing stirs.'

He turned again, to walk on, yet was halted by the overwhelming feeling that someone was right behind him, on his heels.

'Ha!' He whirled round again, an accusation on his lips.

There was no one.

Yet, having turned, he felt the creature must have darted behind him.

He spent the next few minutes turning quickly, trying to catch his tormentor off guard. Though once or twice he could have sworn he saw the wispy corner of a black cloak, he could not fool the creature. It was very frustrating, enough to drive the monk mad. He yelled at his tormentor, his voice bouncing around the rocks, echoing in the wilderness. Still, no matter how quickly he turned, how swift and unpredictable were his actions, his pursuer remained out of sight. Finally, Solomon walked on, trying to ignore the fiend which remained at his heels. Every so often he listened hard, convinced he could hear the soft tread of creeping feet, or the shallow breath of the fiend somewhere down by his hip.

When twilight came the wilderness took on an even more sinister aspect. He came to a stagnant pool, surrounded by elders grey with blossom. Peering into this cluster of bent and twisted wood, he was convinced he could see an old woman's face, looking back out at him. Her eyes were as black as berries and her lacy shawl much like the heads of elderflowers. She seemed to be beaming at him, yet the complexion was so grey the smile was hideous rather than friendly. Once, he thought she reached out with a claw-like hand to clutch at his robe, but when he unhooked himself in panic, he found it was simply a leafless branch moved by the wind.

But he felt the hand of death had touched him.

He hurried on, past the ugly pond with its slimy surface, into a region of high, leafless trees. Here now was a charcoal-coloured forest, bleak as winter. Still his companion was with him, remaining faithfully at his heels, silently gleeful at the torment he was putting Solomon through. Finally, the monk was so fatigued he could go no further. He lay down, sobbing at the base of the brittle trunks and tried to sleep. A large moon came up from behind a bank of spindly saplings. It cast its mellow light down upon the unhappy monk, who even in the night could not escape the dreary landscape into which he had been sent by the sorcerer Mallmoc.

'I hate him now,' mouthed Solomon with seething fury. 'I turned myself to his use, forsaking my lady, and this is how he gives his thanks. To send me back to those I forsook, who will no doubt judge me for my crime of treachery and sentence me. I can expect no more.' His mouth set firm. 'But no longer shall I serve this Mal du Morc. When I shall find my companions again, I shall beg their forgiveness, and promise my loyalties will never more stray, though it be a fruitless gesture.'

These were the noble thoughts that went through Solomon's mind, unaware that his former master was watching him keenly in the same bronze device with which Solomon had provided him. One of Mallmoc's greatest skills was lip-reading and the wizard frowned at what he saw. The monk had been tested and found wanting. The sorcerer recalled the wendigo he had sent to follow the monk. Now that the youth was lost in the wilderness it would be only a matter of time before he died. Yet Mallmoc sought to hasten that death, his impatience impossible to ignore.

'We shall give him his reward,' muttered Mallmoc. 'His usefulness was but a limited commodity in any event.'

That night a huge and savage black dog was let loose on the moors.

When Solomon woke in the morning there was a ray of hope for him. Sleeping upright in the hollow trunk of an old dead tree was a giant. This great fellow wore the tree like an overcoat, his arms threaded through hollow boughs and his hands left dangling at the ends. His legs were somewhere inside the trunk, and his head lolled over the broken top. The giant was snoring gently, his chin resting on the dry bark.

'Excuse me?' said Solomon, though not in a loud voice. 'I wonder if thou couldst be of some assistance?'

The giant continued to snore softly.

'EXCUSE ME.'

The fellow woke with a start. A bird landed on his nose, then seeing it was alive, took off again.

'What? What is it?'

'I wonder if you would be so kind, sire, as to give me direction?'

The giant looked at him for a few moments. Then, first one arm slid out of its branchy sleeve and dropped to the floor. Then the other. The giant then slithered armless out of the trunk. Once standing on the ground he bent down, picked up one of his arms with his teeth and placed the limb back on his shoulder. He did the same with the second arm, but this time more expertly with the hand that was now in use. Intact again, he addressed the youth with the tonsure standing before him.

'Now,' he murmured, 'how can I help?'

'Firstly,' said Solomon, wishing to get on the giant's good side, 'can I be of assistance to *you*?' He pointed to the giant's gleaming boots. 'I was looking at your feet, the toes of which point backwards and outwards. Might I suggest you have your legs on the wrong way round, and possibly on the wrong sides of your torso?'

The giant looked down and laughed.

'Why, I do believe you're right, sir. I can't count the times I've done that this week. I thank you from the bottom of my heart, wherever it is at the moment. I had it on my person yesterday, so I know it's there somewhere. Had I tried to run I would have fallen and perhaps injured myself. So I owe you a debt, traveller, which in one moment I shall attempt to repay. My name is Hollow Ben.'

Hollow Ben then sat down, took off his legs, and put
them on the right way round and on the correct sides of
his body. He stood up again and tested the thick limbs by
walking up and down. The frayed trouser cuffs were
long enough to flap over the thick leather boots. When
he walked they rubbed on the caps, shining them
without effort on the part of the wearer. Eventually he
seemed satisfied, but he checked his fingers as well, just
to make sure he had not made the same mistake with the
upper end of his body.

'There – now, what can I do for *you*?'

'I wish to know which way to go. I'm looking for the
county of Nottinghamshire. It has a gentle landscape,
with a fine river called the Trent running through it, and
a very long straight road over its back. No wait,'
Solomon frowned, 'the road will not be present, this
being Faerieland. Yet Sherwood Forest should be visible,
even here, and a grand castle. You, sir, are several heads
higher than I am. Canst thou see to the next horizon and
give me some clue as to which way I must walk?'

'As to that,' said the giant, 'even from here I can only
see wilderness, but don't worry about that, we can go
even higher.'

He selected a long slender stave from amongst the tall
saplings growing near to the hollow tree. Next he took
off his head, for this giant could clearly dismember
himself with no harm to his person. He placed the head
on the stick, then lifted it as high as it would go. Once up
there, he turned the head this way and that, calling down
to Solomon with descriptions of distant horizons. Finally
a scene was relayed to the monk which he felt he recognised.

'I thank thee. Thou art a fine fellow,' he called up to the giant. 'Thou art a good neighbour to a wayfarer in distress.'

The giant lowered his stick, took his head off the end, and placed the object back on its home shoulders.

'Think nothing of it. But I must warn you. Trouble's on its way. I saw it in the east. A great black hound this way comes.'

'A dog? Is it after *me*?'

'There're no others on the trail and it has intent. I could see it in the cur's demeanour, in its determined run. It'll soon be upon you, wayfarer, and no doubt devouring your flesh.'

Solomon went pale. Was this retribution from his former friends or Mallmoc changing his mind? He could not think that his lady would sanction such a ghastly revenge. Somehow then, the sorcerer had found out that Solomon had again turned his coat. Was he now about to die? Here was the creature, loping over the hill! It was a monster of a hound, with teeth bared, lips curled back. Yes, it would tear him from limb to limb, once it fell upon him.

This last wild thought suddenly gave Solomon an idea. He looked around for a dead branch; seeing none he snatched the giant's arm. It easily came away from the fellow's broad shoulder.

'Hey?'

Solomon gave the arm to the giant, putting it into the hand still attached to his body.

'Please, sire – throw this for the dog, to distract it while I make my escape? My gratitude will be yours for ever.'

The giant frowned, but saw some sport in this activity. 'Why, let's try it then.'

Just as the black hound was bearing down on its victim the giant whirled the arm about his head and tossed it half a league. No dog worth its salt can resist a thrown object, be it stick, slipper or severed limb. Immediately, it abandoned its original goal and set off in pursuit of the hurled arm, yelping delightedly. Solomon shook the giant's remaining hand and hurried away, out towards the green pastures of which he had been informed. Looking back a while later, from a safe distance, Solomon saw the dog and the giant tussling for the arm.

The dog was growling in play, its teeth firmly gripping the fingers of the detached limb. The giant was roaring, tugging on the ball end of the arm, trying to wrest the limb from the hound's grasp. He pulled the dog back and forth, crying, 'Let go, you beast! Let go, and I'll throw it again, eh, sir? What, you would be stubborn with me? Why, I can heave you around like a limp rag, sir, and roll you on your back if I wish. There! How's that. The limb is mine. Here, boy, fetch!' And another great throw had the dog bounding over the moorland, running in the opposite direction to Solomon, whose gratitude to towards the friendly giant was bottomless.

Solomon made his escape over the moors, leaving the dog gambolling with Hollow Ben. He was extremely grateful to the giant, who had come to his aid just as the Good Samaritan had helped the poor beaten man he had found on the wayside. To assist a stranger in need is one of the most honourable of Christian duties, even if it places oneself in peril. Solomon had learned a lesson: one he would not forget until the day he died. Hurrying on, he reached a place of peat hags and deep ditches: a boggy stretch of ground set with standing stones. Here he rested for the night, finding a damp hollow on the mossy ground.

In the morning he set off again, hoping he was going in the right direction. It was with great relief that he came to some grasslands and listened in delight to the thridding of the insects. Here was life and energy! The wastelands were behind him and he need have no fear of loneliness and solitude. Hawks circled in the sky, mice whispered in the grasses, deer thudded the earth with small hooves. True, there was a wolf on the ridge ahead, but this seemed comforting rather than menacing.

The wolf merely glanced in Solomon's direction, then loped off down the other side of the rise. Solomon heaved a sigh of relief, not so much because of the beast, but more because the sun was shining and the world seemed a less threatening place. He reached into one of the many pockets which lined his habit and withdrew a large hunk of bread. This, along with other foodstuffs, had been on his person since he had left Mallmoc. In Solomon's time monks were forever hungry. They attended mealtimes of course, but it was sparse fare and growing young men like him had a lot of energy to replace. Thus, he was like his peers a hoarder. Whenever he could he filled his pockets with supplies. If they should go bad he simply threw them away or gave them to the dogs.

He sat down on the grass and was about to sink his teeth into the bread when a voice behind him asked, 'May I have a bite of that?'

Solomon turned his head, warily, to find a rider on horseback behind him. The rider was of course a faerie, having two small and rather useless-looking wings on his back. He wore a simple white shift and no hat on his head. He sat astride his steed with great confidence. There were no weapons in his hands, nor none that Solomon could see on the horse. This made the youth a little less apprehensive. Still, he remained on his guard, asking, 'Art thou in allegiance with the ulcugga fairy clan, friend?'

To his great astonishment, it was the horse that answered him, not the rider.

'I despise the ulcugga,' replied the horse, curling his lips away from his teeth. 'They are as dirt beneath my hooves.'

'I'm glad to hear that,' Solomon said, his eyes still flicking towards the rider, who indeed seemed rather less animated than the mount. 'I too am not enamoured of that particular group of fairies. Their master, the most horrible Mal du Morc, is intent on murdering me. Here, eat your fill of this bread, for I have some biscuits in another pocket.'

'I would rather have the biscuits.'

So would I, thought Solomon. Yet he reached in and gave some biscuits to the horse. Then he addressed the rider again.

'And thee, sire? Wouldst thou like something to eat?'

'Who are you talking to?' asked the horse, munching on the biscuits.

'Why, your master of course. The fellow on your back.'

The horse whinnied. 'No sense in that, monk. He

won't answer you. He doesn't speak. Sometimes he grunts, in a grouchy sort of way. Sometimes he laughs. On the odd occasion, he will get tearful. But he never talks. I often wonder if there's anything up top, if you know what I mean. Some of my friends reckon they're intelligent, but they are no steeds' masters. We're the masters of *them*, if you know what I mean. It's me who decides what's what.'

'Oh.' Solomon absorbed this with interest. He was, of course, not in the real world. He was in the pagan land of faerie. Things were different here. 'Art thou some strange kind of faerie?'

The horse pursed its lips. 'Strange? I wouldn't call it that. We're simply a kind you probably haven't met before now. Not many folk do meet us. We're a little bit shy and steer clear of society. I'm a horse-fairy. A palomino horse-fairy with, as you see, a white mane and tail, and a golden body. Yes, a genuine horse-fairy. In the same sort of category as a horse-chestnut. That is to say, inedible.'

'Canst thou eat proper fairies then?'

'No,' replied the horse-fairy. 'Why do you ask that?'

'Thee said thee were uneatable.'

'Which is true. My flesh tastes foul. *His* doesn't, but you'd be hard pushed to get me to agree to having him roasted.' The horse-fairy whinnied again and the rider laughed. 'You see, we're symbiotic. In fact, we're two parts of a whole. He isn't merely sitting on me. We're joined together, grafted so to speak, one and the same creature. That's why he never dismounts. He is *me* and I him. Different flesh, as I said, covered with a different skin, but essentially we are one being.'

'A centaur.'

The horse-fairy seemed affronted. 'Certainly not! Is not my rider situated in the *middle* where he should be, rather than at the head? Do I not have a head myself, as well as he? Does he not have legs and is without horns of any kind? Good grief, I'm nothing like a centaur. Spare me. I am, as you observe, a horse with a rider, the only difference being, we are one and the same and exist as a single entity, sealed together.'

Solomon said he was sorry for the mistake and begged pardon.

'Granted. Now, have you any more biscuits?'

'One or two. And a sugar lump.'

The horse-fairy's eyes lit up at the mention of sugar. Solomon gave the creature the titbits, then asked if it knew where to find gnomes burrowing in the earth. The horse-fairy crunched the sugar, saying that gnomes always burrowed in the earth, but if the monk meant those that mined for flints in the south, why he could carry the monk to that very place.

'It'll take a day to get there, but I don't mind walking with you.'

'I have very little food left,' Solomon warned, not wishing to cause offence later.

The horse-fairy looked disappointed, but shrugged its fine golden shoulders. 'Never mind, I'll show you anyway. Would you like to get on my back? I can take you where you wish to go. You say that the sorcerer – you call him Mal du Morc but I know him as Mallmoc – you say he wishes you dead?'

'Certainly. He sent the hound of hell after me, to tear me limb from limb. Now I must escape to my former friends, who were betrayed by me in a manner most foul. I am heartily ashamed for my sin of treachery. Wilt thou assist me in this endeavour?'

'Surely, as I said a moment ago, I'll carry you there.'

Solomon, who had never been on a normal horse, let alone a strange faerie creature, shook his head.

'No, though I thank thee for thy kind offer. I should fall from thy back in an instant. Let us walk together, side by side.'

The horse-fairy seemed angry. 'You do not ride horses?'

'I never have, no. Besides, thou hast one rider already. I think it best I stay down here. I should fall off, for certain. No, no, do not press me. If thou dost not wish to have me as a companion, by all means go on alone, but I would rather my feet remained in contact with the good earth.'

'All right,' replied the other reluctantly, 'we'll walk side-by-side. Now tell me, who baked the biscuits, and where? Was it your fellow monks in the monastery ovens? Ah, your eyes say *yes*. So, I suppose those ovens are not here, in Liöfwende? No. No, they wouldn't be, would they. They'll be back where you came from, which judging from your habit is somewhere in King John's time? Yes? I might see if I can make a visit. What's the name of the monastery? The Holy Retreat of St Bartholomew of Byzantium. It's not actually *in* Byzantium, is it? No, no, of course, you just take the name, adopt it so to speak. Fine, I think that's all I need to know.'

'If whither thou goest, wilt thou take me with thee?' asked Solomon, hopefully.

'I *might*. We'll see.'

As they walked, Solomon continually heard a fluttering sound, like that of a pigeon caught in a tree. Finally, he looked up at the rider, the source of this sound. This creature – or part-creature to be quite accurate – was flapping the tiny wings on his back. It was clearly to attract the attention of Solomon. To the youth's consternation the rider was mouthing a word, silently, while at the same time looking anxiously at the back of the horse's head.

Help! said the rider, his eyes wide. *Help me!*

No sound came out. It was all in the hopeless expression, the moving lips, the terrified look in the eyes.

Solomon turned his head quickly to the front, his heart beating fast. What was this? Was the rider trapped? How could Solomon help him? He certainly looked fixed to the back of the horse. It would take surgery to remove him and Solomon was no surgeon. He professed to be something of a physician, but that was simply because of a knowledge of herbs. A knowledge passed down to him by his grandmother, who had been burned as a witch. He knew from past experience that when you cut something away from the body – a crushed arm or wounded leg – the stump often went green and the victim usually died of a rotting sickness which crept over his body. There was no way Solomon could help the rider. He did not want to fall foul of the horse part of the pair, either. It was a very strange situation.

The flapping continued now, more vigorously, but Solomon chose to ignore the rider's pleas.

'Once upon a time,' said the horse, after a long silence had fallen between them, 'we struggled for supremacy.'

'Who?' asked Solomon, politely.

'Why, the riders and the horses. The horses won, of course, for we were the more intelligent of the two.'

Solomon instinctively glanced up at the rider, who mouthed the word, 'liar'.

'And,' asked a flustered Solomon, 'this battle. Did this battle take place between *all* riders and horses of the horse-fairy clan at the same time? My meaning being, did some horses win and some lose?'

'Ah, you've been looking it up, haven't you? *Most* horses won, but there were some riders who – curse their fairy names – overcame their proper masters. These feral creatures now live in the New Forest. They are but few in number and of such a wild nature it is a wonder they have not dashed out their brains on the low branches of trees. They charge their pony half around, careering through bracken and brake, causing great fatigue. They have no sense of responsibility, no moral reasoning, and will eventually kill themselves all off, of that I'm certain. I'm sad for their better halves, but it will be a fine day when the last of them keels over.'

Solomon looked up. The rider looked furious. He bared his teeth in anger and his eyes rolled in his head. Solomon thought he was going to have apoplexy or some kind of a seizure. The rider's cheeks were purple, his brow was as furrowed as a well-ploughed field and his tongue protruded from his mouth to such a length it must have been straining at the root.

'I really could not make a judgement,' he said, quickly, in order to remain on good terms with both horse and rider. ''Tis beyond my ken.'

'Hummph,' muttered the horse.

Finally they came to woodland which seemed familiar to Solomon. But then, he argued with himself, one woodland looked much like another to a holy man who had spent most of his life in a stone cell. Life at the monastery was all chapel and solitude, prayers and prayers. Any breaks for meals were brief and to the point. You sat down, you ate, you went about your duties again. Matins, vespers, work and sleep. Virtually the only time Solomon saw outdoors was when he worked in the monastery gardens. So the countryside was a bit of a mystery to him. Yet, he was puzzled. Surely he had seen that tree before? The shape of that root which protruded from the ground?

'Have we come in a circle?' he asked the horse-fairy. 'I seem to have been here before.'

'No, no,' said the horse-fairy, rather too quickly. 'Not at all. We are on our way to the place where the gnomes live. I promised to take you there and I will. I always keep my promises.'

Solomon shrugged and decided his companion must be right.

It was here they rested for the night. The creature lay down in a soft spot, leaving Solomon to find his own. The monk was used to sleeping on hardwood beds with no mattresses, even stone floors, and was not fussy where he lay his head. He gave the horse-fairy some food from one of his many inside pockets, ate a little himself, and then fell into a deep sleep. During the night various woodland faerie flitted past, but none that was malevolent. In the morning the youth woke refreshed, to find the horse-fairy up and drinking from a pond.

'Is that water fresh?' asked Solomon. 'I think it looks a little green for my tender stomach.'

'It's all right for horses.'

Solomon decided he was too thirsty to wait for the water of a clear brook. He drank from the pond, which was not so dangerous for him as it would have been for Jack. In medieval times the streams and rivers had been cleaner, but in places where people lived crowded together in towns and castles, hygiene was poor. Solomon was likely to get away with things like dirty water and tainted meat.

They did indeed come across a fresh-water river just a short time later, but by then it was too late. Looking for a bridge, Solomon could see none. The river was fast-flowing and he had no idea how he was going to cross it. He might try to jump it. A really good leap would carry him to the other side. But he was afraid. He was *very* afraid.

In certain respects, like sleeping on stone and drinking dirty water, Solomon had the advantage over Jack. There were many things which did not bother a medieval monk which would floor Jack. But then again, there were other situations where Jack would triumph. Solomon did not know anyone from his own time, including himself, who could swim. There was never any reason to enter water. Learning to swim takes time and effort and a medieval monk's time and effort went into surviving each day. One of his fellow monks had drowned in the moat of the baron's castle. Solomon had seen this accident, had been powerless to help, and it had horrified him.

'How art thou proposing to reach the other side, horse?' he asked his companion.

'Why, I'll leap across,' replied the horse-fairy. And he

did so, with great agility. When he saw that Solomon was not following him, he jumped back again.

'I can't do that,' said the monk. 'It's too wide for me.'

The horse-fairy made a sudden decision.

'I don't usually let people on my back — I have one rider after all — but I'll make an exception for you. Climb up in front of my rider and I'll take all of us to the other bank.'

'Wilt thou do that for me?'

'Surely, monk. Just climb up.'

Scared, but knowing he had to get to those he had betrayed, Solomon was racked with indecision. If he refused the offer he might spend days looking for a ford or bridge. Yet, he felt he was anxious to make his peace with Jack and Spiggot, and to beg Rosamund's forgiveness. He knew really that he had no choice. His knees were trembling and his hands were shaking as he swung himself up in front of the horse-fairy rider and gripped the white mane. The horse-fairy whinnied loudly and pawed the ground. Then he took a long run at the river and sailed over it to land on the other side. All through the short flight Solomon's eyes were wide with terror, but once they landed four-hoofed on the far side, he let out a whoop of delight.

'Success! I have braved the mighty flood and triumphed! The Lord gave me wings and saved me from the tempest.'

Solomon was filled with elation. But at that moment, when he tried to dismount, the rider gripped him with powerful arms. Solomon struggled but the rider laughed, locking his thick-fingered hands before the monk's chest, squeezing him almost breathless.

'Help me, horse!' cried Solomon. 'Thy fiendish rider will not release me. He holds me fast. Thou art the master of him. Tell him he must unlock his arms and let me down.'

'I'll do no such thing,' said the horse-fairy. 'We're almost back at Mallmoc's castle. Once there I shall hand you over to the sorcerer for a substantial reward. I have heard it from your own lips that he wants you, alive or dead, and I shall deliver you alive.'

'Let me go!' cried Solomon, furiously. 'Listen! I shall take thee to where thou shalt have much food.'

'No, no,' replied the horse-fairy, 'I'm not falling for those sort of tricks. Mallmoc will reward me with more than sugar lumps.'

The horse-fairy then began to gallop off, following a groove in the turf to where the castle could be found. Solomon continued to struggle with his captor, who giggled while continuing to hold him fast. Then something cracked in Solomon's chest. The monk gave a yell, crying, 'My ribs – he hath broke my ribs . . .'

The horse part of the horse-fairy called up to the rider, 'Don't crush him just yet. Mallmoc may want him alive.'

The arms around the monk's chest relaxed a little. This gave Solomon his opportunity. He jerked away, sliding downwards in his thick loose robe. The rider tried to grasp him again, but found more cloth than flesh in his grip. Solomon slipped out of the robe, under the rider's arms, leaving his habit in possession of the angry rider. Wearing nothing but a loin cloth, he dropped to the ground and rolled over a tump. Instantly, he was on his feet and running back towards the river. The cracking sound had been one of his thick hard biscuits and not his ribcage at all. He had fooled the horse-fairy.

The horse-fairy was indeed unaware that he had lost his prey. It was true he noticed a change in the weight on his back, but he put this down to his greater speed. Loads always appear lighter as the bearer goes faster. He thundered on, over the turf, following the channel in the earth. His rider cried out, but being without language could not communicate with his other half. On, on, went the horse-fairy, until finally the rider pulled hard on the white mane, and the horse knew that something was seriously wrong.

He came to a halt and looked back, to see a semi-naked figure running back towards the river. The monk in his white skin looked quite different without his robe: his form reminded the horse-fairy of a large maggot with arms and legs. Infuriated at losing his prisoner, the horse-fairy turned and charged after him, knowing he could catch him without difficulty. The rider was screaming hysterically now. No one, not even his other half, could understand what he was saying, but clearly he was upset. As he passed a tree he reached up and broke off a branch. This he began to wield like a club as his horse part thundered on in pursuit of the running monk.

Solomon, gasping for breath, looked back at the horrifying spectacle of the horse-fairy. The bottom half was snorting sprigs of steam from its nostrils as it galloped towards him. The top half was in warrior mode, swinging a thick cudgel, ready to beat the monk over the head. Solomon knew if he did not run for his life he was a dead man. Once, he stopped to wrench some turf from the ground and throw it after his pursuers. The clod struck the rider in the chest and he shrieked indignantly. Then Solomon saw some gorse bushes, with long wicked thorns and yellow flowers, and began to weave amongst them. The horse-fairy followed, quite agile at threading himself between the shrubs. Solomon soon found he was treading on thorns himself and blood streaked his feet. Still he refused to obey the demands to stop. He was a bright young man and he felt if he could just remain ahead of the creature who was chasing him, some inventive method of escape would occur to him soon.

Finally though, he discovered himself tearing down a slope towards the raging torrent he had crossed on the horse-fairy's back. On the other side, kicking his head along like a football, was Hollow Ben. Solomon yelled at him, 'Assist me, Hollow Ben, for I am about to be overcome by a horse-fairy.'

But the giant's eyes were at ground level. Hollow Ben was enjoying a game of soccer using his thick-skulled head as the ball. It was something he did when he was bored. The hair flailed when his boot took a hefty kick at his pate. His head took great pleasure in the sensation of rolling along. Horizons flashed before his eyes: the world jumbled and tumbled. He liked the smells down there, of wild flowers, leaves and forest mast. He enjoyed the feel of the grass brushing his hair and skin as his head rolled along the highways and byways of Liöfwende. He understood no sounds, of course. Any noises that fell on his ears were broken and unintelligible.

Thus he neither saw nor heard the youth whose plight was now dire, so wrapped up was he in his game of kick-head.

Solomon finally ran down the bank towards the river's edge. He could not think what to do. There was the flooding surge in front of him, just as wide as it had been when they jumped it the first time. Now he had the choice of remaining on this side, or trying to jump it himself. He decided that it was not as far to the other bank as he previously imagined. Could he do it? He just might. How surprised the horse-fairy was going to be when he saw Solomon on the other bank! His astonishment would be worth risking life and limb for, would it not? Summoning up all his courage, for he was terrified of the water, he launched himself into the air and over the river.

The horse-fairy stopped and watched with two sets of eyes, amazed that the fearful monk should overcome his terror enough to leap.

Solomon *almost* made it. Had the river been a metre less wide his feet would have found the shore. One of his sandals indeed left his foot and landed on firm ground. But the young monk himself fell short. He dropped into the thundering waters of the raging river, and was immediately pulled under by the current. Drowning is not a pleasant experience but it was a quick death, for he never made the surface to draw breath again. Solomon's last thought was triumphant: that at least he had not divulged the secret of the whirligigs to Mallmoc. The sorcerer was still no nearer to learning why his castle-ship failed to keep a true course during the night.

The monk's pale body was washed downriver. Eventually the current released its grip on him. He rose through the white foam to be washed into a swirling bend which would one day become an oxbow lake. There he lay, looking up with sightless eyes, at the light-blue sky. In death he had regained his innocence and was now bereft of all his spite and jealousy. He was, once more, a young priest.

The horse-fairy ran off, guilt surging through his two bodies, horse and rider, knowing the wrong he had done.

Some time later Hollow Ben passed by. His head was back on his shoulders, but the wrong way round. He was walking backwards an awkward motions, then came across the poor wan corpse. It lay in the lapping waters of the oxbow's shallows. Realising, when he could not use his arms, that his body was out of sorts he turned his head back the right way. Then he lifted Solomon up and stared at him sadly.

'Oh, youth has flitted from him and he is but a shade now,' said the giant. 'His enemies hunted him down like a lone wolf and finally took his life. I shall bury his drooping remains beneath that weeping willow, for they are twins in sorrow, this boy and that melancholy tree.'

And so Hollow Ben scooped away the soft earth from near the roots of the old willow and placed the youth inside a shallow grave. In time the green tree would find succour in the mortal remains of the monk. The plant would flourish in his fertile juices and the worms would come to feed on his flesh and aerate the earth. Death giving to life. Solomon was now in the bosom of the earth, with moles for company. He was as sad, and as glad, as any man who has cast off life while still in his prime.

Hollow Ben left a lily on the mound, to warn any passing faerie not to dig, for the only treasure lying there was ivory bones.

Mallmoc had witnessed the drowning with some satisfaction. He had spent another night wandering aimlessly around the countryside, wondering why he had lost the ability to find his way by the stars. The destruction of the youth was his one bright spot in a very dark time. While to most mortals revenge turns out to be a less satisfying meal than first envisaged, to Mallmoc it was better than a banquet. Something burned inside him like a small fire when one of his enemies came to grief. Solomon had been small fry, but Mallmoc still crowed on seeing the limp body washed by the torrent.

'So die all my enemies,' he muttered. 'May they wither and become less than useless husks of corn.'

Prince Rincortle entered his chamber at this moment.

'My Lord, I have located the gnomes. They are somewhere east of here, in the chalklands. My ulcugga will show you the way. Simply follow after those you see mounted on white steeds.'

'Good,' muttered Mallmoc, 'it must be they are working their magic from underground, but I still wonder how this can be. Do they have a magician as powerful as me? It doesn't seem possible. Yet *someone* is interfering with my calculations, and from a distance.'

Mallmoc told his second-in-command that he would be on the bridge-turret before the stars left the sky.

TWO

Working underground was a dirty, sweaty business and it was not surprising that Jack and Rosamund became very bad-tempered. They snapped at each other all the time. Spiggot and Fen were also at loggerheads, but theirs was a deeper problem and so they simply pretended to ignore one another. The only happy creatures were the gnomes, who took pleasure in digging whatever the circumstances. There's something in the make-up of a gnome that enjoys getting his stubby little hands dirty. The gnome loves to be grubbing around in the soil, content to carry buckets of mud and soil around, but also always on the look out for little treasures.

'Look at this wonder,' cried Jinty, holding up a piece of flint. 'See how it glints in the light of the lamps.'

They were underground, of course, working in artificial light. Rabbit holes provided air shafts for them to work in, but it was still hot and stuffy below the surface.

Jack was very grumpy. He looked up and stared at the piece of stone.

'It's just a lump of rock,' he muttered. 'I don't understand this business of making arrowheads. This is Faerieland.'

'That's because thou hast no sense of mystery,' replied the unperturbed gnome chieftain. 'We like to see stuff go from one side to the other, especially in remote places, like the Arctic Circle.'

'The Arctic Circle? There's nothing there but snow and ice,' expostulated an indignant Jack.

'So? Some of thy snow slips through to us and some of our ice slips through to thee.'

'Fairy snow and ice,' grumbled Jack, 'I never heard such rubbish.'

'Just dig thy share of the dirt, Jack,' growled Rosamund, her face covered in muddy streaks, her normally beautiful hair hanging like damp weeds from her head. 'Thou art playing at red herrings.' She filled the bucket at her feet with a final spit of soil. A humpty gnome dashed forward and took the full bucket, leaving an empty one in its place. Rosamund glared at the gnome, saying, 'A short rest would ease my aching back, if thou wouldst care to let me straighten up before providing yet a further pail.'

This last remark was actually addressed to the bucket gnome but Jack thought Rosamund was getting at him again. He responded angrily by digging much harder and quicker. Dirt began to fly from his spade. Some of it sprayed Spiggot and Fen, who were working nearby, studiously ignoring everyone else, especially one another.

'Hey!' cried Fen.

'Watch it!' shouted Spiggot.

By now Jinty and the other gnomes had had enough of these testy boggarts and their mortals. Jinty suggested the four of them down tools and go up to the surface. 'You're not used to mucking in below ground,' he said. 'Just leave the rest of it to us gnomes. We know what we're doing. You lot are just getting in the way.'

'Nice to know you're wanted,' said Jack in a sniffy voice, but he was relieved to be given the chance to relax. Like Rosamund, his back hurt, his throat was parched with stale air and he felt filthy from head to foot. There was mud in his shoes, mud in his hair and mud in his clothes. He had had enough.

The four of them crouched and sometimes even had to wriggle their way along the messy tunnels. Elastic-bodied gnomes were happily mucking in the dirt, squashing down into themselves when the ceiling got too low for their height, stretching up again when it became taller. The mortals and the boggarts had fixed bodies, which failed to concertina, and so they were at a great disadvantage in mine shafts and tunnels that varied in height and breadth.

Once outside the four companions passed Kling, who lay under a tree watching the butterflies and bees flying from bloom to bloom. He looked relaxed and content to idle away his time in the sun. A straw hung from between his ratty fangs. Removing it, he bid his master's son good day and asked him what was the hurry on so bright a day.

Spiggot glared at the water rat. 'I'll remember you managed to get out of the digging,' he said, darkly.

'Oh, master's son, it was not my choice. For Kling

would have been by your side, matching you sod for
clod. But you know, chieftain Jinty decided that these
claws were not made for digging. What was Kling supposed to do? Defy the laws of the gnomes?'

'Never mind all that, I'll remember.'

Spiggot and the others hurried by the languid water
rat, making straight for the nearest water to wash themselves. This happened to be a river about half a mile from
the mines. It was a pleasant flowing stretch of water,
lined on each bank by crack willows and limp elders.
Water nymphs and dryads were playing in its shallows as
the four approached, but these shy frail creatures scattered on hearing the tramp of human and boggart feet.
There was one being there who did not run, however,
and he became alert and interested, peering out from
behind a curtain of willow fronds at the oncoming group.

About a hundred yards away from the river Spiggot
stopped.

'A waterman,' he said. 'Look!'

Rosamund and Jack followed the direction in which
the stocky arm, pitted with burn marks from red-hot iron
sparks, was pointing. At first Jack could see nothing in
the dense green and shadow of the willow wands, but
gradually he made out a shape. There was a man sitting
on one of the boughs which overhung the river. He was
dressed in rather shabby, old-fashioned clothes: big
boots, a baggy jacket and flannel trousers, a collarless
shirt, a floppy-brimmed hat. There was a red kerchief
with white polka dots tied round his throat, just as
pedlars and tramps once wore. In his mouth was a
straight-stemmed briar pipe, smoke coming from the
bowl.

Jack saw the man reach up and slowly remove the pipe from between his lips. There was the feeling that Jack was being studied. But it was not his appearance that was under scrutiny. It was his inner self. The man was peering into Jack's soul, weighing it, judging its worth.

Jack shivered and grabbed Rosamund's hand. She looked up at him, surprised by his sudden action. He then became a little embarrassed, but decided he had done it instinctively, to protect his friend.

'I don't like that bloke,' he said, nodding towards the willows. 'What's he think he's staring at, anyway? A waterman? Does he own a barge or something? Or is he some sort of official, looking after the river?'

Fen said, 'You should be wary of him, Jack. He's not a real man. He's – what do you call it? One of *our* world.'

'Supernatural?'

'Yes, Jack. Supernatural. The waterman collects the souls of drowned mortals. He keeps these souls in jars, the lids of which are sealed with wax. This in itself is not a bad occupation, for a Liöfwendian, but the waterman has a bad side too, like most of his kind. He will drown you himself, to get at a golden soul. Children in Mortaland used to be terrified of him – they still are in regions like Moravia and Bohemia. These days there are not so many of them and people have forgotten him, but as you can see, watermen have not died out completely.'

Jack stared at the creature. He appeared harmless enough. He could have been someone's grandpa or older uncle. If he had asked Jack for a game of ludo or draughts, Jack would not have been surprised. But then most beings in Liöfwende didn't *look* dangerous.

This one seemed very casual in his movements. Only those narrow piercing eyes were sinister.

'I like thee not, waterman,' hissed Rosamund, at the figure down by the river. 'I think thee a cut-throat, out to steal my soul.'

Jack was suddenly aware that he still held Rosamund's hand in his own.

'I'm with you, Rosy. We'll steer clear of *him*.'

Jack wasn't sure what made a soul worth catching in the waterman's nets. Did one have to be angelically-good, in order to have a golden soul? Was a silver soul just as valuable to a waterman? Jack had never considered himself a 'good' person. He hadn't done anything really evil, or even very wicked, but he wasn't one of those people who are assured of getting their halo and wings when they die. As the waterman peered into his soul, through his eyes, Jack tried to think of all those *bad* things he had done which might tarnish his spirit, making it valueless to any collector of souls worth his salt. Finally the waterman averted his gaze and turned it on Rosamund, which made Jack even angrier than he had been before.

'I'll pulverise him if he touches Rosy,' he muttered.

Spiggot and Fen took the two mortals upriver of the waterman, keeping a wary eye on him. They seemed almost as concerned by the creature as Jack and Rosamund were themselves. Finding a clear bank, where there were no willows or elders, they could see either side of them. No one could sneak up on them without being seen well in advance.

They had their swim, managing to wash off most of the dirt. It cooled them too. However, Fen had been on

guard and had seen the waterman enter the river, sub-
merging with his pipe still lit. She shouted a warning and
Jack was just in time to see the hat disappearing under
the ripples. There was no hissing of the lit tobacco.
When the waterman emerged again, just twenty yards
away, the pipe was still smoking. His head came up just
once, then it slowly went under again, the eyes glittering.
Jack pulled Rosamund from the water quickly, certain
that the creature had seen something more than golden
in his medieval girlfriend. He said so, to Rosamund
herself.

'I thank thee, but I think not, Jack. I have done some
wicked things in my father's house. There are those who
take me for a shrew and would have a wife's scold placed
on my tongue, if I were not the daughter of the most
powerful baron in the land. No, no, it is thee who
attracts the fiend.'

The waterman finally walked out of the river on the
far side, apparently not willing to tackle the two mortals
with their boggart friends. Within a second he looked
dry and comfortable. He turned and stared across at
Jack then grinned, wickedly. Taking his pipe out of his
mouth the waterman pointed to something at his feet,
tethered to the bank. He nodded at Jack, then smiled
again, before reaching down.

'What doth the creature do?' whispered Rosamund.
'Wherefore does he show his teeth like a baying
donkey?'

Jack saw the waterman grasp the line which was tied
to a stake and withdraw something from the flowing
river. It was a keep net, the kind fishermen put their
caught fish in. When the net was clear of the river and

the waterman was holding it up like a lamp, they could
see something – something pale green and struggling in
the meshes – something hideous. It had the features and
the shape of Solomon, the missing monk, but it was as
rubbery and translucent as a jellyfish. A sickly-green
jellyfish. This was not Solomon, but it had come from
Solomon. This was the monk's soul.

Rosamund screamed and put her hands over her eyes.

Jack gasped, fighting for breath, as he realised what it
was that the waterman had in his ghastly net.

The waterman grinned again, tapping the oozing soul
with the stem of his pipe, making it squirm obscenely.

Spiggot took Jack's arm and turned him round. Fen
did the same with Rosamund.

'Don't look,' said Spiggot. 'That's what he wants.'

'He wants to torture you into diving into the river,'
added Fen. 'Ignore him. Laugh, as if you don't care.'

But Jack could not laugh. Neither could Rosamund.
The sight of that green shadow which had once belonged
to Solomon had stunned them. They were mesmerised
by it, even though it was now out of their sight. They
could still see it in their minds' eyes. Solomon's trapped
and yearning soul would haunt their dreams for many a
night to come. They had witnessed real horror and it
would dominate many dark nights and days of rain.

Friends again, united in adversity, Jack and Rosamund
walked back to the mines together. Now that they were
clean and cool they were ready to face the work again.
However, they saw with relief that the gnomes were
organising talking moles to carry on the digging while
they stopped for lunch. One last glance back showed

Jack the waterman strolling back into the river, carrying his mortal prize. He was submerged within seconds, back in his natural habitat, and only a swirl, an eddy, remained behind.

Spiggot and Fen walked behind the two mortals. The boggarts were conscious of their silence towards one another. Each felt they ought to say something, yet being socially awkward creatures, neither knew how to open the conversation. Spiggot was acutely aware of Fen's large but – to him – beautiful feet. He noticed that when her soles touched the ground her hairy toes spread out so that the grass poked through the gaps between them. He kept his head low, pretending to be looking down at the path. He wanted desperately to get on Fen's good side, but was completely at a loss as to how to accomplish it. If he told her about his remarkable exploits as a faerie knight, she accused him of bragging. If he tried to be modest and simple, she laughed at him. It seemed that anything he said went against him.

'Watch out for that root,' he said, his politeness overcoming his shyness. 'You might trip, Fen.'

'I can see it as well as you,' she retorted, haughtily. 'Do you think you are the only one with eagle's eyes?'

'Nay,' laughed Rosamund, wheeling, 'for it is I who have eagle's eyes. Those pixies still have mine own.'

'Yes and we must get them back, someday,' added Jack. 'That was quite bad of you to let the pixies take them, Spiggot.'

This was more than the brave but foolish boggart could bear. Now his best friend was criticising him in front of someone he was trying to impress. He lost his temper and kicked at a puffball, making it burst in a cloud of vile yellow powder the colour of snuff. At that moment Kling came down the path towards his master's son.

'Temper, temper,' said the water rat. 'No need to take it out on dead faerie, is there.'

'No,' Fen added, primly. 'That could have been Boskywod for all you know.'

'I hope it was Boskywod!' shouted Spiggot. 'I hope it was him and now he's just a puff of dust. It gets on my nerves, you keep mentioning him every five minutes. Boskywod, Boskywod. I'll kick every toadstool from here to kingdom come, if there's a chance it will be Boskywod, so there.'

THREE

Jack and Rosamund sat aside from the gnomes, who tended towards joviality at mealtimes and sprayed everyone when they laughed.

'How dost think Solomon was drowned?' asked Rosamund of Jack. 'Dost thou believe the waterman caught him?'

'I don't know, Rosy. Maybe it was an accident. Could Solomon swim? No, I thought not. Maybe he was just trying to cross at a dangerous point and got washed away?'

'Mayhap that was a waterman's trick!' said Rosamund.

'You mean, that *wasn't* really Solomon's soul?'

They both pondered on this and there was a moment when they might have believed it, yet deep down they felt the realisation that they were fooling themselves. The truth had been there to behold. The waterman could not have known that Solomon was their friend. He simply showed them, as any fisherman would, that he was not going home empty-handed. *They* might have escaped his hook, but there had been an earlier catch. Solomon had drowned, either by accident or design, and nothing would change that.

'He wasn't a bad bloke,' muttered Jack. 'I was jealous of him, of course, because of his history with you, Rosy. But that was just stuff. I didn't really hate him, you know.'

'Wast thou jealous, Jack?'

'Couldn't help it. He kept going on about how he'd known you a long time before I had, and how he was your suitor. That's enough to get anyone going, isn't it? I wanted to flatten his nose for him. But – but he's gone now, so none of that matters. I'm sorry, Rosy.'

'Sorry? Why dost thou pity me?'

'Well, you and him, you *did* have a history.'

'But we were not lovers, Jack – he was my tutor in singing and the arts – but that was all.'

Jack felt relieved. Despite all his protestations he had still felt a niggle of doubt about the pair. Now he was reassured.

'I think I'll sleep up here tonight, Rosy. Under the stars. How about you? It's so stuffy under the ground.'

'I think this is a good idea, Jack.'

The pair spoke to Spiggot and Fen, suggesting they did the same.

'We could have one of our little campfires,' said Jack, 'just like we used to before we became moles.'

So it was agreed, they would remain above ground. Kling was not enthralled about this arrangement. He was enjoying himself at the moment, being the only one to stay on the surface, guarding the cart with all its treasures. He knew if Spiggot stayed up he, the water rat, would be running around like a servant, fetching and carrying. But his grumbles brought no rewards. The four companions would join him for that night. The gnomes were informed and Jinty was all for the arrangement.

'Do thee good,' he said. 'Get a bit of fresh air into thy lungs. As for us gnomes, fresh air is bad for us. Sort of chills the lungs and gets caught in the windpipe. We like well-used air, comfortable air that's been swallowed and exhaled lots of times before, nice and warm and browned in the oven of someone else's chest. Familiar air, that's been breathed before. It feels safe to us gnomes, well-breathed air. It doesn't have an edge to it.'

Thus it was that Spiggot, Fen, Rosamund and Jack remained above ground, and the unfortunate incident occurred.

Mallmoc was at screaming point. Each night he felt he had solved the mystery of his poor navigation and each morning it was revealed that he had not. His frustration was taken out on the poor slaves he kept in his castle-ship. He had no use for their talents as metal-workers any more, since his iron vessel was now complete, but he could not bear to release them. They were abject creatures, who cringed before his raging person, and he derived great satisfaction from seeing them tremble. He was one of those tyrants who enjoyed every aspect of unlimited power. It gave him just as much pleasure to crush a butterfly under his heel as to torture a mortal or faerie.

In order to relax a little, Mallmoc had a diversion. In his chambers there were several pets which he enjoyed feeding. There was a strange giant owl which perched on a dark corner shelf. A large nameless snake he had conjured himself from hellish regions curled around the leg of a table. A spider the size of a soup plate with legs like those of a crayfish scuttled across his desk. A huge white slug he had found in the same place as the snake left a trail of slime on his books. A vile yellow bat which had escaped from some maniac warlock's laboratory attacked the lamps.

'Ah, Prince Rincortle,' he said, suppressing a snarl for the ulcugga – especially the royal ulcugga – were one race of faerie whose pride he had to keep stroking, 'thank you for coming to see me.'

'My lord,' murmured the fairy prince. 'You wished to speak with me.'

'Yes, yes.' Mallmoc paced the floor of his chamber. 'I've been thinking. I've been trying to decide who exactly is responsible for thwarting our plans. At first I believed it to be the boggart, Spiggot, son of Gnomon. Yet I cannot think that is right . . .' He paused in his speech to dangle a live mouse by the tail in front of the spider. Four jaws opened in the spider's bulbous hairy form and took the squealing mouse whole, crunching it like a sweet. The last thing to disappear down the arachnid's gullet was a wispy tail. 'What I *now* believe,' continued Mallmoc, pointing to the slug so that Prince Rincortle would not step on it, 'is that the youth is responsible. I mean that creature who flits around after the baron's daughter. What does he call himself?'

'Jack, my lord. As in Jack-the-giant-killer.'

'Yes, well that young man believes himself an engineer – and well he may be. Boggarts know nothing of the black art of *science* and clearly the creature who has the knowledge to turn us from our course is well versed in science. It must be this Jack, must it not? We had that boy in our clutches once and let him go. I must capture him again. Or better still,' the bat swooped and snatched a canary from the sorcerer's fingers, carrying the fluttering unfortunate creature aloft, 'have him assassinated. Do we still have those renegade gnomes, the ones who hate their current chieftain?'

'Wolfsbane and Kurse? Yes, they are here.'

'Send for them, if you will, Prince Rincortle.'

The ulcugga did as he was asked and soon two rather lumpy-looking gnomes with bulbous noses and eyes like prunes stood before the sorcerer. They looked into his face expectantly, knowing he had a mission for them at last. The pair felt they had been rotting away, forgotten, in the lower regions of the castle-ship. Hopefully this was to be a mission which took them out into the world. The castle-ship was becoming rather claustrophobic.

'Take your weapons,' said Mallmoc. 'I want you to plunge steel into the heart of a mortal youth. Be certain of your target. I want no failures. Lure him into a false sense of security, then strike like adders. Am I understood?'

'Where shall we find him, lord?' asked one of the gnomes, eagerly.

'Why,' said Mallmoc, smiling, 'amongst your own kind.'

Their faces dropped. The one who had not yet spoken, Wolfsbane by name, now voiced his doubts.

'But we will be taken captive by Jinty and forced to justify our past actions as well as this assassination.'

'That's not my concern. You will do your work and escape retribution if you can. If not,' Mallmoc shrugged, 'it is nothing to me. Why, did you think it should be?'

'No, no, my lord,' said Kurse, hastily. 'The responsibility is ours, naturally. We take the consequences if we are caught. But this will be like walking into the lion's den. Jinty will have our hides.'

Mallmoc was about to get impatient with these fools when his eye caught that of his snake and he changed his mind.

'I'll tell you what I'll do. I'll make you immortal, invisible and invulnerable. How's that?' He reached into a drawer and withdrew some blue dust, which he scattered on their heads. 'There, it's done.'

'But I can still see my hand,' said Kurse, looking down. 'And I can see Wolfsbane . . .'

'Ah, yes – you may see yourselves and each other, because you are both in the same spell-bubble, but those of us outside that bubble are unaware of your presence. We cannot see them, can we Rincortle?'

The fairy prince's eyes seemed to looking right through the gnomes.

'Where are they, my lord?'

'Precisely. You, my two assassins, are now protected from sight, from harm and from death. No one can touch you. Go forth and murder, with impunity. Do not concern yourselves with your enemies. They will be powerless against such powerful magic. Go forth and *destroy*.'

The two gnomes, convinced they had a barrier

between them and any foes they might meet, left the chambers.

'Idiots,' Mallmoc muttered, after they had gone. A joke occurred to him and he told it to Rincortle. 'Two gnomes have been sent forth to kill, but they are stupid creatures. Do you know why?'

'No,' said the prince, 'but I have the feeling you are going to tell me.'

'Because they are ass-ass-ins. Get it? Ass, ass. Two donkeys.'

'Ha-ha,' said the prince, in a flat, lifeless voice. 'I do love the humour of mortals and warlocks.'

PART FOUR

Rosy's story, Jack's tale

ONE

Wolfsbane and Kurse set forth as ordered by their master. Mallmoc had seen to it that they were both well-trained as assassins. Wolfsbane carried a slim sword known as a rapier in a sheath that was hidden down his back. The blade rested in the hollow of his spine. He had only to reach up and behind to grasp the hilt and withdraw the deadly weapon. Kurse was an expert with a slingshot. He could hit an oak leaf at twenty paces with a pebble. Both creatures walked with a sort of swagger unaffected by other gnomes, feeling themselves special amongst their own kind. They had adopted the mode of speech used by Mallmoc and his ulcugga and this too set them apart from other gnomes.

'I'm glad these are mortals we have to kill,' said Wolfsbane. 'It doesn't seem right and proper to destroy other gnomes.'

'But we would do it, if we were told to,' answered Kurse, hastily.

'Of course, of course.'

While Wolfsbane replied he glanced nervously at the leafy trees that rustled in the breeze, in case Mallmoc had any watchers and listeners hidden there. The sorcerer was infamous for recruiting and training creatures to spy on his own secret army, even on his own spies and assassins. There were layers and layers of such creatures. You were never safe, for Mallmoc's devious intrigues and designs could not be unravelled. Wherever you were, whatever you were doing, Mallmoc was listening and watching you. His eyes were hidden in grassy knolls, his ears in the bushes of shrubland. Most of his minions had learned never to take Mallmoc for granted, always to be on their guard. Wolfsbane and Kurse were new to the forces of evil, but they were learning very quickly.

A rabbit hopped out of a hole ahead of them, oblivious to the presence of gnomes, who were generally rabbit-friendly. The fact that he took no notice of the pair confirmed to the gnomes that they were invisible.

Kurse took out his sling for a practise shot.

'Put it away,' growled Wolfsbane. 'We're on a mission.'

'I still don't see why I can't pot that rabbit.'

'Because you'd be wasting time. You know what Mallmoc thinks of time-wasters. Stay focused on our assignment.'

Kurse gave the rabbit a passing glare and stuffed the slingshot into the pocket of his hose.

Later they came across some thrum, gnawing at the roots of some oaks and elms. Kurse glanced at his companion.

'Oh, all right, then,' sighed Wolfsbane. 'You won't be happy until you've loosed a few stones, will you?'

Kurse happily took out his slingshot and began killing the snarling savage faerie from Gilscipe. When his thirst for slaughter had been slaked, Kurse put his slingshot back into his pocket and hummed a tune. Wolfsbane, glad that his companion had got the twitches out of the way, also began humming.

The pair continued over the downs. The soft warm summer air was full of butterflies and dragonflies, glinting like jewels. In the tall grasses, whispering harvest mice were making their homes. Gaily-feathered birds decorated the trees and bushes. It's a beautiful morning, thought Wolfsbane, feeling contented. Just the sort of morning for an assassination. Had it been raining, or the ground covered in winter snow, it would not be such a pleasant task ahead of them. Rotten weather always spoiled things like picnics or assassinations. No task is pleasant in the rain. One worried about one's nice shiny blade going rusty. And in the winter weather one's hands froze on the hilt of the rapier.

No, no, this was good. Clear skies, the sun on your back, the soft dry grass under your feet. Of course, underground was better. A gnome preferred an earthen roof over his head to the sky anytime. But if one *had* to be in the open air, this was the sort of weather to be out there.

Wolfsbane was in no great hurry to do the deed and report back to Mallmoc. Savour the moment, that was his motto. Savour it like a nice juicy worm wriggling on one's tongue. Such contentment was rare.

*

Jack woke with a start and knew something was wrong right away. Rosamund, despite being a gentle maid, was a light snorer. Jack always chose to sleep on the far side of a bush, hoping that the leaves would filter out the sound of her whistled breathing, but it never did. He had finally dropped off in the early hours, the sound of sleeping Rosamund in his ears.

Yet now he could hear nothing.

He rose and looked on the other side of the gorse bush. The space where she had lain the previous evening was empty, the grass flattened to her slim shape. Not far away, tucked in the roots of some trees, were Spiggot and Fen. Fen was using Kling, who was also there, as a pillow. All three were fast asleep, the dew still forming on their clothes or fur. Jack looked at the position of the sun and decided they would not be up for at least another hour. Boggarts were not sluggards, but they rarely rose until the sun had let go hands with the edge of the Earth.

'Rosy?' called Jack, softly, thinking she had gone into a nearby spinney for something. 'Rosy, are you there?'

There came back the faintest of sounds.

Jack walked towards the spinney.

'Rosy, is that you?'

Again, a whisper, a rustle.

Jack was unsure what to do.

'Look, Rosy, are you decent? I don't want to . . .'

At that moment, a fox swaggered out from the undergrowth. He glanced at Jack with evident dislike.

'Do you mind?' muttered the fox. 'I was engaged.'

'Sorry,' replied Jack, as always taken aback by a talking animal, even though he should expect it by now.

Some of them did, some of them didn't, that was the trouble. If they all had the power of speech he would get used to it, but for the most part they were dumb creatures. Only the odd one, like Kling, had the power of human speech. Nothing was consistent in Liöfwende.

'You – you didn't see a girl in there, did you?' he asked the fox.

'No, I didn't. I have no desire to see a girl. I have no wish to exchange idle chatter with a boy, either.' The grumbling tone continued. 'Can't even go behind a bush without being interrupted.'

The fox trotted away, over the next rise.

Jack wandered around, not knowing what to do. It was not like Rosamund to go off somewhere without telling him or Spiggot. She knew how dangerous Faerieland was for the lonely stranger. He went down to the nearest stream, of which there were countless numbers in Liöfwende. There he washed and drank. When he had finished he inspected his feet. His shoes had long since worn through and he was using bark sandals made for him by Kling. The straps were fashioned from reeds which actually cut into his skin a little, though they were better than nothing.

A shadow fell over him. He looked up startled.

'What are you doing up so early, Jack?'

It was a lumpy-looking Fen, blowsy from sleep, with her wild and wiry dark hair sprouting in every direction from her head. She wore a pink ribbon, given to her by Rosamund. Rosamund had tied it in a bow, but the ribbon now hung limply undone from the end of one of Fen's tresses. Fen's big brown eyes were liquid though and comforting to look into.

'I was looking for Rosy. She seems to be missing. You don't know where she's gone, do you?'

'No, Jack, I don't. Look though, those are her wet footprints in the grass on the other side of the brook! Aren't they? I can't think they would belong to anyone else, they're so small and dainty.'

Jack stared. 'Fen, you could be right.'

'I'm sure I am.'

'Look,' said Jack, making a sudden decision, 'Rosy's obviously wandered off in the night. I'm going to have to follow those prints and find her. Tell Spiggot, will you? Ask him to send Kling after us, because I'm likely to get just as lost. Kling's good at tracking, or he should be with a hooter like he's got. Now where's Kling's cart?'

'Over there, in the shadow of the rock.'

Jack ran to the cart and retrieved a sack which contained his magic crossbow and his pair of silver fairy shoes. He threw the sack on his shoulder and set off, tracking the footprints.

Fen was worried. She called, 'Jack, are you sure you should leave the camp too?'

'I can't let her get too far,' he said over his shoulder, 'she might just have set off. Those prints in the dew look fresh. She might only be over the next hillock. I'm off, then.'

He jumped the brook and set out at a smart pace, following the damp depressions in the meadow. Rosy, Jack told himself, could get into all sorts of trouble in such turbulent times. She might run into the ulcugga, or even Mallmoc himself. Certainly the sorcerer had agents all over the landscape spying for him. Jack had to find her before Mallmoc did. The sorcerer would not let her out of his clutches a second time. Look at what had happened to poor old Solly. Drowned away and now a waterman's catch.

Why Rosy had gone, he couldn't imagine, but there were all sorts of enticing faerie about. They came to you glimmering with light, beckoning with silver fingers, and it was hard to resist. They led you off to hazards unknown and left you there. Or took you to their lairs where they tried to get the secret of the mortals out of you. All faerie believed that mortals knew what 'death' was and refused to believe that it was just as much a mystery to human beings as it was to faerie folk. Faerie despised secrets, unless they were their own secrets, and couldn't bear to be on the outside. They *had* to know. It was in their nature. Jack had spent much time in Liöfwende trying to convince elves, pixies, goblins and the like that individual mortals only found out about death once they had died themselves.

TWO

By mid-morning, Jack had still not had sight of Rosamund and he was now extremely worried. The dew had dried under the hot sun but luckily the grasses were long enough to follow her trail. Jack had kept a wary eye out for ulcugga on purple dragons or horses, not even knowing whether he was heading in the direction of Mallmoc's castle-ship or not. He had encountered several faerie folk, mostly goblins, and asked them for information. Most shook their heads, but one or two goblins asked for crooked sixpences and then told Jack a pack of lies. He had learned to recognise when goblins were lying. Their noses twitched violently and they dribbled.

At noon he came to bank of wild flowers whereon sat the most beautiful female fairy he had ever seen. She had a picnic laid before her on a pure white linen tablecloth. Spread on the cloth were all kinds of sweetmeats and

rising like a church spire from their midst was the tallest
bottle of pink wine imaginable. The scented sweetmeats
smelled delicious and Jack's mouth began watering.

He could not, however, take his eyes from the maiden.
She had a pretty heart-shaped face with pouting pink
lips and a brow of ivory. There were silver lines painted
like a tiger's claw marks down one side of her face and
her eyelids bore a tasteful amount of silver shadow. The
eyes themselves were magenta, with silvery sparkles
flashing from them. On her throat was a black tattoo of
a flying dragon with its tail streaming behind it.

Jack noticed dimples appearing in her cheeks when
she smiled. She wore nothing but a shimmering shift that
came down to her knees, while her golden hair tumbled
about her shoulders and fell almost the same length. Her
ankles were trim, her knees were pert, her calves were
exquisite. One could say the same of her wrists, elbows
and forearms. In short, she was perfect.

She beckoned with a curled enticing finger.

Jack sighed, heavily. 'Alas, I cannot,' he said in his
best faerie dialect, 'for I am searching for a lost mortal.'

'Just for a moment, or two,' she said, smiling. 'Even
searchers must refresh themselves from time to time.'

Her voice was the tinkling of tiny glass bells.

Jack was charmed of course and fought within
himself to stay true to his task.

'Young lady, I must go on,' he said, firmly. 'Please do
not tempt me further. You would be doing me and the
one I seek a great disservice. Let me go, I beg you. Once
I find her, we shall come back here together. Then I shall
be pleased to partake of your picnic.'

A glistening tear coursed down the fairy's cheek.

'Thou dost reject me,' she said. 'I thought thee kind, but thou hast a heart of stone. All these years have I waited for someone like thee to come along, a knight who would whisk me away to fair climes. Now that I have found thee, now that the Fates send thee to my bosom, thou hast no use for me. Go then . . .'

'No, no, you don't understand,' said Jack, finding that, in spite of himself, he was sitting down by the cloth. He tried to get to his feet, but each time he thought he was there, he found himself sitting again. 'If my time were my own I should be pleased – *more* than pleased – to join you in this feast. Just a half-glass, if you don't mind. What is it? Elderberry?'

'We fairies call it summer wine.'

'Well then, just a half-glass and no more.'

Jack drank the summer wine and immediately felt light-headed. He attempted to recall his objective in coming out here. To find Rosamund! That was it! Rosy had wandered off and lost herself in the woodland. Yes, he had to look for Rosamund, so only one more glass of that wine and he would have to be on his way. If Rosy was lost, that was her fault not his, and she would have to wait until he was good and ready to look for her.

'What is thy name?'

The voice came to him as if in a dream.

'Jack.'

'Jack, Jack, I love thee, Jack. Thou hast me in thy thrall.'

She leaned forward and kissed him on the lips. A quiver of joy went through him. He had never felt such a thrill. That single kiss was like a drug. He needed more. He had to have more. He would die if there were no more kisses like that one. So, he stole one back, and another. She responded by raining kisses on his cheeks and brow, on his neck and ears, until he was drunk with them, drunk with fairy love. His thoughts floated lazily from his head, up into the ether. There was some distant concern, for something, but he could not grasp it and pushed it aside with a happy laugh.

'More wine!' he cried, thrusting forward his goblet. 'More wine for the king of the meadows.'

'Art thou yet a king?' she trilled. 'Art thou an emperor?'

'I'll be what you want me to be. I'll be ruler of the universe if you like. Just give me some more summer wine, and indeed some more of those delicious kisses.'

'Thou shalt have all that thou dost desire,' she cried. 'Thou art my beloved Jack, whose classic features are as divine as any deity in heaven, whose complexion is as soft and downy as the floating dandelion seed, whose hair makes his head look like a coconut doormat.'

'Beg pardon?' he said, frowning, hearing something that didn't quite sound like a compliment. 'What did you,' he hiccoughed, 'what was that last remark?'

'I said we must be together always,' said the fairy, now dancing round him in a confusing shimmer of silvery light. 'Always, always, always.'

Jack burped. 'Well, I dunno about that – *always*?'

'Will you not love me for ever?'

Jack's head was beginning to hammer in the midday sun.

'Did I say I loved you at all?'

He wasn't sure. Maybe he had, maybe he hadn't. He didn't really want to be rushed into a quick decision.

'Let me sleep on it,' he said, lying back, spilling summer wine all over his face. 'I need a few minutes' shut eye to think.'

Another fairy then appeared, coming up over the hill-side.

'Who is this, my daughter?' boomed the male fairy. 'What dost thou with this mortal?'

'Father, he is my wondrous Jack. We are betrothed. He and I are linked. See, he made me this daisy chain, which I wear like a crown upon my brow. He has tested the buttercup under my chin and found it glowed yellow. We shall be wed in the light of the morn's moon, when the grass blades spear the jewelled dewdrops. I shall be his fairy wife and he shall be my mortal man. We shall be happy, Father. Give us thy blessing?'

'He appears to be a comely youth,' said the elderly fairy, 'in spite of his bowlish hair.'

'Yes, Father, he is, and he has drunk a prodigious amount of the summer wine.'

'In that case, my children, thou hast my blessing.'

Jack was half-asleep, but he heard the words and they went through him like a lightning bolt. Marriage? Who had mentioned marriage? Certainly not him. Surely it was the first he had heard of the word. And why was he sitting here drinking wine, while Rosamund might be in terrible danger? What was he thinking of? He sat up, eyes wide open.

'I have to go,' he said. 'I must leave.'

'We both must go, Jack – but after the wedding. See, my father has gone to inform the woodland fairies of our forthcoming nuptials. They shall be making merry soon, crushing the berries for the making of more wine. They

shall be gathering in the harvest of golden wild corn for
the making of our wedding bread. They shall be crushing
the herbs and scenting the forest through and through,
so that our heads swim with scents. Flowers will be
strewn on the woodland paths, the amber sap of the pine
taken to make beads for my bridal necklace, and frost-
white thorns for thy crown, Jack.'

'No!' he struggled to get to his feet, while her cool
hand stroked his fevered head. 'No, no – I must find
Rosy.'

'I shall give thee rosy lips as a present for the groom. I
shall give thee many presents, many gifts beside. The
golden eyes of a lion shalt thou have, my dear Jack.
Thou shalt also have his silver claws and teeth for thine
own. I shall give thee deserts in which to roam at night
and forest in which to hunt me down in dark shadows.
Thou shalt be my tiger, my leopard, my panther. We shall
roll in the summer grasses like mares at play. The winds
will be our companions, our playmates. When we rest
white doves shall be our pillows. Our nights will be blue-
black satin studded with sapphire stars. Cockerels will
crow blushing notes to wake us in the mornings. Oh
what delights thou hast in store, my beloved Jack, when
we are wed, when we are wed . . .'

'Stop talking nonsense,' cried Jack, alarmed. 'You're
making my head spin. I can't think straight.' He stood
up. 'I'm going. I'm sorry, but I am. I never promised you
anything. You just got me merry on that summer wine.'

'Go? How canst thou go,' her sweet voice said, 'for I
can run faster than any mortal born. I shall catch thee,
Jack, and bring thee back.'

He stared at her, still a little befuddled by the constant

flow of her charming words and the residue of the wine. He knew now that he had been tricked: enslaved by this beguiling fairy. He might as well be in manacles and chains, her hold was so strong. And Jack had been in Faerieland long enough to know that what she said was true. He could never outrun a fairy, even a slight female like this one. What was he to do? She had trapped him, as many a mortal had been trapped, by melliflous murmurings and sweet summer wine. How many warnings were there in the poems he had read at school, against tarrying with such a deadly female? They were legion. Yet gullible youths like him still fell into the sugared clutches of a captor.

'What is in thy sack, Jack?' asked the fairy, plucking at his burden. 'Hast thou a present for me?'

'Oh, this?' Jack replied, miserably, still trying to think of a way out. 'Just a crossbow and some silver shoes.'

'Some silver shoes?' she cried, jumping to her feet and eagerly dancing around him. 'Thou hast brought me a gift of silver shoes? Dost thou know I *love* silver? It is my favourite colour, my favourite metal. A gentleman must have his gold but a lady must have her silver. Give them to me.'

Jack hated himself for what he did next, but he knew it was the only way he was going to escape.

'Why – why yes, a – a wedding gift.'

'Oh Jack, let me see, let me see.'

He opened the sack and took out the shoes. Shoes he had found in the heather in Scotland, where the most feral of fairies lived. They were savage folk up there in the Highlands, with their red hair and wild ways. Many were the lures, the traps, they left lying in the grasses.

Jack had found several of these traps. Most he had thrown away, or given to the seelie and unseelie courts, who knew what to do with them. But the silver shoes he had kept, for a rainy day. Well, it seemed that contrary day had arrived. The sun was shining outside, but inside he was all black clouds and rain.

'They're yours,' said Jack, wincing within. 'Try them on.'

The silver fairy took the silver shoes. They seemed made for her. They were exactly her colour and her style. She slipped them on and they covered her feet with not a fraction of an inch to spare. She stood up. They dazzled in the sunlight. She danced, and danced, whirling around Jack, laughing her tinkling laugh, until suddenly she grimaced and fell to the ground, groaning, reaching down to pull the shoes from her feet.

'They crush me!' she cried. 'They squeeze my toes.'

Jack was up and running. He felt as guilty as a man who has just wounded a butterfly, but he knew his life was at stake. He had to find Rosamund and this fairy had lured him into a trap. Well now the trap had turned and it was she who was caught. When he glanced back he saw that she was limping away, towards the forest. Her father and his fairy folk would soon have those shoes off her feet, Jack thought. In the meantime he had to be gone, away over the hills, out of their reach.

THREE

Rosamund had risen just before the dawn, her senses drugged with sleep. She had wandered down to the stream to get a drink. The last stars were fading in the sky and the ragged hem of the night was showing above the horizon. Rosamund kneeled down and flicked water on to her face, before quenching her thirst. Then she said a little prayer, as she always did in the short lonely hours, for Jack and herself in this strange world.

When she opened her eyes there was an elderly man in view. Not far away on the other side of the brook stood a broken oak. The roots had been eaten by the thrum and it was now a dying plant. Rosamund saw the elderly man reach inside the tree and pull something out: something green, which struggled a little like a fish taken out of water. The man, a corpulent looking gentleman accompanied by an ass, had a huge bag. The struggling thing was put inside the bag and the bag sealed and slung on the ass's back.

'What dost thou?' cried Rosamund. 'Wherefore dost thou steal from trees?'

The old man glared at her. 'I steal nothing. This is my work.'

With that he climbed on the ass's back and prodded its rump. The beast dutifully ambled forward with its load.

Rosamund was fascinated by the man, who had skin like bark and hair and eyes as green as willow leaves. She had noticed that there was moss growing out of his ears and his nose was merely two knotholes in the bark of his face. Since it would be a couple of hours before the others awoke, she decided to follow the old man on the ass, convinced she could return before they missed her. She was unable to sleep anyway and would only have lain awake, impatient and frustrated with the others for being so fast asleep.

She strolled along behind the ass, careful not to get too close and arouse the old man's ire, until the pair reached a cave in a cliff. There the rider dismounted and relieved the ass of his burden. The animal wandered off in search of fresh grass on the edge of a woodland.

Rosamund stayed back, in the shade of some trees, until the old man had been in his cave for quite a while. Then she approached.

Peering inside a strange sight met her eyes. There, several lines were slung across the roof of the cage. On these lines were dozens of hangers. Draped neatly over these hangers were what first appeared to be ironed clothes. Indeed, the old man had a flat iron which he heated every so often on a fire near to where he stood. Then he took a crumbled garment from a pile in a basket on the floor. He would iron this 'garment' before threading it through a hanger and hooking the hanger on to one of the lines above his head.

Suddenly, the old man looked up and caught sight of the spy.

'What are you doing here?' he growled. 'Mortals are not permitted to enter this cave.'

'I beg pardon, kind sir, but I was curious. Why dost thou iron such a vast number of vests? All of the same green hue? Thou must surely be the cleanest man in these forested parts, to have so many vests to wear. One a day for a whole year, I would wager.'

He held one of his 'garments' up to the light.

'This? This is no *vest*. This is the spirit of a dead tree.'

Placing the tree-soul down on the iron board he took up a lamp.

'Look!' he said, holding the lamp high.

Rosamund gasped. There at the end of the cave were hundreds of shelves. On these shelves were stored thousands of such souls, folded neatly like bedsheets. They were all varying shades of green.

'I've been working hard of late,' grumbled the old man, putting the lamp back down. 'Those thrum have killed so many of my charges.'

'You have to rescue the spirits of the trees?'

'I do indeed, and store them here in the dark and cool, until a new tree grows and is ready for its soul. Unlike you mortals, trees are not born with a soul, nor can they develop it. They have to use second-hand souls, from their ancestors. Of course, again unlike mortals, these souls never become blemished or stained. There is no taint to the life of a tree. That makes such a business possible, even for one man such as myself.'

'May I touch one?'

The old man was not sure, but eventually he nodded.

'All right, but be very careful, mind. Handle it as you would a delicate leaf. Don't press with your fingers or you'll leave a mark.'

She stroked the one he had been ironing last. It was flimsy and wrinkled up at her touch.

'Careful, mind!'

'It feels like silk,' she said. 'The finest silk from Far Cathay.'

The old man's eyes narrowed. 'You're not thinking of stealing one, are you?'

Rosamund was shocked. 'No, not I. Who would commit such a terrible crime?'

'Oh, there are those who would – who *have* done – to wear them like shifts for the pleasure of receiving compliments. Or to gratify their own selfish needs for a feeling of infinite happiness. Being tree spirits there is purity in them. They contain intrinsic tranquillity. That is to say that when you put one on, a feeling of security, contentment and utter peace descends upon your own soul. No more worries or concerns. Just calmness.'

'When thou dost tell me that,' confessed Rosamund, 'it does sound desirable. I should like to be forever calm and peaceful.'

'But·they know not what they do, these soul-stealers. Some of these tree-spirits are as ancient as flora itself. They were formed in the dark trunks of cycads and tree-ferns, in some long-forgotten prehistoric era. Once nature decided there were enough of them, they ceased to grow more, but there were literally millions of trees then inhabiting the Earth.'

'And the danger is?'

'Child, child. Anything *that* old has gathered to itself secrets, dark, unhealthy secrets, which could never be borne by mortals. Anyone from the family of mankind soon sickens and dies when they learn such arcane things from their garment. They die happy, of course, for they are peaceful and unconcerned by worldly subjects, matters of the flesh. But theirs is a dreadful fate, for even after death they cannot share their knowledge. Imagine bursting with profound mysteries and being unable to divulge them!'

Rosamund agreed. 'True, for I cannot hold a secret more than a few moments, before I tell it to one of my trusted companions. There is something about a secret which wishes to unfold itself and make itself known to the commonwealth.' She placed the tree spirit down on the ironing board again and said to the old man, 'Thou hast a sacred trust.'

'I have indeed, now if you'll excuse me, I have a basket load of ironing to do . . .'

Rosamund left the old man to his chores and set about returning to where she had left her friends sleeping. When she got back to the camp however, she found Fen and Spiggot wringing their hairy hands.

'Where have you been? Have you seen Jack?' asked Fen.

'Why, no, is he gone?' she replied.

'He set out after you,' Spiggot explained. 'When we found you missing this morning we thought you'd been enticed away from the camp and Jack went after you, following your footprints. Now we've found you, we've lost Jack . . .'

Rosamund said, 'Shall I seek him out?'

'No, no,' cried Kling, entering the fray, 'then Jack will come home and we'll have lost you again. We'll all have to wait till he comes.'

Rosamund agreed to this, but when Jinty came to ask for workers she refused to go below until Jack returned. Spiggot and Fen also said they could not work until they had sight of Jack. Jinty did not mind this so much. He felt the gnomes could get on with digging far better without mortals and boggarts. He went back down below to supervise the earthworks, which were now progressing at a rapid pace. It would not be long, perhaps just another day, before the trap was ready for the castle-ship.

During the morning, two gnomes arrived at the mines.

They tried to sneak past Rosamund, who cried, 'Whither goest thou?'

'Eh?' cried one, somewhat distressed. 'You can see us?'

'Of course I can see thee.'

'By cracky,' said the other, 'we was lied to again . . .'

'Who told thee lies?' asked Rosamund.

'Eh – oh, no one. No one in partic'lar. Now that we're here, Kurst, we might as well get the job done, visable or not.'

'I suppose so, Wolfsbane.'

They were amazed to see the work that was going on. They asked if this was a drive to root out all the flints in faeriedom, but as soon as they were recognised they were dragged up in front of Jinty. The gnome chieftain was not pleased to see them.

'What? The two rebels back?' he growled. 'I seem to remember you plotted to overthrow me as chieftain of the clan last time I saw thee. Rebels. Rioters. Revolutionists. Did I not banish thee?'

'Yes,' replied Wolfsbane, quickly, 'but we seek forgiveness.'

Jinty stroked his chin. 'A gnome, *forgiving* someone. That would be a new thing.'

'Please, Jinty,' pleaded Kurse, 'we really have mended our ways.'

'And where hast thou been in the meantime? Organising revolts against me with other gnome clans? Fomenting unrest? Stirring the pot?'

Wolfsbane replied, 'We have been living in the forest, off berries and roots, seeking repentance. Many is the night we have lain under the stars, longing to be back underground again. The starlight has withered our skin, has tanned it an unhealthy hue as you can see. The days were, of course, spent in the company of rabbits and badgers, sharing their homes. Our hearts were heavy, the treachery bearing down on them the whole while. Yet, I believe we have cleansed ourselves, Jinty, and we come hat in hand. Give us some penance that we may earn our way back into our own home.'

Jinty frowned. Could he believe these two? They had always been trouble-makers, always seeking the wrong ways to power. He could do with another four hands at the spades, it was true. Yet how could he trust such devious creatures as Wolfsbane and Kurse, who had cause such turbulence in the past? It was a difficult decision to make. A little time was needed.

'Come back after the vertical noon, then wilt thou have answer.'

'Thank you,' said Wolfsbane, humbly. Then, casually,

'I have heard there are two mortals with you? Is that true? I should like to meet the one called Jack, for I've heard great things about him amongst the faerie.'

'Jack? He is not to be seen at the moment.'

'Oh, how disappointing. Where can he be found?'

Jinty stared at the two stunted gnomes.

'Why this sudden interest in common mortals?'

'No real interest,' replied Wolfsbane, smoothly. 'Curiosity I suppose. They say he is seven feet tall.'

'Nothing of the sort,' snorted Jinty. 'Just a normal youth.'

'Oh, my mistake then. We'll, ah, wait up on the surface for your decision. Please take your time.'

The two gnomes left and went above.

Well out of earshot, the two would-be assassins spoke.

Kurse said, 'Now what?'

'He's obviously not here. We have to find out where he is, idiot. Look, there's a mortal over there. That must be the Rosamund Rincortle spoke about. We'll ask her where he is.' He raised his voice to a honeyed note. 'Oh, mortal, could we have a word with you, please?'

'Oh, gnomes. Art not thou at thy work?'

Wolfsbane said, 'Ah, no, Jinty sent us to look for Jack. He – he wants a word with him, if you please.'

'Jack is not here.'

'Oh dear,' said Wolfsbane, looking round nervously, 'Jinty will be upset – can you tell us where we can find him? Jack, I mean?'

'Alas, he wandered off in the early dawn and has not yet come home to us – but when he does I shall send him to Jinty direct.'

'Wandered off?' growled Kurse, gruffly, sticking his nose in Rosamund's face. 'Wandered off *where*, girl?'

'Dost thou speak with such rough manners to a lady?' said Rosamund, surprised. 'Thou art a dolt.'

Kurse pushed his face even further forward. 'Who are you calling a . . .' But Wolfsbane flicked his ear, stopping him short. 'Ow!'

'I trust you won't speak to the lady like that again, friend gnome,' said Wolfsbane, 'when the lady is only trying to *help*. My lady, in which direction was Jack heading when he left? I only ask so that I can pass on the information to my chief, who is worried about him.'

'Well, *that* way.' She pointed. 'But I'm sure he'll be back soon.'

Wolfsbane took off his hat and swept it down as he bowed. 'Thank you, my lady, and forgive this oaf, his mother was a toad and his father was another. What can come of such a union except a . . .'

'Toad?' she finished for him.

'Exactly!'

When Wolfsbane had pulled him aside, Kurse said, 'Who are you call a toad?'

'Shut up, fool. Now, the girl pointed that way. We'll follow the direction and ask questions of those we meet. It won't be long before we have this Jack. Then if your pebble doesn't kill him stone dead – that's a little joke – my rapier will still his heart. If you draw out the vowel in *still* it sounds like *steel* – and that's another joke. I think I'm getting almost as good as the sorcerer at jokes. What do you think, Kurse?'

'I think I want to get this job done and get my just rewards.'

FOUR

Rosamund stood watching the two strange gnomes for quite some time. With her sharp eagle's eyes she was able to view them from quite a long way off. They seemed to be arguing as they left and she was puzzled at why Jinty would send them after Jack, when he was so short of workers. In fact, Jinty came up from under a short while later and asked where 'those two blamed gnomes' had gone.

'That way,' said Rosamund, still keeping them in view. 'There they are, on the horizon.'

'Cannot see 'em,' muttered Jinty, squinting hard, 'haven't got thy perfect vision. They said they would go to work.'

'Thee did not send them after Jack?'

'No, why would I do that?' said Jinty. 'I need workers.'

'That's what I thought,' Rosamund murmured. 'Who are they?'

'Rebels that were banished some time ago. Normally gnomes are gentle creatures, like me, but occasionally we have bad eggs amongst us. Which race of creatures does not? I didn't think we would ever see those two again, but they asked for my forgiveness for past misdemeanours.'

She left Jinty standing there and set off at a pace after the two gnomes. She was now highly suspicious of their motives. Why would they lie to Jinty and why would they want to find Jack unless it was to do him some harm? Things were clearly wrong here and the baron's daughter had enough grit to decide she was going to do something about it. When Rosamund wanted to move, she could move. In her time, girls were either pallid weak things that pined away in towers, or they were tough creatures, determined to get what they wanted out of life. Rosamund was in the latter mould. She had battled with a bullying father for years and she was no victim. She was also as fit as a horse, having insisted on doing training with her father's knights, rather than languishing away weaving a tapestry in a cold cell.

'So,' said she, trudging after the pair, 'thou believest that thee can better Rosamund, daughter of Guillaume de Arundel, dost thou? For shame, recalcitrant gnomes! I shall tear out thy tongues and use them for shoe-ribbons. I shall pull off thy ears and use them for counters at chequers. I shall wrench off thy noses and use them for . . .' Here her inventiveness failed her and she had to be content with her basic boiling anger.

With her eagle's eyes, courtesy of the Cornish piskies, she was able to keep the two gnomes well within sight. They, however, having but normal gnomish eyes, did not know they were being followed. Rosamund followed doggedly after them, watching also for signs of Jack.

It was coming on evening, the twilight time, when Rosamund spotted Jack. He was ambling in his usual absent-minded way back towards the area where the mines were being dug. The two gnomes did not seem to have noticed him. They were busy arguing again and in any case their eyes were not as sharp and penetrating in the gloaming as were Rosamund's.

How was she to warn Jack, however? The gnomes and Jack were heading directly towards one another. If she yelled, Wolfsbane and Kurse would hear her too. She simply hurried on, hoping to avert any harm. It could be, she told herself, that she was wrong. Perhaps the gnomes were perfectly innocent and intended no crime. She hoped so. She prayed so. She could not bear it if anything were to happen to Jack. Already she had lost Solomon, drowned away in the river. And her feelings for Solomon had been nothing compared to her feelings for the strange Jack.

Now the gnomes had stopped. They had spotted Jack coming towards them. Another exchange occurred between them that, maddeningly, Rosamund could not hear. The pair advanced on Jack.

Jack saw the two gnomes appearing out of the red gloom of the fine evening. Here at last were faerie he could speak to without fear of them being minions of Mallmoc. He was in a state of desperation now, trying to locate Rosamund, and just talking with others would help to calm him.

'Hello,' he said, walking up to the pair, 'can I ask you a question?'

The larger gnome smiled a toothy smile. 'Why, sir, what are you doing out on the road at this hour? Don't you know there are brigands and footpads in these parts?'

Jack unslung his crossbow, hanging down his back, and flourished it in the faces of the two gnomes.

'Why, I have this to defend myself,' he said, 'so there is no need to worry on my account.'

The gnomes appeared to view the crossbow with some apprehension, but Jack said, 'Oh, I didn't mean to alarm you.'

The biggest gnome suddenly smiled again. 'Oh, you know, we are but gentle gnomes and easily frightened. See, I too have a weapon. This rapier at the ready, to ward off any attackers.' He flashed a slim blade in the red light of the dying sun, swishing it close to Jack's throat. 'Together we should be safe enough. Shall we walk alongside one another?'

Jack stepped back, slightly uncomfortable, but decided the gnome was just showing off, as faerie were wont to do.

'That's very commendable, but all I wish to know is, have you seen a maiden around here? She's got sort of strange eyes.'

'The eyes of an eagle?' said the smaller gnome.

'Yes, yes,' cried Jack, eagerly. 'You *have* seen her.'

'Not too long ago,' said the bigger one, looking over his shoulder. 'She's safe and well, tucked up on a mossy bank, ready to sleep the night away. We can take you to her, if you wish.'

'That would be great,' gabbled Jack, so relieved. 'This way, is it?'

He stepped out quickly, eager to find Rosamund. The

two gnomes were close behind him. When they had not gone more than twenty paces and were under the shadow of a tall standing stone, Jack felt a touch on his shoulder. At the same time there came the sound of a screech owl, out in the evening, which startled him with its resemblance to Rosy's voice.

Jack turned in time to realise that the gnome was steadying himself. The creature's hand was on Jack's shoulder as he tried to drive the rapier into Jack's heart. Jack gave a cry of alarm and leapt backwards. The assassin's blade fortunately missed its mark. Jack's backward leap destroyed the creature's aim. Instead, the blade went into his shoulder. Jack lashed out with his crossbow in self defence. He struck his attacker on the head.

The gnome fell backwards into a ditch. He let out a horrible scream. Jack soon saw saw why. During his fall the gnome's rapier penetrated his own chest. The chubby fellow rolled down to the bottom of the ditch. When he reached the bottom he lay stone still. The blade of his own weapon was sticking out of his chest. He was obviously dead.

The second gnome let out a shriek of anguish and ran off. Jack was in pain now. His sight was growing misty. But it was clear enough to recognise a figure appearing on the next rise. It was Rosamund, running towards him. The second gnome was directly in her path and Jack saw the creature take something out of his pocket and whirl it above his head. What was that? A slingshot? Was he aiming at Rosamund? There were several obstacles between Jack and the gnome, including trees and rocks, but he had to stop the creature from hitting Rosy with his deadly missile.

Jack levelled the crossbow and released the trigger. As always, the bolt changed into a harrier the second it left the bow. The raptor weaved in and out of the obstacles, heading towards the running gnome. Still whirling his slingshot above his head, the gnome must have sensed danger, for he turned at the last minute, just as the hawk changed back into a bolt. The bolt struck him full in the chest and bowled him over, dead as his friend.

Jack felt sick. There was no great elation in his victory. He was simply relieved that he had survived with just a flesh wound and that Rosamund was still alive and well. She reached him, running into his arms, only to let out a cry of anguish.

'Thou art hurt! The fellow has wounded thee. A curse on them, both, for they were but cowardly assassins and worthless creatures.'

'I'm – I'm all right, I think,' he said, feeling a little dizzy. 'What about those two? Are they both – dead?'

Despite himself, Jack had the hope that they too might just be wounded, though from the circumstances he didn't think to get off that lightly.

Rosamund said, 'No, they have been sent to another place, Jack. They have changed already, to the plants that fit them after death. That one out there is now some kind of ragwort, the worst of wild plants not even edible by cattle —' She crossed to look into the darkness of the ditch, which with her wonderful eyes was revealed to her clearly ' —and this one a prickly ditch weed. We have no need to concern ourselves about them. They are gone to a place they deserve.' She made Jack sit down and began tending to his injury. 'Oh, thou art pricked by the dastard's blade. No poison, I think, for the wound seems to be flowing clear and red.'

Jack's head swam. He had not thought of poison. Now his heart began hammering in panic.

'Are you sure there was nothing on the blade?'

'Believe me, Jack, my father's apothecary knew everything there is to know about poisons. He taught me all, in order that I might protect my father at mealtimes and when tending his wounds. I see no signs of such in thy wound – no strange discolouration or fiery action. No, no, this is simply a sword wound. Once we clean it and put on a poultice, thou need not fear the green rot. I have been versed in medicines by a friend of my father's, a Knight Hospitaler, one of those who offer assistance to wounded knights on the road to the crusades. Fear not, for thy Rosy is at hand.'

She smiled him such a dazzling smile of confidence and love that Jack almost melted on the spot.

'You know everything, Rosy,' he said, weakly submitting to her ministrations.

'Not *everything*, dear Jack – simply more than thee.'

'Oh, I say . . .'

'About *these* matters.'

'Right, of course. About wounds and things.'

Once she had him bandaged with a strip from the bottom of her vest and some herbs she had searched for and found, he felt a lot better. The darkness had come in now and they had to find a place to sleep. Not that it bothered them to sleep out in the open in Liöfwende, for they were used to it. The nights were rarely cold and the moss was always soft. They discovered a good patch and lay down.

'Jack,' whispered Rosamund, 'thou art very brave.'

'Not a bit of it,' he confessed, looking up at the stars as he spoke, 'I just reacted, that's all. I wish I was brave. Now *you* – you came out after me, even though those gnomes were obviously bad 'uns.'

'Oh, I know *I'm* brave, Jack. It was thee we were unsure about.'

He was quiet for a moment, then he said, 'You're teasing me, aren't you? Well,' he gave a great sigh, 'I'm not as great as you think I am, Rosy. I have to confess when I went out looking for you I got sidetracked. This beautiful fairy, see – she gave me summer wine.'

Rosamund was up and standing over him, hands on hips.

'Summer wine? Did you marry her?'

He sat up so quickly his shoulder was shot through with fiery pain and he went giddy again.

'Marry her? Of course I didn't marry her. But she delayed me a lot. I would have found you a lot sooner . . .'

'Found *me*? I think not. I found *thee*.'

'Whatever. Anyway, this female was bewitching. I mean, really bewitching, Rosy. When I looked into her mauve eyes I almost drowned, honest. I couldn't help myself. She gave me these things to eat, little sticky cakes that tasted of honey, and this moreish wine . . .'

'Summer wine.'

'Yes, exactly. Well, before I knew it her father was there and she was telling him we were going to be wed.'

'So, thou *didst* marry her.'

'No, no. I ran away.'

Rosamund's anger disappeared immediately. She

laughed in what Jack thought was rather a coarse voice
for a young lady.

'Thou fled?'

'Yes. I gave her those silver shoes, to make her feet
hurt so that she couldn't follow me, and ran off. That's all
there was to it, I swear, Rosy. I've never felt so merry in
all my life. That was some potent wine, that stuff. My
head aches even now, when I think about it.'

'Thee had a lucky escape, Jack. Many is the knight
who has woken on the cold hillside, regretting that he
had stopped to partake of summer wine with the belle
without mercy. She would have stolen thy soul, Jack,
and used it for a rag with which to wash greasy dishes.
Such fairies have no compassion. They lay their traps
and wait for gullible youths such as thyself.' Rosamund
kissed him on the cheek before returning to her mossy
spot. 'Jack, thou art such a sweet boy. I love thee more
than ever.'

He felt warm and good inside. He couldn't quite
figure out what he had done right, but he wasn't going to
delve any further. Rosy was pleased with him and that
was all that mattered. And here they were, together, she
safe and sound, and he safe and almost sound. Just the
little wound in his shoulder, which was burning like the
blazes now that he thought about it. No wonder he felt
warm! His shoulder was like a furnace! Oh well, try to
get some sleep, and deal with everything else in the
morning.

FIVE

By the morning Jack had a high fever. Rosamund was now sure that the assassin's blade had been dirty. One didn't need to tip the steel with a toxic substance when a filthy blade would give the victim blood poisoning. Rosamund was unsure what to do. Jack was in no condition to walk. He was groggy, unsteady on his feet and liable to collapse through weakness at any moment.

'I must find someone to help me,' she said, dipping a rag into cool water and mopping Jack's fevered brow with it. 'Someone strong and able.'

At that moment a giant came over the hill, whistling a merry tune and kicking his head along the ground. When the head rolled past Rosamund it gave out a little cry. The giant then got his toe under the head, flicked it up in the air, kneed it up to his shoulder, which nudged it sideways. It landed squarely on the neck and the right way round, too. The manoeuvre was carried out with a great deal of skill. Jack had told Rosamund about a football team called Arsenal and she wondered if this giant belonged to such a wonderful team.

'Excuse me, ma'am,' said the giant. 'I didn't mean to alarm you. I know you mortals are not used to the antics of Hollow Ben.'

'How knowest thou that?'

'Because Solomon told me.'

Rosamund stepped back. 'Thou art the villain who drowned our priest.'

'No, no, indeed. He drowned himself, I think, by trying to cross the fierce flood. He was being chased at the time by a horse-fairy. Was he your friend? I'm sorry. We had some nice talks together. I hope he's changed into something beautiful, like a lily or a rose.'

'Being mortal, I think we do not change.'

'Ah, pity.'

Rosamund stared at the giant and found herself believing him. He was too amiable a fellow to go around killing monks. Just at that moment Jack groaned and rolled over. Rosamund let out a sigh.

'Ah, sir giant, dost thou know any person hereabouts, faerie, mortal or mythago, who might help me? I must carry my poor ailing friend to the gnomes, that we might be given assistance.'

'Why, Hollow Ben will help you. He doesn't look too heavy. A mere stripling. Let me do it for you. I'll carry him as gently as a mother carries her baby.'

'But,' the maiden pointed out, 'you have no arms.'

Hollow Ben looked down at himself and saw this was true.

'Oh, my, I forgot to put them back on again. They'll

still be lying down by the last brook, where I dipped them in a pool to cool the hands. You wait here, little maid. I'll be back in just a short while.'

Hollow Ben ambled off. In quite a short time he was back again, swinging his arms proudly. 'I'm going to lose them one of these days,' he confessed, as he picked up Jack. 'Then I'll be sorry. They're quite a good pair and they fit me exactly.'

'It must be, for surely thou wast born with them?'

Hollow Ben stopped and thought for a moment.

'You may be right. Now, which way do we go, young maid?'

'That way, I think. Yes, that was the direction from which Jack came.' Jack moaned again. 'Hurry, we must find a good physician, for my dear friend Jack, who is sorely in need. I shall treat him on the way with any woundwort plants we might find, but he needs expert attention.'

Hollow Ben strode out. Rosamund had to run to keep up with his walk. It took them half a day to reach the mines, which were now ready to sabotage Mallmoc's castle-ship. The giant was a long way ahead of Rosamund at this point, with a limp Jack draped in his arms.

Spiggot and Fen came rushing up to Hollow Ben and demanded to know why he had broken their Jack.

'For shame, giant!' cried Fen. 'Pick on someone your own size.'

'No, no,' puffed Rosamund, finally catching up. 'Hollow Ben carried him here. Jack was wounded by an assassin's blade and now has a blood-fever which will carry him off if we do not get help. Where is Jinty?'

'Jinty we do not need,' said Fen, emphatically. 'Place him on the ground, giant, and leave him to me.'

Hollow Ben did as he was asked, then stepped aside in case his clumsiness should cause any more injury amongst the folk around him. He went and sat on a stump nearby, taking off his aching arms with his teeth and hanging them in the boughs of a tree to give them a rest. He was quite pleased with himself. It was not often he got the chance to help mortals, or faerie for that matter. When such occasions came round, they left him feeling warm and good inside. He hummed a tune, quietly to himself.

Fen went to work on Jack with some female boggart magic. Boggarts were not renowned for their magic, nor indeed were gnomes, for both faerie were more physical than spiritual. But this was Liöfwende and everyone who came from here had *some* skill in the magic arts. Certainly the boggarts had healing skills, for metal workers are always hitting their thumbs with hammers, or dropping anvils on their toes, or burning their fingers on red-hot iron. Male boggarts were forever running to their females with an injury which the mother, wife, sister or daughter then had to make better.

Septicaemia, or blood poisoning, was a state which boggarts often brought upon themselves. Purifiers and clarifiers of the blood were needed. Fen had to chase down the poison, block its passage, dilute it, render it impotent. Fen took charge, sending Spiggot and the gnomes out into the woods and fields to look for various herbs and fungi.

'It's a good thing you put that woundwort poultice on his injury,' muttered Fen to Rosamund, 'or that red line would be well on its way to his heart by now.'

She pointed to the ugly vein that traced the poison through Jack's body towards his softly-beating heart.

Jack sat up with a start, his eyes staring wildly.

'Inform the Pentagon we need Black Star cover!' he
cried. Then he lay back down on his bed in a hot sweat,
murmuring, 'Julia Roberts, yeah, Julia Roberts.'

'Methinks the poor boy is passing mad,' said
Rosamund, 'to utter such strange words and names.'

Rosamund was now dabbing a cool, damp cloth on
Jack's forehead again. She was anxious and worried
about him, but Fen's ministrations made her feel better.

'Dost thou think thee might save my Jack?'

'I hope so. Indeed, I'm sure I can. I have treated many
a wound worse than this and brought the victim out of
his fever.'

Fen tried to sound confident, but she was not sure
how strong mortals were at resisting illness. Jack had
to *want* to live. There had to be some fight in him, some
determination that he was going to get better, no
matter what. A boggart was a sort of blunt faerie.
When a boggart was injured he did not lie down and
whimper: he shrugged and gritted his teeth. Now
pixies wailed and elves snivelled, but for the most part,
all faerie were pretty tough when it came to illness and
injury. That's why changelings lived so long, even
when they had been given to mortals to look after.
They sort of wasted away, rather than keeled over and
died.

Yet this Jack seemed to be made of the right stuff.
Certainly Rosamund was, but Fen was only half-con-
vinced that mortal males were as strong as mortal
females. She was inclined to think not. Not when it came
to illness. Oh, sure, they could lift logs and throw rocks,
but could they withstand the ravages of disease as well as
their other halves?

Spiggot came running back with his arms full of leaves, roots and bits of bark.

'That,' said Fen, picking through them, 'but not *that* or that – Spiggot, what did your mother Quagmarish ever teach you? Ah, yes, good – you brought this herb. Well, that's something. Go out and get some more of it. Can you remember where you found it? I hope so. Off, off.'

Spiggot did as he was told, wondering how female boggarts managed to get so bossy when it came to situations like this.

'Can I help?' asked Hollow Ben. 'I could lift him up so the gentle breeze gets under his frail body.'

'You could,' said Fen, 'but don't forget to put your arms back on first.'

Hollow Ben retrieved his arms and then knelt down by the patient. He lifted him up about a metre off the ground. Now the breezes were able to reach every part of Jack's body and cool him. Rosamund patted the giant's shoulder to show how pleased she was with him.

All the rest of that evening, and part of the next day, Jack underwent the closest ministrations by Fen and Rosamund. Hollow Ben could not bear to watch someone who was so sick, so he left them and wandered off again on his own. It was not that the giant did not care. On the contrary, his heart was so soft it could not withstand the blows of emotional pain. If sorrow battered at this great organ too much it might cease to work at all.

Halfway through the morning Jack opened his eyes.

'Oh, I feel awful,' he groaned. 'Rosy, I think I'm done for.'

Once Rosamund had seen that Jack was on the mend

all the worry lines and strain went out of her face. These
contours of anxiety were replaced by a clear expression
of indifference. There was no sympathy from Rosamund
Guillaume de Arundel. Only the sort of cold briskness of
a state-registered nurse. Her eyes revealed an impartial-
ity which shocked Jack.

She immediately began berating him for being so self-
indulgent.

'Get a hold of thyself, Jack,' she growled at him. 'Pull
thyself together. Stop whining in self-pity. Sit up while I
give thee some chicken gruel.'

'My mum,' muttered Jack, 'used to be ever so nice to
us when we were ill as children.'

'Thy mother is thy mother. I am thy nurse. Fen is thy
physician. If we spent time feeling sorry for thee, Jack,
we would not be able to make thee better. Thou art a *man*
Jack, so act like one. I care not of course,' she added
airily, as she fed him gruel with a spoon, 'whether thou
recovers or passes on to another place. There are many
Jacks in the world for us Jills.'

His eyes were ringed with black and his face was as
pale as newly-ground flour.

'I don't believe you,' he said. 'You do care.'

'Open up. Wider. There. Not I, Jack. Thee must have
me confused with some other. Thou art simply the
patient and I the curer. Wider still, this spoon was made
for a large gnomish mouth. There, swallow. Why, thy
eyes water. Art thou weeping because there are no fond
words from me, Jack?'

'No,' gargled Jack, 'the soup's too peppery!'

Rosamund laughed at this. She continued to feed him
and once he had finished he fell asleep again. Fen

nodded at her, as if to say, the fever has broken. He is now safe. Rosamund's eyes went misty and soft again, now that Jack was not there to see them. In her world females had to protect themselves with such wiles, or they would not last long. A knight soon grew bored of a wilting maiden and threw her in the tower. It was only the ones with spirit that survived, that came through to a free old age.

'Now,' said Jinty, with a council of his gnomes, 'you say Jack was attacked by those two gnomes who were here before?'

'Yes,' explained Rosamund. 'I followed them, hoping they would lead me to him. Thank the lord I had these eagle's eyes and was able, not only to keep them in sight, but to warn Jack of their nefarious intentions.'

'Wolfsbane and Kurse,' said Jinty, shaking his head. 'I knew they were bad, but not *that* bad. Gnomes have never been assassins before, even if they were banished. It just shows you how evil Mallmoc is, that he can turn a gnome into a killer. What a fiend he is. Well, we're all ready for him now. I understand he's discovered the reason why he has been unable to find his course. Prince Rincortle found the whirligigs stirring up the earth spirits. So he's on his way back here again, we being in direct line with Sutton Hoo. Now it would be a miracle if he came sailing right through this field, just as we want him to. It's likely he'll come near, but we have to lure him into the trap, just as a mortal hunter might lure a wild beast . . .'

'Well,' said Spiggot, 'I understand they often ∂rove wild beasts into their traps.'

'That's as maybe,' said Jinty, 'but thou dost not ∂rive

sorcerers. Thee may entice them, thee might lead them, but thou dost not push them. We have to get some bait. We need something to make the warlock come this way and try to cross this field. Any suggestions anyone?'

Rosamund put her hand up. 'Yes, Jinty,' she replied. 'Jack and I have spoken on this matter and we have a plan.'

PART FIVE

The War of the Shadows

ONE

'So,' said Spiggot, folding his spark-pitted arms, 'what is this plan of yours, Rosamund?'

'A barrier in front of the field.'

All present looked at Rosamund as if she were mad. A barrier? Jinty scratched his head. Fen looked mystified. Spiggot looked from one face to another, loath to commit himself at first. But then, when he saw that the rest of the faerie around him were as puzzled as he was, he spoke.

'I don't think you understand, Rosamund,' he said. 'If we build a barrier in front of the field, Mallmoc will see it. If he was indeed heading straight for our trap, he will then avoid it.' Spiggot smiled gently. 'I'm sure you mortals mean well, but you have no deviousness in you. Now, let's all try and think of a *sensible* scheme.'

''Tis a scheme with *much* sense,' said Rosamund. 'Is it not so, Jack?'

Jack nodded, croaking in a weak voice, 'Listen to Rosy.'

'Show us the sense,' Fen suggested. 'Then we'll listen.'

'We build a barrier of logs and branches just as wide as the meadow we have mined beneath,' explained Rosamund. 'We build it prodigiously large. Formidable to behold. But in the secret knowledge that Mallmoc's castle-ship could smash through such a barrier without damage to itself. Mallmoc sends dragon-outriders ahead of him, does he not? Ulcugga riders?'

'Yes,' said Jinty and Spiggot, both at once.

'Well, then, they will see the barrier from the air and assess its strength. They will report to the sorcerer. Mallmoc will know that such a barrier will not stop his castle-ship. They will report to Mallmoc who will think we are trying to stop him going across the field. His arrogance and pride will make him want to show us how powerful and unstoppable he actually is. He is vain about his potency. Thus Mallmoc will head for the barrier of a purpose, to show us in what disdain he holds our puny efforts to prevent his progress. He will go out of his way to smash through our barrier and reduce it to kindling-sticks because he likes to destroy things and he likes to show off.'

Spiggot stared at Fen. Fen looked at Jinty. Jinty suddenly let out a yell of triumph.

'Yes! He will do it.'

Spiggot folded those nut-brown arms of his again. 'Perhaps,' he said. 'But we're assuming a lot, aren't we? This plan could work, but we need another lure. How soon could you gnomes build something that looks like a siege catapult? A nice big one that looks as if it could cause some damage? It doesn't actually have to work properly.'

'Oh, we could knock one up in an hour or two by the flower clock,' said Jinty, pursing his lips. 'It wouldn't be a good *working* machine, but it would look the business. We could use timbers from old mines. And the spoon thing could be fashioned from an old bucket.'

'What we need, then,' said Spiggot, going into his busy-busy mode, 'is a big catapult which we place some way behind the barrier. Myself and Jack, if he's well enough, and a dozen or so gnomes will man the catapult as if we mean to use it.'

'But,' pointed out Rosamund, 'won't you be caught by the ulcugga when they come riding up on their horses?'

Spiggot shook his head. 'When Mallmoc smashes through the barrier to get at the catapult, we'll bolt for the nearest entrance to the gnome underground passageways. Once we're down inside the burrows the ulcugga will never follow us. Like all fairies, they're terrified of being caught in confined spaces beneath the earth. They'd get slaughtered, one by one, if they tried to enter the subterranean world of the gnomes.'

'They would, too,' muttered Jinty, nodding darkly. 'Good, well, that's the plan, then. Let's get to work.'

Soon the landscape was a hive of activity. The siege catapult was knocked up and set in place. The timbers used to give it shape were only loosely cobbled together, but from a distance no one could tell it was not the real thing. Indeed, the catapult was in place and seemingly manned by a group of gnomes when the first of the purple dragonriders flew overhead. The ulcugga in the saddle looked down and saw a feverish army of gnomes

dragging dead boughs and logs in an attempt to form a
barrier across the entrance to a large field. There had
been some effort also, by the gnomes, to camouflage the
catapult with leafy branches.

The dragonrider noticed that once he had been
spotted, the boggarts, mortals and gnomes below seemed
to panic. They began running about like frantic ants,
fetching thorn twigs from the forest and adding them to
the barrier. Every so often they looked up at the circling
dragon and pointed, shouting urgent orders to 'Hurry'.
Jack, now on his feet but still extremely weak, shook his
fist at the dragonrider, and gestured that he should
come and fight. The ulcugga smiled and shook his head.
He was not going to be enticed from his duty that way.
He was going to report to his master immediately.

'So,' muttered Mallmoc, stroking his chin, 'they have
built a barrier.'

'Yes, my lord,' said the fairy. ''Tis prodigiously large.'

'In order to protect a field weapon.'

'That is how it seemed to me, my lord. But the weapon
is merely one that flings fireballs and rocks and such.
Nothing to harm our mighty vessel. Indeed, the barrier
was tall but not impregnable. It could not withstand our
vessel. There is nothing they have which could stop our
progress.'

'And at the moment our set course would take us two
hundred yards to the right of this meadow?'

'It seems so, from the air, my lord.'

After the fairy had gone, Prince Rincortle said, 'Are
you thinking what I'm thinking?'

Mallmoc nodded. 'I have reports that Puck has now

gathered an army of fairies and is heading our way. It might be expedient to show that army who they are dealing with. We might teach them a lesson that there is no barrier, indeed no weapon, however large and strange to Liöfwende, that can stop Mallmoc's mighty land iron-clad. I'm sure that mortal engineer thinks he is very clever, building his barriers and siege machines. We'll show them just how clever he isn't. Change course. We'll smash through that barrier and crush their puny weapon.'

Spiggot, armoured and armed, shining like a precious statue in the gleam of the morning sunlight, stood with sword in hand. Fen and a dozen gnomes had remained with him, watching the terrible castle-ship ploughing through the turf towards them. Flints and other stones flew out from the bows of the land vessel, striking tree trunks. Sods of earth splattered against the bushes it passed. Divots were flung high into the sky. Dirt, grit and other debris rained upon the fields through which it passed.

'Here it comes,' muttered Spiggot. 'Get ready to run.'

Once more the boggart was pleased that it was light fairy armour that he wore, which would not hamper his retreat.

'We're ready,' said Jinty,' aren't we folks?'

The gnomes had edgy feet. They could see the beauti-ful but dreaded ulcugga fairies riding in their hundreds on either side of the ironclad. Others swarmed behind these riders, the infantry which was bringing up the rear. Those ulcugga could swamp the small contingent of gnomes and boggarts and obliterate them without a trace.

Jack had still been too ill to join the defending force, though he had pleaded to be allowed to. Rosamund would not hear of it and she and Kling had taken Jack to the burrows where the gnomes lived. Spiggot had told Jack that he did not think any less of his friend for that. Kling, that able water rat, had taken Jack and Rosamund on the cart, along with their other possessions, leaving Spiggot looking as if he was ready to do battle with the sorcerer.

Spiggot pointed. 'There's Mallmoc!'

The gnomes looked up. They could see the sorcerer in one of the castle's towers. He was gripping a crenellation with crooked hands, laughing as goblins, elves and other faerie in the region scrambled to get out of the way of his craft. A goblin pedlar lost his pots and pans when he woke from sleep in a ditch to find the castle-ship almost upon him. He left the spot in panic, then turned to see the iron monster squash his wares. Dejected, the goblin pedlar simply stared up at the grinning sorcerer. He might have voiced his hate if the ulcugga had not been riding by. When they had passed he took off his green pointed cap and flung it at his feet in disgust.

'It's almost at the barrier,' murmured Fen. 'Get ready to run!'

'I'm ready, I'm ready,' answered Jinty.

The prow of the castle-ship crashed into the barrier of logs and branches. The logs were simply pushed aside like twigs. The branches cracked and crumpled, going under the iron bows of the castle. The craft cut through them with its ploughshare prow. Cracked branches went spinning through the air. Logs were reduced to slivers.

The astounding weight and power of the craft ensured its onward progress.

Pushing aside the remnants of the blockade, the castle-ship entered the meadow.

'Run!' cried Jinty, as the ulcugga surged forward through the gap. 'Run for your lives!'

Spiggot, Fen and the gnomes needed no further bidding. They fled. However, Spiggot could not help looking over his shoulder as Mallmoc's great shout of despair went up. He saw the castle-ship dive nose-down into a huge black pit in the earth as the worm-holed meadow collapsed beneath it. Great showers of stones and rocks fell upon the ulcugga riders and infantry. The terrible ironclad dropped like a monstrous heaving beast into the hole it had made for itself. The shock of the impact flung Mallmoc from his turret out on to the turf, under the hooves of the panicking ulcugga mounts. He scrambled to his feet, seemingly unhurt, but looking quite bewildered.

Then the castle-ship let out a horrible scream, as if it was indeed a wounded animal. Now the escaping boggarts and gnomes all stopped and turned to witness the scene. Some of the iron plates in the castle had split their welded seams on impact at the bottom of the pit. Steam hissed through fissures. Hot coals from hell's scullery within were flung forth. Fire was spurting out through gaps in the hull and walls. Flaming lumps of coke and charcoal were shot from furnace mouths like shells from cannons. They made beautiful fiery arcs in the air before falling to Earth.

Molten iron from the foundary cauldrons came pouring forth as red-hot lava from a volcano. It oozed into Mallmoc's chambers destroying books, charts and documents. The vessel's lifeblood was draining away, dripping down into the damps soils beneath. The great castle-ship's belly had burst upon the impact and the hot air trapped within pipes and boilers now shrieked through widening cracks, frightening the birds. Fountains of boiling water sprayed over the landscape and fell on ulcugga fairies. Turrets fell and towers dropped with loud clanging noises. The whole vessel was collapsing, falling in on itself, dropping apart.

Then, out through wider gaps in the plates, ragged mortals and grubby faerie came pouring forth. They were pale creatures, having been locked away from the light of day for many a year. Some dodged between the confused ulcugga troops and scattered for the woodlands on the horizon. Others ran full pelt for a nearby river ford, to splash across its shallows and away over a stretch of moorland. Spiggot knew these were Mallmoc's slaves. He had been one himself once. Fen and the gnomes cheered the escapees.

Ulcugga riders went after the slaves, but there were too many of them. Some of them grabbed branches and knocked the ulcugga fairies out of their saddles. Others attacked single fairies in groups of a dozen or more, yet more others were anxious to ensure their own freedom, for the ulcugga began to rally. Soon, Mallmoc's hated fairies organised themselves and began the recapture of the escapees, rounding them up like cattle. Clearly many *had* got away, but Rincortle was going to make sure *some* were caught.

Finally, a squadron of the Ulcugga cavalry turned their attention to Spiggot and his allies, who began running like mad for the entrances to the gnome warren.

TWO

Spiggot, Fen and the gnomes managed to get to the entrance of the underground passageways before being ridden down. Spiggot stood facing the charging fairies, hacking at their lances when they came too near. Then he, too, was gone, down into the darkness of the burrows, where no ulcugga would follow. The sound of Mallmoc shouting in despair and anguish was the last thing that Spiggot heard from the surface. He allowed himself a great sigh of satisfaction.

Later they were all gathered together for a feast in the earthen hall of the gnome chieftains.

'To our triumph and success,' cried Jinty, raising a goblet of elderflower juice. 'Eat, drink and be merry!'

A loud cheer went up and the gnomes began hammering on the tables with their spoons and forks. Spiggot grinned at Fen. Jack, propped up in a tall-backed chair, smiled at Rosamund. They had won the first round. Of course, it was not the end of the battles they would have against Mallmoc, but at least they had stopped the fiendish sorcerer from reaching Sutton Hoo. They ate and drank for an hour or so, some of the younger gnomes becoming rowdy as the banquet went on. Then Jack and Spiggot excused themselves to go and investigate what was happening on the surface.

There was a hollow tree on a hill. One could reach the inside of this tree from the gnome burrows. Through a hole where a branch had once been Spiggot and Jack had a good view of the meadow. Steam was still rising from the hole in the middle. Swarming round the pit were ulcugga fairies with ropes, trying to use their horses to drag the castle out. It was an impossible task, of course.

'If they used beam engines and pulleys, they might get somewhere,' muttered the Jack, the engineer coming out in him. 'But even then the weight of that iron castle-ship must be tremendous.'

'They won't use engines,' replied Spiggot. 'They won't even *think* about it. Fairies hate engines. One of the reasons they hate them is because they have no understanding of them. If you gave them one of your derricks or cranes right now they would simply be mystified by its use.'

'Does that mean they'll *never* get that castle out?'

'No,' replied Spiggot. 'It's not that they're not clever. They are. And so is Mallmoc, of course. Mallmoc is a genius when it comes to magic and the dark arts. They simply need a great deal of time to organise themselves and think their way out of this trap. Give them a week and they'll have it out and repaired enough to be ploughing towards Sutton Hoo again.'

'But I don't understand *how*,' insisted Jack, 'if they don't use lifting equipment.'

'Well, Mallmoc may divert a river and float it free. Or he may conjure up a volcanic eruption and push it out with lava. Or he may magic up an earthquake which slides it out. Now, you see, Jack, I am not particularly clever at all, but I can think of all those ways.'

'Well, a week won't help him. The Irish, Scots and English fairies from the North will be here very soon. They'll defeat the ulcugga and then we'll be free to deal with Mallmoc.'

'It's not as easy as that, Jack. I wish it were.'

'What's to stop it?'

'Why, the battles between the ulcugga and the other fairy clans will be long and complicated. That will buy Mallmoc some time. You see, fairies don't fight like mortals, Jack. They don't ride hard into each other and start bashing away with clubs. They don't march in columns to a given place and then charge at each other with swords. They sort of dance around one another, weighing up the odds, avoiding any direct contact. There might be one or two skirmishes on the edges, but nothing serious. It's a wary game of one army circling the other army, not getting too close. It's the art of fighting without fighting. They won't close with one another just like that. Oh no. They'll taunt one another from a safe distance. Then the taunted side will give chase, the taunters will run, and the two groups will go back to their camps at the end of the day without any real encounter.'

'That's daft!' cried Jack.

'No, no, it's *sensible*. Any battle such as mortals fight

would diminish the fairy clans drastically. You must remember fairies don't spawn like mortals or boggarts. It takes centuries to build up to the fairy numbers that inhabit our world today. Millennia, even.'

'Breed would be a better word,' muttered Jack.

'Sorry?'

'We don't *spawn*, we breed.'

'Sorry, Jack, didn't know that was a sensitive issue amongst you folk. Anyway, you understand what I mean? In any case there has to be a shadow war before the proper one takes place.'

'A shadow war,' repeated Jack, wearily. 'All right, Spiggot, what's a shadow war?'

'The fairy clans will send in their shadows to fight each other, just to get the measure of who might win and who might lose. It's a dreadful thing, Jack, if your shadow does not come back. Folk lose sight of you for a while, until you grow another one. I mean, your shadow defines who you are, doesn't it? Without light and shade, you become invisible.'

Jack shook his head in bewilderment.

'Isn't there ever any outcome? Do these Mexican stand-offs last for ever? Or is there eventually a fight?'

'You see!' cried Spiggot, 'You even have a name for it. Some of your battles must be of a similar nature.'

'Not the ones I know. Anyway, answer the question.'

'Well, I suppose there will be a clash of sorts in the end. Not a full onslaught by either side, but a sort of clannish battle of the bravest of the brave.'

'What do you think, about a tenth of the whole?'

'Something like that, Jack. We're talking of numbers that will not deplete the population if one side starts getting the upper hand. We don't want any massacres in Liöfwende.'

'Not even to save Liöfwende itself?'

'Not even to do that. Rather we spend the next ten thousand years under the thrall of Mallmoc, in a muddled mix of two worlds – mortal and faerie – than wipe out the fairy clans. Once their numbers fall too low they might die out altogether. You remember that mad fairy we once met on the edge of a moor? If they were slaughtered the survivors would all turn to lunatics, Jack. They might seem strong to you now, while they are here in numbers, but actually their minds are fragile. They would shatter like glass and their species would disappear from the face of the Earth.'

'An endangered species, eh?'

'Could be.'

Jack peered out through the hole at the busy ulcugga. From here they looked numerous and mighty strong. He knew they were vicious creatures when they wanted to be. Almost as cruel as the one who led them at this present time. Was it because Mallmoc had them in his thrall? Had he enslaved their minds? Perhaps the ulcugga could be taught to be good faerie if they were given another chance? Spiggot had once said that the ulcugga had not been quite as bad before Mallmoc arrived in Liöfwende.

'So, the shadow war comes first?'

'Yes.'

'Will you send your shadow out?'

'No, Jack – only the fairies can do that. But I shall be amongst the bravest of the brave, when the real fighting comes. Will you?'

'I dunno,' replied Jack, honestly. 'I'm not sure if I'm one of the bravest . . .'

'Well, it will be your choice, Jack. No one will force you to go.'

'There might be pressure on me, psychologically. I mean, if you all go. If Rosy decides to go. Then I'll have to, won't I? I mean, how could I live with myself afterwards if none of you came back? That's how a lot of kings and rulers and governments have got their citizens to fight as soldiers in wars, by shaming them into joining. Didn't you know that?'

Spiggot was dumbfounded. 'No, I never thought of that.'

'I didn't think you had. Of course, there are those who feel the need to fight because of their beliefs or because they wish to defend their country. Some less savoury: because they want their country to rule over others. Or there are mercenaries who fight simply to earn money. There are all kinds of reasons why men become warriors. But those who do fight often look down on those who refuse to fight, taking the moral high ground.'

'You mortals *are* devious, in the way you think. I just thought, well, Kling *definitely* won't go out and fight. That's his choice.'

'But he's a water rat . . .'

'He's still a creature, one whose world will tumble down around him if Mallmoc gets his way.'

'But water rats don't have to answer to anyone, do they? Other water rats won't hold them in contempt.'

'No, I suppose that's true. Can we go back now, Jack? My mind is spinning with your debating. I need a drink of water.'

The pair of them returned to the chamber they had been given. Rosamund and Kling were already there, sorting out who was sleeping where. Jack marvelled at how calmly Rosamund took everything. He was in a whirl of bloodheat, what with all they had been through that day. Of course, he knew he had only just come out of a state of delirium, caused by the blood poisoning from the rapier, but still he admired her. She was one of the toughest characters he had ever met, which seemed strange when you looked at her, for what you saw was a delicate peaches-and-cream maiden.

'Are you all right, Rosy?'

'Why, yes, Jack,' she laughed, placing a bundle of hay in one corner, the last empty corner of the chamber. 'Now, here is thy bed, stripling. I have made it nice and soft for thee, so that thou sleepest sound tonight. We want no bad humours to visit our Jack and give him nightmares, do we? Rosamund shall be over there, in that corner, if thou dost need water. Thou art not a strong youth at the present hour, Jack, and need thy rest.'

'You're a brick, Rosy. I am knackered.'

'A brick?' she laughed again. 'Would that I were a stone and then I would be senseless to all this bloody conquest. Yet, we shall prevail, of that I am certain. Thou art my knight, Jack, and give me strength.'

No, thought Jack, Rosamund would never understand if he decided he would not follow Spiggot into battle. She was a warrior's daughter, from a time when warriors ruled the Earth. There were no governments with ideals, no democratically voted representatives, no fast-talking politicians in Rosamund's time. In those days might was right and you did what you were told by the strongest baron in the region, or you lost your head.

Jack's shoulder was beginning to feel sore again and he did as he was told and went to bed. He lay there, half-dozing, for many an hour it seemed, listening to the low drone of conversation between his friends. It was calming, that sound of talk. It made him feel secure and peaceful. Finally, he dropped off into a deep energy-reviving sleep for several hours.

THREE

The next day, Spiggot and Kling slipped out in the early dawn to meet with Puck. Soft balls of cloud were drifting across an indigo sky above as the two creatures sneaked through brake and fern. A bogle flew overhead on a nightjar, stark against the blueness. Perhaps that was the same one who had brought Spiggot the message from Puck that morning?

It was difficult for Spiggot to believe, on such a pleasant sunny day, that Liöfwende was a country torn by war. To the east he could see smoke curling from chimneys: probably a boggart village, for who but a metalsmith would have a fire going on such a day? From one hill they looked down upon some reed beds on the edge of a pixie's mill pond. There were elves there, gathering the reeds, probably for the roofs of their dome-shaped houses. Warblers flew out as the elves cut the stalks with their tiny sickles, angry at having to build new nests, new homes.

There would, of course, thought Spiggot as he scrambled along trying to keep up with the four-footed water rat, be creatures who had no idea of the crisis the world was in. Solitary individuals who kept their own counsel and remained isolated from society would have no idea that they were about to be plunged into the dark shades of war. Creatures like the Urisk and Redcap. Jack-in-Irons of course, and Jimmy Squarefoot. Then there was the Glaistig, Jenny Greenteeth and Peg Powler, will o'the wisp. All creatures of pond, weir, wood and hill, who were ignorant of the affairs of Faerieland.

'Come on, master's son,' muttered Kling, scrambling through some gorse thorns without managing to scratch himself, 'you're dreaming again.'

Robin Goodfellow, as Puck is also known, was standing in the mottled shadows beneath a hornbeam tree. He was almost invisible in his leaf-green jacket and hose, with his pointed green cap and long owl's feather. His shoes were of bark and his belt of split reed. Sharp of nose and hollow of cheek, he looked very severe to the worried Spiggot. Spiggot climbed a rise and then stepped forward to meet the electric and normally effervescent creature familiar to both worlds, Mortaland and Liöfwende.

'Good day to you, boggart – and to you, giant vole.'

Spiggot and Kling returned the greeting. Then Spiggot said, 'Have you brought the armies of fairy?'

'They are just over the hill,' replied the immortal with the narrow elfin face and star-bright eyes, 'in their hundreds. There are the tylwyth teg, the unseelie and seelie court, the tuatha dé, the Northumberland fairies and many others. Some are mounted, some are on foot.

They come in shining armour and padded jackets, with long lances and short swords. There is enough glitter and glister to blind a mole. They are at your command.' Puck's eyes narrowed. 'Use this time well, son of Quagmarish and Gnomon, and do not fail or the otherwise respected smithy race of boggart faerie will be held in contempt for all time thereafter.'

Spiggot gulped, aware of the great responsibility.

'I'll try not to,' he said, aware of Puck's eyes searching his face keenly for signs of weakness. 'I will do my best.'

'The lad's up to it, Puck,' said Kling, putting a forepaw on his master's son's shoulder. 'Kling will help him through.'

'Vole, I know you well and expect no less than perfection.'

Now it was Kling's turn to audibly gulp and Spiggot realised that the pair of them were in great awe of Robin Goodfellow, who had been the mighty Oberon's sidekick and advisor for several centuries.

'Besides,' Spiggot said, 'you'll be here too, won't you, Puck, so we can turn to you for advice?'

'Not I,' came the reply, the folded arms firm against the bony chest. 'Puck is no coward, but this is a battle for the fairies. I can sour milk with the best of them and even fight single combat, but I am no warrior amongst warriors. Puck has always and forever been a lone creature. My work is done: the clans are gathered and waiting. The day of command belongs to you, Spiggot, and you alone. Be wise. Be astute.'

With that, Puck left them, to circle the Earth, as was his wont.

Spiggot girded his loins and prepared to meet the

fairies. He had not worn his armour, of course, because it was bright and shiny and there were ulcugga skirmishers abroad. One had to remain with the camouflage of forest-wear while travelling across country.

Yet when he went over the hill it was obvious to him that the fairies did not believe in camouflage of any kind. It was a dazzling sight, with light leaping from speartip to sword hilt, from bridle bit to helm crest. There were peacock feathers in abundance, and feathers of the black crow, the white owl, the striped partridge and the red pheasant. There were cloakskins made from grey-cowled wolves that had died a natural death and snakehide shoes fashioned from sloughed adderskin. There were standards of cockwattle scarlet and banners spun from spidersilk. Bronze and copper armour was everywhere, blinding in its brilliance. There were the shed antlers of deer and the horns of goats, banded in silver, patterned in gold. Beautiful shields, embossed with the owner's heraldic symbols, hung from the flanks of horses, and spears were stacked like sheaves of corn amongst the mounts.

Such a sight took Spiggot's breath away with its magnificence!

He walked down amongst the fairies, some of them so fierce-looking in their battle array they would stun a wild beast. He was aware of the jingle-jangle of bridle-irons, the justle of small saddle-bells, the whisper of silk and satin on metal. His sense of smell was assailed by the perfume of fragrant fairies: those who could not bear to travel far from their native lands without taking heather, or lilac blossoms, or lavender with them to remind them of their homes. Underlying these odours was the scent of damp hay laid out for the animals to eat in the morning's rest hours.

All eyes were on Spiggot as he walked through the fairy ranks. Most fairies were at least a head taller than a boggart and they looked down upon him. Could he command them? These magnificent creatures, some from above the borders of the North, others from across the Irish Sea? Doubts attacked him now as he sought out King Cimberlin and Prince Xinixia of the Northumberland fairies.

At last he saw the pair, standing with Chieftain Cragfeggian of the seelie court, from Thristlac, and Fearghus of Eri-innis, king of the tuatha dé. These were three of the most powerful fairies in Faerieland and they turned and acknowledged the common boggart as he approached.

'Spiggot,' said King Cimberlin. 'How is your father, Gnomon?' He turned to the other two clan rulers. 'You know Spiggot's father is the best armour-maker in the whole of Liöfwende? I have never known a boggart with hands like Gnomon. His works are renowned.'

'I ken the smithy,' replied Cragfeggian, 'and mah ain claymore was fashioned by this very boggart, to be admired by all.'

Spiggot felt as if he could burst with pride on hearing this. His own father, known beyond the borders of the land!

'I too have heard of him,' said Fearghus. 'His name is whispered in the storms that cross the seas to Eri-innis.'

'Well, Spiggot,' continued Cimberlin, 'are we ready?'

The brown boggart nodded his black-haired head in affirmation.

'I am a ready boggart if you are ready, fairies.'

This remark had every head turning in the camp. Delivered in the deep timbre of a smithy, it sounded like one of those sayings which last forever. Sayings such as used by the first man to step on the surface of the moon, or by a general before an unequal battle. Spiggot knew at once that he had said the right thing. A murmur went up around him, from the lips of those who might well have held him in contempt not so long ago. It was the sort of remark that inspired confidence in those unsure of their victory. Respect. That was what flowed towards Spiggot from all sides. He received approving looks from all three leaders of the fairy clans who stood close by him.

'Of course,' added Spiggot, 'we must fight the shadow war before the real one, but I think we have fierceness on our side.'

The shadows of the gathered fairies shimmied nervously in the light from the sun.

'Let us hope so, boggart, for the enemy have the numbers,' said Prince Xinixia, who had so far been silent. If anyone doubted the ability of a boggart to lead a fairy army, Spiggot knew it was him. 'But enough of the talk, it is time we sent our shadows forth, to do battle with those of the ulcugga.'

A great shout went up amongst the fairies and their shadows suddenly detached themselves and swept over the hill, dark and dangerous in their hundreds. The fairies then took on false shadows, so that they should remain visible to one another and to their visitors. When the last real shadow had slid over the brow of the hill, a quiet peace descended on the camp. The leaders of the three clans said their farewells to Spiggot and told him they would meet again once the shadow war was determined.

Prince Xinixia was walking away when an emboldened Spiggot called to him.

'You don't think I'm good enough, do you?'

Xinixia turned and stared at him. 'Good enough for what?'

'To lead the fairy army.'

Xinixia was one of the most handsome fairies that had ever lived, but he could sneer with great ugliness.

'What I think,' he said, his hand on his sword hilt, 'is immaterial. My father rules and what he says is law. But I will say one thing. Do not for one moment believe you were chosen for your prowess with a weapon or for your ability to lead where others could not. Do you honestly think you are better than *me* in battle? Or most of the fairy warriors here? Any one of them could cut you down in a second. You know that.'

'Then – then why was I chosen?'

Kling clutched at his master's son's garb and tried to pull him away, murmuring, 'Don't ask that.'

'Why?' said Prince Xinixia. 'Why? Use your intelligence. If I or my father led these fairies and the battle was lost, we would be broken rulers. The same with any of the other clan leaders.' Xinixia's eyes suddenly took on a rare softness. 'Boggart, I have nothing against you. I too believe your father is one of the most brilliant armourers in all the kingdoms. You could have followed him in his art and craft, for there is no one like a father teaching a son, to pass on such skills. Perhaps you could have surpassed him in talent: become an even greater smithy than he? Who knows.'

'So – so,' croaked Spiggot, his voice cracking, 'you think I've been put here as someone to blame if it all goes wrong?'

'Sadly, yes – yes I do.'

Spiggot stared around the fairy nations. They were extremely attractive creatures, quite lovely. Those with wings had painted them with the colours and patterns of butterflies – painted ladies, commas, peacocks, vanessas, red admirals, tortoiseshells – and those without wings had decorated their faces with the black-and-turquoise bands of damselflies. Every other faerie from boggart to spriggan was envious of the fairies. Every other faerie wanted to be a fenoderee, or tylwyth teg or seelie court. The fairies were to be envied for their beauty and splendour.

Yet, they were also shrewd, cunning creatures, often completely selfish, seldom without intrigue and double-interest. Spiggot knew this and reasoned that Xinixia was probably right. He was no doubt being used by the fairy nations as a figurehead which could be thrown to the wolves if things went wrong. But he also reasoned that if things went right, he would go down in the books as the greatest non-fairy who had ever existed. He was willing to take the chance of being either the fool or the hero.

'Thank you for telling me that, Prince Xinixia,' said Spiggot. 'Nevertheless I intend to stay with the plan. You're wrong, you know, about me having the potential to surpass my father at his work. No one could do that. He is unique, a genius, and I could never match his skill. It will be a long time before Liöfwende produces a boggart metalworker to match Gnomon and I'm certainly not that boggart.'

'As you say,' said Xinixia. 'I just didn't want you to be under any misapprehensions. They'll discard you, you know, once it's all over.'

'I expect them to,' replied Spiggot. 'That's what fairies do.'

Spiggot and Kling then made their way back to where the gnomes were waiting to hear from them. Spiggot could not resist a detour, though. He had to see how Mallmoc was coping with his accident. Looking from a treetop, the boggart could see that he wasn't, not well at any rate. The ulcugga had hitched their horses to the craft and were still trying to haul it out that way. But theirs were no heavy horses – wagon horses – they were thoroughbred light horses. They were not born to pull; they were born to race like lunatics across meadows. Mallmoc was getting nowhere.

FOUR

The war between the shadows allowed Jack time to recover from his recent wound. Like others, he went up to the surface to watch the shadows do battle with one another. It was a perfectly safe occupation, so long as he didn't run into any *real* ulcugga. The shadow war was extremely interesting, being bloodless yet exciting. There were a number of aspects about it which Jack had not thought of before the battles began.

Shadows were extremely fast-moving. They slid over the landscape at alarming speeds, sweeping over hills and along valleys bristling with shadow-weapons. If they were caught unawares by the enemy they often slipped into other shadows: those of tall rocks and trees.

Jack once saw what he believed to be the great Irish fairy chieftain Fearghus's shadow. It was coming alone up a rocky depression on a moor when it encountered a whole squadron of ulcugga shadows. Fearghus's shadow immediately leapt into the shadow of a tall tor and, of course, disappeared from view, for one shadow laid over another is quite invisible. Jack pointed this out to Rosamund, who was also fascinated by the war.

'He's in there,' said Jack, pointing. 'That tall one with the funny notch in the top.'

'I see it, dear Jack,' answered Rosamund. 'Is he safe?'

'I think so – we'll have to wait and see.'

The ulcugga shadows surrounded the high rock and seemed content to wait until the sun moved. Jack believed they were hoping that the change in position of the rock-shadow would reveal their foe, for shadows within shadows often become drowsy and in danger of falling asleep. It was something to do with being swamped by shade. If Fearghus dropped off, it was quite likely the rock-shadow would move away from his position and expose him to the dark blades of his pursuers.

However, Fearghus's shadow, like his owner, was a wily creature. He obviously remained awake because the ulcugga were disappointed. When noon came the ulcugga were mere inkblots clustered around the rock, the sun being directly overhead. Fearghus had been biding his time for this moment. He waited until the dark shape of a flying eagle came through the rock-shadow. This silhouette was larger than himself in the midday sun, having spread wings and tail. Fearghus's wraith slipped inside this black haven and escaped across the moor hidden from sight. Jack and Rosamund knew what he had done only when they saw him leave the eagle's shadow and his squat silhouette raced away to the north. The ulcugga remained where they were, convinced they still had their prey trapped.

When the evenings came it was the battle of the giants. Long, tall shadows of fairy warriors strode the landscape. They were fainter but quite lean and danger-ous-looking. There were battles on the plains and skirmishes in the woods. On the flatlands it was a show without impairment, but the forest fights were quite dif-ficult to follow with the naked eye. Dark shapes slid from tree-shade to tree-shade and it became almost impossible for the watchers to see what was going on.

'I once saw a shadow-puppet show,' said Jack, 'when I went on holiday to Bali.'

Rosamund and he were sitting on a hilltop, viewing the countryside below. A gentle river meandered between some faerie villages. Beyond them was a range of purple hills. Shadow-warriors had flitted into those hills and were now lost to the view of the two mortals.

'Bali? I do not know this name.'

'Ah yes, it was probably called something different when you were living in Mortaland. Or maybe it wasn't, but it hadn't been visited by Europeans then. Bali – well, it's a tropical island, part of Indonesia. That is, it's in the south, over the equator – oh hell, I'll show you sometime on a map. The thing is, Rosy, it's quite exotic. They have these figures of their gods and heroes cut out of leather. Puppets. *Wayang kulits* they call them. They're worked by hand so that they throw shadows on to a white sheet. You sit in front of the sheet and the shadows of the figures look real. The show often involved battles between the gods and heroes, just like this lot.'

'Thy world must be quite wonderful, Jack.'

'Not really. Sometimes it's awful, sometimes it's good. Just like anywhere, really. And I'm sure the *wayang kulits* were being used in your time, Rosy. You just didn't know about them, that's all.'

Rosamund took Jack's hand in hers.

'Dost thou think, dear Jack, that someday thou wilt be able to show me thy world?'

This idea made Jack quite excited. To take Rosy home! He would love to have her visit his mum and dad. And his older sister, Debbie. What would they make of this beautiful princess, with her long glossy hair and grey eagle's eyes? She was stunningly beautiful, Jack knew that, and he knew he was not the sort of youth who captivated such women. Yet Rosamund said she was in love with him and he had no reason to doubt her. No reason except that he was a rather unprepossessing youth – or at least, until now everyone had told him he was. They didn't use that long word of course, but there were other shorter ones equally as damning.

'I'd like you to see my world too, but it would probably frighten you, Rosy.'

'Pah! After Faerieland I should not be afraid.'

'That's true, there's many a strange thing here. Stranger than fiction, as they say. But where I come from it's all noise and people. You've never seen so many people. And there are horseless wagons made of metal that flash along the roads at tremendous speeds, with people inside them. And giant ships of steel that carry hundreds of people. Metal birds that carry hundreds more. Boxes – we call it TV – with talking pictures. Machines called computers that can almost think. I'm not sure you would like it there, Rosy. It frightens *me* when I think of it.'

She nodded. 'Perhaps I *would* be just a little afraid,

Jack – but with thee by my side I should not be *terrified*.'

This made him feel rather good and he told her, 'If we ever get the chance, either to go to your time, or to mine, I think we should take it. Just for a visit, not to stay. I'd like to see what it was *really* like in medieval times. Do you think your mum and dad would take to me?'

'I have no mother,' she said, matter-of-factly. 'My father locked her in a dungeon and she died of rat bites.'

Jack was, of course, dreadfully shocked by this information.

'What did she do to deserve a fate like that?'

'She gave birth to *me*. My father wanted a son and heir.'

'But – but that's not a crime.'

'Oh, my mother wasn't locked away because she committed any crime, Jack. It was just my father's will. He was angry with her. He wanted to punish her, but not badly. And he told me he wept prodigiously when she died. It was said that he went personally to the dungeon and slaughtered the rats with his own sword. He also killed the jailer for letting the rats get out of hand. He was very angry. I think he loved my mother very much and he was especially annoyed that he had to kill her brother after she passed away because her family demanded to be handed back the dowry lands in France. That made my father very angry and he went to war with my mother's brother and slaughtered his kin.'

'Sounds as if your dad is in a permanent rage.'

'Sometimes I think it is so. Has thy father never imprisoned thy mother, Jack?'

'Well, he locked her in the loo once, when she lost her temper and threatened to throw his golf clubs in the bin.

But that was only for five minutes while he hid his clubs and he wished he hadn't done it afterwards. He didn't hear the end of it for a week. I suppose all families have their ups and downs.'

Rosamund nodded. 'Has he not starved her to bend her will to his own, when she has become wilful?'

'Nope. Not to my knowledge.'

'Then he cannot love her, for where is his passion?'

'Passion's not something I would accuse my dad of having,' said Jack, thoughtfully, 'unless it's when he misses a two-foot putt.'

Jack was appalled at what went on in Rosamund's time, but he could not tell her that.

'Didn't he ever marry again – your dad?'

'Oh, yes. Several times.' She counted on her fingers. 'Now the first after my mother was beheaded by the king himself for fomenting plots against the crown; the second was sent home after it was found she was already with child; the next caught the pox and died; and now there is one who hates me for she is just my age and a spiteful vixen. She winds my father around her finger like a blade of grass, but I have her measure.' Rosamund's eyes narrowed frighteningly. 'Mayhap I shall have her in the tower yet. Methinks she would have it hard to deny she is a witch.'

'A witch?' The hair on Jack's neck stood on end. 'What makes you think that?'

'Why, she has bewitched my father, has she not?'

'But that's just normal – an older man besotted with a younger woman.'

'And she has a pet cat . . .'

Jack thought it useless to continue the argument.

'Heck, Rosy, I've never heard of such a dysfunctional family!'

Jack said this but he had the horrible feeling that this kind of family for a baron's daughter was quite normal for the time. Had she been a peasant, of course, things would have been just as nasty for her but in a different way. She would have been raised on cabbage-stalk soup and have dozens of brothers and sisters. She would have lived in a filthy one-room hovel, would have been married at twelve and worked to death by the age of twenty. He shuddered. The modern world was not the best place to live in, but it was a case of better the devil you know.

'I know not what this means.'

'No, and it's better it stays that way. I *never* want to go back to your time, Rosy. I know it's home to you, but it sounds like hell to me.'

In fact, thought Jack, the only place the pair of them could live together, with any sanity, was Liöfwende. He began to see that if they were to stay together they could never go back to either world, the modern or the medieval.

Their conversation was interrupted by Spiggot and Kling coming to join them.

'The shadow war is almost over, Jack,' said Spiggot, gloomily.

'Don't say we've lost?' cried Jack, jumping to his feet.

He had seen the shadows coming back to their owners. Many of the dark silhouettes had been wounded. Some had missing arms or legs. One or two returned, minus their heads. The owners of these shadows were greatly annoyed of course, for though they could use the limb with the missing shadow they couldn't actually *see* it. They were liable to whack someone round the head accidentally while simply gesturing. And from the other side, speaking to someone without a head was really weird.

The whole business was very strange.

Kling said, 'Looks like a draw. Has anyone got any chocolate on them? Kling hasn't tasted chocolate in a week. Kling is thinking along the lines of rose and violet cremes. Can you all search your pockets . . .'

Jack ignored Kling's obsession with food.

'What does a *draw* mean? Does it mean there'll be no more fighting? Or does the serious stuff start now.'

'The serious stuff starts,' replied Spiggot, plucking a stalk of grass and chewing it. 'I have to lead the fairies into battle. I'll be killed, of course, but I knew that all along, ever since I put that armour on for the first time. He who lives by the sword dies by the sword. I'll be a puffball by sunset. I want you to promise me, Jack, that you will not kick me. I wish to enjoy my time as a fungus, for a while at least, until some wild beast eats me.'

'Now let's not get ahead of ourselves,' replied Jack. 'You may get through it intact. You're a fine warrior, Spiggot. And you'll have a bodyguard of fairies, of course.'

'They'll abandon me, once the fighting starts.'

He really did have the blues, poor Spiggot.

'We shall be by thy side, Spiggot,' cried Rosamund, leaping to her feet. 'We shall be thy bodyguard. We shall be thy housecarls and form a war-hedge around our lord and half-king, Spiggot. We shall call ourselves "the Immortals" and die protecting thee. We shall hew down the heathen churls who name themselves the ulcugga and their bodies shall be strewn over the landscape. We, thy loyal thanes, will keep faith with angels, and make certain that thee leave the battlefield unscathed. Many of us will die, but our lord will live. We who have great gust for fighting, we thy hearthsharers with our ash-spears shall be thy fence to ward off all-comers.'

'By cracky, Rosy, you give a good speech,' said Jack, admiringly.

FIVE

The shadow war was over. As Kling had predicted, it was indecisive. A real battle would have to take place to settle the issue. Spiggot, as the warrior-in-chief, was the one who called for a council of war. The tribal chiefs, the royal personages, the princes and the prelates of the fairy world gathered together in a woodland glade lit by shafts of sunlight. Jack and Rosamund had been invited along as observers. Spiggot told them they were strictly forbidden to speak, that being the prerogative of faerie.

Spiggot had to overcome his awe at having to open the meeting – known as a witenagemot after the Anglo-Saxon parliament – before speaking. His knees were shaking a little and his tongue seemed twice its size but he managed to welcome all the fairy kings and princes, the chieftains from over the border and over the sea. It helped that he was wearing his suit of golden armour, which gave him stature.

'You will notice,' he told the fairies, 'that I have placed the traditional wind egg in the centre of our circle.'

Spiggot had already explained to Jack and Rosamund that a wind egg was a fresh hen's egg without its shell. It is held together only by a delicate membrane, a skin so thin the egg trembles in the slightest breeze. The egg wobbles like jelly and is of a distorted shape, similar to a balloon full of water which has been left to rest on the ground. If this egg broke before the end of the meeting everything they had discussed would be abandoned and the war would be over. All the fairy nations would go back to their homes and trust to luck that the world would right itself.

No one knew where this ritual came from, but like most faerie rites it was strictly adhered to.

(At other witenagemots, those opposed to war had been known to blow on the egg when they thought no one was looking.)

'Good,' said Spiggot, striding around in the centre of the circle, working up his courage, 'I suggest we go straight into the fray . . .'

'Excuse me,' murmured Jack, 'but if you're not careful you'll step on your wind egg.'

Spiggot looked down anxiously, aware of the amused smiles on the faces of many of his audience.

'Jack,' he said, 'I told you – mortals are not supposed to speak at the witenagemot!'

'Sorry. Just thought you ought to know.'

'Be quiet!'

'Yes, sorry.' Jack nodded around the circle. 'Very sorry. Won't do it again.'

Spiggot was now standing stock still. Jack had told

him that when speaking in public he should choose one member of the audience to stare at and address his speech to that one person or faerie. Jack had told him to resist the urge to look round at all the faces. If he did that, Jack had said, he might become panicky or confused by the multitude of expressions that met his gaze. Thus he chose a seelie court out of the ring of faces. This fairy chieftain had ragged ribbons tied to his wild red hair and a face as grim as a flint mineshaft on a bleak day in February. The creature's features were lean, mean and glinty-eyed, with just a trace of malice about the mouth.

'I, er, so – yes, as I said, I think we have to go straight at them.'

The fairy he was staring at spoke.

'Just you an' me, eh, boggart?'

'No, no. *All* of us.'

'Then why look at me?'

Miserably, Spiggot took his gaze from the Thristlac fairy's face. So much for Jack's advice.

'No, really. I know we have this traditional way of fighting – that is to circle the enemy, avoid any major conflicts, and just skirmish around the edges. But I think for once we have to forget the old ways and really get down to it. We have to stop Mallmoc from repairing his castle-ship, his ironclad. If we just flit around, not really engaging the enemy, we'll allow him all the time he needs.'

The breezes had picked up and the wind egg was wobbling dangerously in the middle of the circle.

'First,' said King Cimberlin of the Northumberland fairies, 'we need to work a bit of magic. We can't fight on open ground. That's not the way we do things. We need our thistle forests and thorn brakes.'

'Well, that's taken as read,' replied Spiggot. 'The thistle forests and gorse brakes, of course. Will you do it now?'

All the fairies present bowed their heads and concentrated. This was something they could do only by their combined efforts at magic. Something they only did together, in situations of great menace and threat, like this one. Jack and Rosamund heard a sort of rustling sound, quite a noisy one, coming from all around the real forest. Through the gaps between the trees the mortal pair could see that the fields beyond were sprouting giant thistles and thorn bushes. All manner and varieties of purple-headed thistles — musk, woolly, welted, spear, creeping, cotton, stemless, melancholy and meadow thistles — these had all sprung up as high and spread as wide as oaks. This was also true of the gorse and other thorn bushes, though they were not quite so high and had a broader girth.

It was a great jungle of thorns and spikes out there, which would make warfare such as mortals fought quite impossible. Any army on a vast scale would be broken up into smaller groups of warriors. There would be no famous charges by the cavalry, no sweeping line of soldiers in massed attack, no massacres on a grand scale. Instead, there would be many small pockets of fighting and the war would be fought in corridors of spikes, down avenues of sharp points, in small clearings hemmed by gimlets.

Only elves and pixies were fond of open warfare and look what had happened to them in their battles against the ulcugga!

'Right,' said Spiggot, 'there we have it. Our forests of thistles and thorns. Now we can go out and fight.'

Jack was looking anxiously at the wind egg, which
was sort of flattening itself like a blob of water about to
run away. The sun was still streaming through the green
canopy, but Jack could feel the meteorological pressure
building up. The day was turning hot and humid, with a
denseness to the air. He felt they were in for some stormy
weather. Perhaps when fairies went to war the weather
turned foul? They were into *atmospheres*, the faerie, and it
would not surprise Jack if thunder and lightning accompanied the fighting, the skies reflecting what was
occurring on the Earth.

'Whoa!' cried Jack, standing up. 'Look, fairy kings
and what-not, I know I'm not supposed to speak, but
heck, this is no way to plan a war.'

'Have ye ever schemed up a war yerself?' asked a
Thristlac warrior. 'D'ye ken whut tae do?'

'No, but I've read about it, seen it on the telly, and I
know you need a bit more than just "Go out and get
'em!" Will you let me speak, just this once?'

Spiggot was staring at his friend, horrified.

'A mortal, speaking at a witenagemot – Jack, Jack,
please.'

But the fairy kings and princes were not as horrified
as the boggart. It was they who made the rules and they
who broke them if they wished. They muttered amongst
themselves that they were inclined to listen to the mortal
youth.

'After all,' said King Fearghus, 'mortals invented war.
Even if this youth hasn't fought in a war, unfortunately it's
in his blood. I should not be happy to have such blemish
on *my* spirit, but since we have this mortal here amongst
us perhaps we should listen to what he has to say.'

'Right,' said Jack, 'well, you need two essential things to ensure your side is successful – good communications and command of the air. Have you got them?'

'Good communications?' murmured one group.

'Command of the air?' muttered another.

Clearly they had no idea what he was talking about.

'Fine,' Jack continued, 'I'll tell you what I mean. You must make sure that any bridges *you* need remain intact and that any bridges the enemy need are destroyed. Also you need to be able to rally your troops in a particular place at any given time. In the old days we used to use bugles and drums to do this and have a flag to rally round. What do you think?'

A wizened old fairy spoke. 'The trolls are on our side, so the bridges are secure. As to blowing trumpets and bashing drums, why, only the pixies and elves do that.'

'What about whistling?' interrupted Rosamund. 'Can thee whistle like this . . .?' And she stuck two fingers in her mouth and let out a high, shrieking whistle that was liable to burst Jack's eardrums. The eyes of fairies, who had sharper and more delicate hearing than mortals, went alarmingly wide. 'Can thee do that?' asked Rosamund, cheerfully. 'If not, I can teach thee.'

'I think,' said King Cimberlin, shaking his head to free his ears of the ringing noise, 'we would prefer to yip or yelp. We are better at yipping than – than we are at whistling. And we are quite dramatic yelpers when we wish to be.'

Several fairies let out high yelps and yips to prove these words. Admittedly, these sounds were not so loud and piercing as Rosamund's whistle, but for fairies, just as effective. Rosamund looked a little disappointed, but she bore it well. Jack nodded to her, as if to say, given the choice *he* would have chosen whistle over yelp and yip.

A fairy from Eri-innis then tied a long flowing purple chiffon scarf to the end of his lance and held it high.

'Here is our banner!' he cried. 'Rally to me, or to the bearer of the same, if and when necessary.'

'Good,' cried Jack. 'Very good. Now, command of the air. We know the ulcugga have six dragons they can use. But I don't recall them flying very high. They seem to sweep low over the fields. Can they go higher?'

'They don't like to,' answered the same Irish fairy who was carrying the banner. 'It hurts their heads and gives them the frights. Faerie dragons are not good with heights. They tell me they get the urge to curl up in a ball and drop like a stone to the ground if they go above anything higher than an elm.'

'What about those fairies who have wings?'

'A hop, skip and jump, like a chicken, but no long or high flights,' explained Spiggot. 'A fairy's wings are more decorative than useful.'

Spiggot was glared at but all knew he was speaking the truth.

'Right,' said Jack, slapping his palm with his fist, 'then we'll get command of the air using *kites*.'

'Kites?' cried the fairies, in unison. 'What kites?'

Jack replied, 'We'll make them. I spent half my boyhood making kites out of brown paper, bits of wood, and string. Box kites, traditional kites, all sorts. I'll work out some designs. We'll get in some elves in to make them, they're good at craft. They might be fed up with fighting but I'm sure we can persuade them to give us a hand with this project. We'll need to get some done today, so I suggest we contact the elves as soon as poss.'

'But,' said Spiggot, speaking for the all the faerie present, 'how will kites help us?'

Jack said, 'Why, we'll make each one big enough to carry a fairy. Mortals have such kites in the Orient — man-carrying kites. We'll make fairy-carrying kites. And also,' he cried, something else coming to him, 'we'll make some smaller ones to fly in a ring around the area where the ulcugga are concentrated. These won't have pilots. They'll just be ordinary kites. Then if the ulcugga try to fly on their dragons they'll get tangled in the strings. We'll get command of the air with bits of paper and string — you see if we don't, and the ulcugga will be grounded!'

'Aye,' cried a Thristlac fairy, 'the youth has brains!'

They all cheered.

Spiggot looked a little crestfallen. His thunder had been stolen from him by Jack. Now Jack went to his friend and lifted his armoured arm.

'And in Spiggot,' said Jack, 'we have a marvellous leader, a great warrior, whose arm is strong and whose heart is stout.'

Another great cheer went up and Spiggot's face now wore a sunny smile.

'Finally,' said Rosamund, 'the maid has an idea, too. My father was once attacked by a force much greater than the one he commanded himself. The day before the battle he made his men polish their bronze shields until they shone like mirrors. When they eventually faced the enemy, the foe were confused, seeing not only my father's warriors before them but another massed army in the glistening shields. Of course, this was but a reflection of the foe's own ranks and though they knew it, it was hard for them to gauge the number of troops they were fighting against. When they charged, the warriors in the shields charged too. When they angrily waved their weapons, the warriors in the shields waved theirs. It was all a bit unsettling, causing the enemy to be uneasy. When my father's men put up a fierce resistance, the enemy soldiers fled the field, eager to run at the first opportunity.'

'Mirror shields!' cried Spiggot. 'We shall magic up some *real* mirror shields. Three cheers for the maid.'

And the greenwood rang with yips and yelps.

After the last fairy left the glade the wind egg broke apart in a splurge of egg white and yolk, dribbling over the mossy ground.

PART SIX

War amongst the prickles

ONE

Not that Jack had fought in a war of any kind before now, but he still felt this war amongst the giant spikes and prickles was very strange. There were long green avenues overhung with bristling leaves. *Deadly* leaves, with dagger-long spines that could run a man through as easily as a rapier. Jack was not on a horse but those who were had to beware. Some of the purple heads of the thistles were heavy, making the plant bend low over the ground, increasing the danger. In other areas a single giant gorse might spread over an area as large as basketball court. There were huge fluffy seed-balls rolling like tumbleweed in the narrow straits between the rows, which might sweep a person off his feet and carry him into a bed of spikes. This was indeed a strange place in which to fight, where natural hazards beset both armies. Thistles and gorse bushes do not choose sides in a conflict.

Jack and Rosamund had both witnessed some heavy fighting in the green alleys, between their own fairies and the ulcugga. Lance met shield and arrow met helmet. Everywhere was the glint of burnished bronze and the flash of polished silver. Sometimes there was a gleam of gold, when a king came on to the scene. Mostly the fairies fought in packs of six or seven, with a lord of some kind at their head. Where larger numbers gathered there was danger for the foe who ran into such packs, but there was also danger for the pack itself, for it was easily discovered from the air.

Jack saw it as his job to supervise the flying of the kites. He was having a little trouble with the pilots of those kites. The individual fairies did not mind who went up aloft – as long as it was not them!

'Right, you – yes, that fairy there – I want you to grip those leather handles with your hands and put your feet into the stirrups.'

'Me! Why me?'

'Because you're next.'

The fairy would start backing away. 'But I don't want to be next. Let *him* be next. He was next, actually. I don't know how I got to the front of the queue. He must have slipped behind me.'

The second fairy would now begin protesting.

'I never did. You big fat liar. You've been in front of me all the time.'

Jack, exasperated, intervened. 'Never mind, while you've been arguing we've managed to get *two* kites ready. You can both step into one each and be up there above the thistles in no time.'

'But – but my twin brother is already up there. In that

one, the yellow one. It's not good to have *both* brothers in mortal danger.'

'Come on, this isn't *Saving Private Ryan*. Anyway, fairies don't have brothers. They just appear from the mists of nowhere, so my good boggart friend tells me. Get your feet in the stirrups. Here, let me help you. Rosy, you get that one. Right, there you are. You won't fall out of that. Now, if you could stop shaking for five minutes we could get the windlass working and have you in the air. All right, you gnomes on the windlass – start reeling him out. That's it. That's it.'

Gradually, the gnomes winched out the cord which was attached to the kite. The wind got under the spread of the sheet and the kite began to rise aloft, a terrified fairy clinging to its underside. Until it was in a steady breeze and fairly stable, the kite darted back and forth, occasionally threatening to nose-dive into the ground. During this episode the fairy passenger would be speechless and numb with fear. Once glider and flier – white knuckles, white face, white trembling knees – were high enough, the winching stopped and the cord was then cut. Seven or eight gnomes held on to the cord, taking it to the nearest tree and anchoring it there. Just once they accidentally let go of the cord and the kite with its unfortunate terrified fairy was swept up into the blueness, never to be seen again on this side of the ocean.

'I feel guilty about that one, Rosy,' said Jack, watching the escaping kite and its passenger getting smaller and smaller in the sky, until it resembled a dandelion seed on the wind. 'He had a right to be scared.'

'Poof!' snapped Rosamund. 'Is he a soldier or isn't he? Such-a-one should be prepared for the unexpected. The trouble with these fairies is they have no fine lady to fight for. Noble knights of my time are more concerned with losing their honour than they are their lives.'

Rosamund had no sympathy with those who were not prepared to lay down their lives at the drop of a winch handle.

Once they were airborne the kites made a wonderful display. They had frames made of willow wand and were skinned with light fabric. Their tails were plaited fern leaves which snaked around the sky. It was true, too, that once the kite had been anchored the flying fairy was happier too. They started to call down the information, about where the enemy legions were clustered, where the foe were gathered and hiding, where the columns were marching, where the squadrons of cavalry were galloping. Jack had runners down below which he sent off with messages to the allies, as they sought out the pockets of ulcugga and routed them.

And indeed it was the allies who took the fight to the ulcugga and not the other way around. With their dragons grounded by a ring of kites (the first of which had got hopelessly entangled in the strings and had fallen to Earth with its hapless rider) the ulcugga were on the back foot. They were riding this way and that, through the long green passageways between the thistles and gorse, and getting hopelessly lost. They had no idea where the allied groups were gathering, they were attacked by savage trolls every time they attempted to cross a bridge, and most of the trees were against them.

At last the trees had come down on the side of the allies. For a long time they had not been able to make up their minds who was *actually* responsible for the release of the thrum from Gilscipe. Trees, of course, are for the most part incapable of gathering together and discussing such things, and coming to a decision. They have to let the wind carry messages for them, as the bogles carry messages for the faerie.

Now the rooted ones, who joined the Earth to the sky, had decided that – yes – it must have been Mallmoc who stole the locking-stone to the magic cairn. Thus whenever ulcugga rode beneath them, the oaks and elms would drop their branches a foot or two, and sweep the enemy from the backs of their horses. They dropped their spiked horse-chestnut grenades, a thousand at a time, on the heads of the ulcugga. They raised a root or two to trip them up as they went by. They blew bees from their knotholes into the faces of the foe and waved their branches to warn the kites when the enemy were approaching.

The trees were incredibly useful to the allies, in their leafy way.

Spiggot staggered into the kite camp about noon, his shoulder bleeding from a deep wound. With a cry of, 'Oh, my . . .' Fen rushed to his side and caught him just as he swooned. She and Rosamund removed his armour and began applying healing herbs to the wound. Before long, bandaged and sipping hot soup, Spiggot was almost as right as rain again.

'What a battle I have had,' he said. 'Me and my brigade met seven ulcugga in a hollow down by the river. I was at the front, riding Kling, when this fairy knight came at me with a levelled lance . . .'

'Oh, where is the dear Kling?' cried Rosamund. 'Is he dead?'

'No, no,' grumbled Spiggot impatiently, annoyed at
the interruption, 'he's down at the other camp, eating
chocolate. No, *Kling* was all right. It was me who was
lifted from the saddle and dumped on my posterior. Then
another ulcugga came thundering up and slashed at me
with his sword. As you see, it caught me on the shoulder.
But I managed to grab his foot and throw him from his
mount at the same time. He ended up in a bunch of
nettles, yelling blue murder. I think we captured him.'

'Well, now you are safe,' said Fen, 'and can leave it to
others.'

Spiggot got to his feet and started to put his armour on
again.

'No, I can't!' he cried, alarmed that Fen would prevent
him from going out again. 'I'm the commander-in-chief.
I have to be out there with my troops, guiding them,
giving them inspiration. They need my encouragement.'

'You are not fighting again today,' said Fen, emphatically, standing on his sword and refusing to budge. 'You
can go out tomorrow.'

'You can't tell me what to do. I'm . . .'

'Yes, we know, commander-of-the-cockroaches. Be
that as it may, I told your mother I would not let you do
anything stupid. Going out just after you've been
wounded comes under the heading of stupidity. You will
do as you're told and like it. Rosamund, take that helmet
away from him.'

Rosamund could be just as firm as Fen. She grabbed
the golden helmet with its sweeping owl's plume, and
stuck it in the branches of a tree.

'There. It'll be fine tomorrow, dear Spiggot, but not
today.'

'Jack?' cried the assailed boggart. 'Help me?'

'Sorry, Spig. No can do. When the womenfolk decide that's it, well – that's it, I'm afraid.'

The rest of the day was pretty scrappy, as far as the battle went. Reports were coming in from the kites above, and from riders and foot soldiers who returned to the main camp, that things were going well, but there would be no unchallenged victory today. The ulcugga were having a hard time of it but they were by no means defeated. What was more they had started conscripting eagles and falcons and were regaining command of the air. Theirs was a more precarious method of flying, since they had to hang on below the raptor birds by gripping the legs above the talons, but there were ulcugga prepared to take the risk. Some of them were dropping into thorny realms from horrible heights. To keep them aloft Mallmoc promised pink gobbets of soothing balms as remedies for thorn wounds to any ulcugga who fell into briar patches, thistle clumps or gorse bushes.

When night fell and the stars came out, weary fairies began to sneak back into camp. They all had their stories, of course, of terrible ordeals, narrow squeaks and trysts that went wrong. There were those who never set an eye on the enemy, but had been wandering the avenues of thistles and gorse bushes the whole day without encounter. There were those who had been attacked by skaggs, those terrible wild creatures who had come up from the depths of the Earth with the thrum. There were those, of course, who would never return, whose comrades had left them a fungus on a forest floor waiting to be eaten by bird or beast.

Everyone had a tale to tell, and there's nothing fairies like better than recounting a story.

Just before they all went to sleep, Puck, their intelligence agent arrived. He had been out gathering information about the enemy. This he imparted in hushed and important-sounding tones. Then he flew off again, into the night, to girdle the earth and gather more of the same.

TWO

Jack had pins and needles in his legs. He wondered if it were the power of suggestion arising out of all the prickles that were in his world at the moment. When you spent your whole time avoiding sharp points it was no wonder that such things as pins and needles should play on your mind. Thus he decided to turn in early and get a good night's sleep if he could.

It seemed to him that no sooner had he laid his head on the pillow of hay, someone was shaking him awake.

'Jack, Jack.'

It was Fen, kneeling by his soft mossy bed.

'Wha—' he said, thickly. 'Wha–what is it?'

'We have to make a raid.'

He was still not quite with it. When Fen said 'a raid' the idea of a fridge came immediately to mind. Were they going to raid the fridge in the middle of the night? It wouldn't be the first time Jack had been on such an expedition. Yet – yet this was Faerieland. There were no fridges here.

Jack went up on his elbows. It was deep into the night, he could sense that, with all the sleeping bodies around him. All else was peaceful. Yet here was Fen yelling about some sort of raid. Well, not *yelling* exactly, but certainly bothering him.

'I don't understand,' he said.

'You, me, Rosamund and three gnomes. We have to go and try to undo what Mallmoc has done today. We have to stop him repairing the damage to his castle-ship. We have to *sabotage* it.'

'We do?'

'Yes, get those sandals on.'

Jack strapped on the bark sandals Rosamund had made for him just two days ago. He was hard on shoes, was Jack, and went through them as if they were made of cardboard. Once he had splashed some water on his face he felt a little more like action and joined Fen and Rosamund. The three gnomes with them had shovels and picks. Jack felt that a handful of plastic explosives might do a better job but of course there was none to be had in Liöfwende. None that he knew of, at any rate. Not that he would know how to handle explosives. What they needed was an Arnie Schwarzenegger.

'Who knows the way?' whispered Jack, thinking that once they got there he would be able to gauge the situation more accurately.

'Me, sor,' said a gnome, touching his forelock. 'I be the way-finder, if it please ye.'

With that the three gnomes set off, expecting Jack, Rosamund and Fen to follow at a rattling pace. They did so, remaining very unsure of the swiftness at which they were travelling. They were inclined to think that a raiding party in the dead of night should be sneaking around, jumping at shadows, creeping through the thorns.

'I expect you asked me to come along because of my engineering experience,' whispered Jack to Fen. 'I must admit it comes in useful at times like this.'

'No,' came the candid reply, 'Rosamund asked for you.'

He felt flattened by this remark. 'Oh, and that's the only reason I'm here – because Rosy wanted me?'

'Yes – well, no – not really. Anyway, we'll see what you're made of, mortal man, before the night is through, won't we?'

'I suppose we will.'

Jack didn't feel he had to *prove* himself, though. Not to this lumpy female boggart, he didn't. Rosamund knew his worth, of course, and he had no need to impress *her*. Well, should his engineering skills be in demand, they were there for the dredging. It could be that by the end of this night little Miss Fen might have to swallow her pride and grant him praise.

The swiftness of their walk was not kept up the whole of the way. Once they drew nearer to the ulcugga lines the guides became more wary. And as they moved through the giant thistles, around the monstrous gorse, Jack kept treading on squashy bits on the ground. In the moonlight he could see that these patches were darker than the rest of the turf. He wondered if they were in a boggy region. He mentioned this to the gnomes.

'No,' replied the one with the shovel on his shoulder, 'that's dead shadows you'm treadin' on.'

'Dead shadows?' whispered Jack to Fen. 'What does he mean?'

'The shadow war was fought hereabouts,' came the reply. 'You're stepping on severed limbs and topped heads. And fully-fledged but dead shadows, of course. This place is a shadow graveyard.'

Jack felt queasy in his stomach and watched where he put his feet from then on.

Finally, though, they were crawling through the grasses on their stomachs, as they got closer to the pit which had swallowed Mallmoc's castle-ship. There in the moonlight they could see hundreds of sleeping ulcugga, their horses in corrals not far from their camp. There was a great deal of clanging and clanking when they approached, but even this noise ceased after a time. No doubt the workfaerie who were repairing the castle-ship had been told to soldier on through the night, but once they were sure that Mallmoc himself was resting they had called a halt.

When all was quiet save for snores Jack and Fen went forward to see what could be done about sabotage. They crawled to the edge of the pit and looked over. To Jack's consternation the ironclad looked as if it were ready to leave. A ramp had been built of packed earth, which sloped gently upwards out of the hole. Rollers made of logs had been placed on the ramp. The signs of efficiency and competence on the part of Mallmoc's workers was rather depressing for the allies.

However, there were also some encouraging signs. The main thing being that the castle-ship itself had been patched-up rather hastily. It was no longer as strong as before. Its plates had once been welded together, but now rivets had been used to put the iron plates back into place.

'Well I don't know what those gnomes are going to do with their picks and shovels,' murmured Fen. 'D'you think they could dig that ramp away before morning, Jack?'

Jack almost laughed out loud. 'Not a chance.'

'No, I didn't think so. It looks so strong, that castle, doesn't it? I wonder we even thought we could do something to stop it.'

'Yes, Mallmoc knew what he was doing, making a movable fortress from thick plates of pig-iron – but, purely from an engineering sense, you understand, it's not as strong as it used to be. If we could pull out a few of those rivets the whole thing might fall apart again.'

'Rivets?'

'Thick iron bolts that hold the thing together.'

'Oh. We call them clinches.'

'Looking at the rivets it seems to me that Mallmoc's workers haven't hammered down the heads on both sides. What they've done is frozen the rivets just before they've been put in the holes. When you freeze metal it shrinks. Naturally it swells again as it warms. Thus you will understand that the rivets are very tight in their sockets.'

'I'm not daft, I'm a smithy's daughter.'

'Ah, well – there you have it,' said Jack. He had been thinking he had to simplify his explanation for a faerie, but of course boggarts worked with metal all their lives. She might not have heard of rivets, since faerie armourers were unlikely to use them at their particular craft. After all, they weren't boilermakers. But she did understand the properties of heated iron. 'You see the problem.'

'Yes,' said Fen, 'but if we reversed the situation, we might loosen the rivets and get them to drop out.'

'Reverse the situation? You aren't suggesting we go down there and heat the plates. I think someone would notice if we started lighting huge coke fires and hammering away at metal, don't you? Anyway, if you heat the metal around the rivets they'll get hot too and that defeats the object.'

'But what if we were to freeze the rivets again?' Fen was quite sure of her science. 'Wouldn't they shrink and drop out?'

Jack stared at her nutbrown features in the moonlight. 'Wow, Fen – you're not just a pretty face, are you?'

'I think you've said that before.'

'No – well, look – can we call old winter's song?'

'Bring in the ice and snow, you mean? Not really. The fairies can do that, but of course the ulcugga are fairies too, and they would simply bring back the good weather straight away. We might jump backwards and forwards from summer into winter and get nowhere.'

'What we want is something more specific,' murmured Jack. 'Some sort of machine to freeze each individual rivet. A device of some kind which sprays out frozen oxygen.'

They went back to the gnomes and Rosamund. Fen explained the situation. Rosamund came from a time when machines and devices were not the first thing that came to mind with such a problem. Hers was a world of mythical characters and legendary creatures.

'Jack Frost's fingers,' said Rosamund, immediately. 'Can we find Jack Frost this night?'

One of the gnomes spoke up excitedly. 'We can't get

hold of *him*, personally, but his nan keeps a spare frost wand for him. She lives in a cave not far away from here. I could go and ask for a loan.'

'Jack Frost has a wand?' Jack said. 'Extraordinary!'

'Not really,' replied the gnome. 'Every workman has tools of his trade.'

'Yes but – oh, never mind – go and get it.'

Off went the gnome, with one of his pals, and he returned shortly with the wand in a long wooden carrying box.

'Grandma Frost says to be very careful with it. It's the only spare her grandson's got.'

'I shall treat it like my own,' said Jack, 'if I had one, that is.'

The wand was very, very cold. They found they had to use a thick glove of bark to hold it. Even so, each one of them had to hand it over to another after a few minutes, so that they could warm their numbed hands. All six went down into the pit, *crept* down, single file. The workfaerie had gone up to the lip to sleep, to be in the fresh breezes so they were able to do the deed without fear of someone nearby waking. It was a relatively simple task to touch a rivet with the tip of the wand, wait a second, then watch the rivet fall out of its socket and drop to the earth.

'Wonderful,' murmured Jack. 'Magic engineering.'

They worked through the night, almost until dawn. One after the other the rivets left their holes and the iron plates became loose. They had to leave the odd rivet in or the whole thing would collapse on top of them, but that was all right. Mallmoc would need more days to put things right, even though the castle-ship looked intact.

When they felt they had done all they could, they put the wand back in its box and prepared to climb out of the pit. At that very moment, one of the heavy loosened panels peeled away from the main hull of the castle-ship. Shrieking and grating, it leaned towards the group, threatening to flatten them. Jack could see that the whole lot was now falling apart under the strain of its own weight, held by but a few rivets.

'Run!' cried Jack. 'Quickly!'

The six scrambled up the bank of the pit as gravity wrenched the ironclad apart with its sure hands. When they reached the top they ran for their lives, dodging between waking ulcugga. Fortunately the fairies had no time to gather their wits or they would have caught the whole group. Behind them, the castle-ship was falling to pieces with a terrible noise that added to the confusion. Jack could hear Mallmoc's horrible voice, screaming at his fairies, ordering them to capture the saboteurs at any cost.

Jack grabbed Rosamund's hand and together they skipped through the night, running fit to keep ahead of the wind. Mounted ulcugga were soon in pursuit, but the forest of thistles and teasels hampered the chase. The two mortals managed to duck and weave in amongst the thorn bushes, keeping just a little ahead of their would-be captors. It was an exciting run, with the enemy just on their tails, but these were two quarry the ulcugga were not going to catch on this hunt. Dawn is a time of dancing shadows and one can flit like a phantom through twilight and fool the eye of the hunter. The ulcugga were often sidetracked by other movements, of birds and beasts, and frequently went off at the wrong tangent to track their prey.

The noise of the chase obviously woke the allied fairies too. They realised the ulcugga were abroad again. The battle which had halted the previous day now commenced with a new dawn. Jack and Rosamund got back to the main camp safely. They laughed when Spiggot came running up to them, as they told him of their success.

'You should have seen it, Spiggot – it fell to bits and is in a sorry state now,' cried Rosamund.

'Yes, yes,' replied the suddenly pale boggart. 'I understand all that – well done, well done. But where is Fen?'

Jack suddenly felt very guilty. He looked around. Of course, they had not had time to watch out for everyone running from the scene. Jack imagined that Fen had escaped with the three gnomes.

'Oh, she'll be here, very soon,' assured Jack. 'I saw her reach the edge of the thistle forest before we did. I'm sure she's all right.'

But he spoke without conviction in his voice and Spiggot let out a wail of dismay as the three gnomes strolled into camp alone.

THREE

'You left her *behind*?' cried the distraught boggart. 'You ran off *without* her?'

'They didn't say that,' said Kling, who obviously felt they needed arbitration in this argument. 'Kling heard what they said. It was all confusion and every water rat – sorry – every man for himself. It just so happened – as I understand it – that the three gnomes and the pair of mortals were separated.'

'Fen was *ahead* of us,' explained Jack. 'I thought she'd be here before us, Spig. I'm sorry. She was running so fast. I guess she must have tripped or fallen into the hands of the ulcugga. They were everywhere. We only just managed to avoid them.'

'Oh yes, *you* avoided them,' snapped Spiggot, bitterly, 'but you left my poor Fen to be – be butchered by that mad sorcerer.'

'Hold on, hold on,' intervened Kling, 'we don't even

know if she's been caught yet. She might still be wandering the landscape.'

One of the gnomes now came forward, his head hanging low.

'Excuse me, sor, I see what occur. The boggart was swep' up by un ulcugga knoight. Took her, he did, back to the warlock. We'm were hidin' in un hollow oak, just a-watchin', us three gnome. I then seen the warlock call forth a giant spider, to weave a webby shroud around the boggart maid, just as iffen she were a fly caught in a cobweb. She'm now hanging from a dead tree bough near to the warlock's castle-ship, spinnin' on the end of a long silk thread like a dead-weight plumbob on a line.'

Spiggot put his face into his large callused hands and sobbed for a moment.

Jack said, 'I'm going to get her back . . .' He started heading for the forest of thistles, but Spiggot's face came out from his hands. He yelled, 'No, Jack, wait. Come back.'

Jack paused in his stride.

Spiggot said, 'That's what he wants – Mallmoc. He's setting a trap for us and using Fen as bait. Don't give him what he wants.'

'But,' said Rosamund, 'we cannot leave her in his thrall.'

Jack came back. 'Spiggot is right. This has to be planned very carefully. Lateral thinking is needed. We have to outwit Mallmoc, not fall in with his schemes. What to you think, Kling?'

'Me? Kling is just a water rat – but, Kling thinks the master's son is right for once.'

Spiggot glared at the water rat, but did not argue.

The three gnomes mumbled their apologies and com-
miserations and left the four friends to work out the
boggart maid's destiny.

'Well, here's a fine to-do,' Spiggot said, miserably. He
sat on the ground and the two mortals, exhausted by the
night's work, sat down alongside him. 'I have to fight
today. It's expected of me. You two will have to work out
a way of getting her back. It won't be easy, that's for sure.
Mallmoc has already killed Solomon. He won't stop at
trying to kill the rest of us. His hate knows no borders.'

'We'll do our best,' Jack told him, putting a hand on
his muscled shoulder. 'I'm sorry she has become a casu-
alty of war.'

Spiggot nodded, then stood up and asked Kling to
help him strap on his armour, 'Now that Fen is not here
to do it'. In fact, all of them helped and when he was
ready, Spiggot rode Kling out of camp and into the fray.

'Well,' said Jack, looking at his medieval girlfriend,
'where do we start, Rosy?'

'Rest, first, dear Jack. Then our thoughts shall be
clearer. There must be no mistakes with that dark lord
this time.'

'I agree — my head's very muzzy.'

'My brain also is overheated, much like Greasy Joan's
iron pot, and needeth keeling before further use.'

They curled up near each other on the moss and fell
asleep. Jack's dreams were full of wild flowers and butterflies. He was running over grassy knolls, hand in hand
with his best girl, calling to the hills and the saluting the
birds. No bad dreams for him. It was only on waking
that he remembered it was daymares he should beware
of, not nightmares.

Rosamund was already awake and pinching her cheeks.

'Why do you do that?' he asked.

'To give myself colour,' she replied.

Jack remembered that make-up, in Rosamund's time, was in short supply. No rouge? Well then, nip the cheeks a little to make them red.

Around them they could still hear the sounds of battle raging. There was some satisfaction in knowing that Mallmoc was rooted to the Earth still and unable to advance on Sutton Hoo. But what to do about poor Fen, before she was subjected to a worse fate than being cocooned? Jack set his mind to work on the problem, trying to think sideways as well as straight.

'Why do you think Mallmoc used a giant spider, Rosy?' asked Jack. 'Why not do the job himself? I'm sure he's capable.'

'Methinks, Jack, that Mallmoc is of such an ancient age that he can no longer shape-change. He cannot trust to the reassembling of his body. Shape-changing requires great energy from three of the five elements – fire, earth and air – and this can be damaging to a body which is merely dust held together by constant magic.'

'The other two elements being . . .' asked Jack, curious about this medieval idea of science.

'Water and metal, of course.'

'Right. Anyway, what I was wondering was whether we could get the giant spider to work for *us* – steal his own handiwork, so to speak? What do you think?'

'On the whole,' said Rosamund, tapping her lip with her finger as she considered this, 'spiders are not bad creatures. Some are afraid of them because of their creeping nature and frightening visage, but in fact they do keep the castle clean by the eating of insects injurious to man.'

'That's very astute of you, Rosy,' Jack said, impressed. 'It's not even something that people of my time would recognise.'

'Jack, I know thee think me primitive, but primitive does not equal ignorant.'

'Yes, sorry Rosy, you're quite right. I shouldn't assume too much. Well now, where does that leave us? Do you think we could use the spider?'

'It would be difficult to turn a spider, once he is in the thrall of a sorcerer, no matter how good a spider he may be. No, the spider is not for turning.'

'Could we get our *own* spider?'

'Perhaps.'

The discussion went on, but no real conclusions were reached. When Spiggot came back to camp, helmet in hand, to have his shoulder rebandaged, they were no nearer to a solution. Surprisingly, Spiggot did not chastise them for this state of affairs. He simply nodded in a grave way and said he too was thinking on the matter. They roasted some crab apples over a fire and sent him back out again in the afternoon still thoughtful.

By evening there were signs that the allies were gaining control of the landscape. As in all fairy wars the number of casualties were few. Having to fight in narrow corridors hand-to-hand, having escape routes near in case the battle was going against them, kept the encounters brief. There were, of course, some fairies who would never ride horses again. There were others who would no more see their homelands. Warriors of Eri-innis and

Thristlac. To be killed on foreign shores makes death — or in the case of fairies the transition to vegetable life — that much more dreadful.

Yet things were happening to the good. The ulcugga were gradually being pushed back to the castle-ship. They were being denied control of the air by the allies and the kite-borne fairies were continually revealing enemy positions and pockets of resistance. Forces were being rushed to these regions and the furious defences of the ulcugga were being overcome, the occupants expelled. Jack was much heartened by the stories which were coming back to the campfires, of a running foe.

Here in camp the fairy warriors sharpened their swords on whetstones, finding a new silver edge for the next fight. Brindled mares were led to ponds to wash and were then lovingly, personally groomed, for a fairy thinks as much of his horse as does a human rider. Leather scabbards and belts were polished. Breastplates had their dents hammered out by willing boggarts and gnomes. Helmets were likewise treated and new feathers — owl, pheasant, partridge, goose — replaced the old and bent plumes.

Once a fairy had completed his ablutions and had primped and preened himself and his horse, he strolled about the camp talking quietly with companions, his vanity impelling him to present the picture of a handsome creature in shining body armour.

And handsome they were, Jack had to admit. Their vanity did get up his nose somewhat, but that was the mortal in him. Fairies did not themselves see any virtue in modesty. Humbleness and modesty were horrible character traits to the supernatural beings of Liöfwende,

Thristlac and Eri-innis. They shuddered when such
words were mentioned. They were in fact beautiful creatures who regarded display as being more important
than emotions. Love, they knew not. Showing affection
and regard was considered all right in its place, but first
Hey, look at me.

Those with long golden hair and flawless complexions,
slim but lithe and strong, immaculately dressed and
with eyes that put the stars to shame, flaunted the vision
of themselves. Others, Northerners with red hair, ruddy
skins and of a more muscled frame, were equally
desirous to parade. These fairies often unsheathed their
swords and showed their prowess with swishing blades
during their promenade. They regarded themselves as
worthy, rather than fine and noble, and their method of
walking was the sturdy stride, not the mincing gait. Then
again there were those with light frames but a dark dis-
position, from across the seas. These fairies danced or
skipped across spaces with the agility of a fawn, greeting
friends with a nod and a wink, thrusting forth a dancer's,
not a wrestler's, hosed leg.

'Look at them,' grumbled Jack to Spiggot, as he
helped his boggart friend remove his helmet. 'Blasted
show-offs.'

Spiggot's face was covered in sweat, his matted black
hair stuck to his forehead.

'Oh, don't be too hard on them, Jack. They don't have
a lot to do but love themselves, you know. They have no
trade like I and other boggarts do. They play no real
games, like chess or backgammon. They have no affinity
with machines and devices, which seem to keep you
mortals occupied. They do some sport, it is true, but not

to fill their time. They are constantly bored, Jack, and bored creatures interest themselves with themselves.'

'Don't they play *any* games? I've seen them dancing.'

'Revels, yes. Wassailing, of course. Wayzgoosing, conversazione, any pastime with a "z" in it. But no board games. They do have a peculiar active game they play with a ryepeck, an owlet and a small fish, but I'm not sure of the rules and would have a hard time explaining it to you.'

'What's a ryepeck?' asked Jack, seizing on one of several words which were unfamiliar to him.

'A pole for a punt. I would have thought you might have known that, Jack. Have you never propelled a punt on a river?'

'Never.'

'And I thought mortals punted all the time.'

'Only those who attend Cambridge University.'

'Oh.'

Jack felt they ought to get back to more serious issues.

'Spiggot – about Fen . . .'

The boggart's face went dark and moody for a second. Then he looked up at Jack. 'Don't worry, Jack – I've worked it all out. I have a plan. It's a very subtle scheme and should work a treat.'

These words did nothing to allay any fears in Jack's mind. When a boggart used the word 'subtle' something was likely to go wrong. Subtlety was not normally in a boggart's vocabulary. But he smiled at his faerie friend in an encouraging way and asked to be appraised of the plan.

FOUR

All was not well in Mallmoc's house. In fact, the sorcerer was close to despair. The older one gets the harder it is to take setbacks. When you are so old that you cannot even remember who your mother was they become monsters of the conscious mind. Misery, too, at an ancient age, is such a worn and tattered emotion it doesn't even have an interesting side, let alone a good side. Many people enjoy the bitterness of misery. Mallmoc had wallowed in it so often it had nothing to offer him. It was just another ragged emotion which he wore with total apathy.

'How can these puny mortals and their idiot boggart have so much luck?' he moaned to Prince Rincortle.

'Perhaps,' answered the ulcugga prince, 'it is not luck?'

'Of course it's luck,' snarled Mallmoc. 'They're not clever creatures. They have less than half my flair. The boy is naïve, the maiden is a simple savage and the boggart is a bumptious moron.'

'Yet they have managed to stop us, lord.'

Rincortle was plainly willing to give his opponents their due. As an ulcugga he was not one to belittle his foes. Those who regard their enemy as inferior get no satisfaction from beating them. What pleasure does one get from stepping on a bewildered beetle? None. It is too easy. Ulcugga enjoyed having worthy opponents, so that their victory was sweet. To overcome a foe that is formidable and challenging is pleasanter by far than crushing an enemy that anyone could beat.

'One of the cleverest of their tricks,' added the prince, 'was to use mirror shields. My fairies are greatly unnerved by having to attack their own reflections. I wish I had thought of it. Too late now.'

'Never mind all that now,' the sorcerer said. 'We must work to stop their games.'

He swept across the chamber, the tail of his long red gown following in his wake, his black battered top hat sitting high on his head. Mallmoc in his black-and-red was a formidable figure. On his head – physically attached to his temples – was a set of antlers. These horns which swept out like wings from Mallmoc's hairline, were very intimidating. Even Rincortle, who was very seldom concerned with fear, felt uneasy when Mallmoc wore his horns. He knew that the sorcerer derived some sort of mortality surge from the antlers, which had been stolen long ago from a shaman, a creature who was now remembered only by a charcoal picture on a cave wall.

'We must find a way of breaking the pact between those mortals and their boggart,' mused Mallmoc.

'I feel it is too late for that,' replied Rincortle. 'My ulcugga fairies have been unable to hold the lines. Your great land ironclad is once again in pieces. It were better if you considered a line of escape. Let us go to the Midlands, to the heart of ulcugga country, and consolidate. Let us take our losses and regroup – perhaps in twenty years or so . . .'

'Twenty years?' snarled Mallmoc. 'I have not got twenty years.'

'You could have centuries, if you wished. I am as eager as you to gain control of the two worlds, but we are on the verge of present failure. You know what will happen to the ulcugga if the other fairy clans defeat us utterly. We will be banished, like the cloche-fée, doomed to live in that lifeless, airless region between the worlds of mortals and of faerie. It would be like having to live in the cavity walls of a house, being neither outdoors nor in. If we retreat now we will have enough strength to withdraw behind our Midland dykes. We still have enough of us left to hold our earth-ramparts.'

Mallmoc groaned. 'Not now. I have *had* centuries. I have had millennia. My mind crumbles. I have not the will to wait longer. I must gain control of the two worlds now, or I will drown in despair. Do you think they will come to rescue the boggart maid? She dangles from the leaning tower of my ruined vessel, crying out to be rescued. Why do they not come?'

'They suspect a trick. They know you wish them to come.'

'That has never stopped them before now. *Knowing* that it is a trap. They have rushed into the jaws of death before now.'

'Yet they have grown more canny, more wise.'

'Damn their souls,' cried Mallmoc, raising his bony arms. 'But I know you are right. We will brave the next few hours, hoping for a change of fortune, then if it still appears we will be defeated – why then, we will retreat; myself to another era, and you and your fairies to the Midlands. You will remain there and await my return. There is something I must do before then, however. I am not safe without a certain object. I must fetch it from its hiding place. Once it is in my hands again perhaps I can rouse myself from this slough of despondency. It has never failed me in the past.'

Prince Rincortle left him alone. Mallmoc wrenched the antlers from their sockets. For a few seconds there were bloody holes where they had been, but these crusted over within a short space of time. While the process of healing took place he dressed in a plain dark suit with a white shirt and dark tie. He replaced the battered top hat with a black Homburg. The sandals were removed from his feet and shoes and socks put in their place. He looked like a businessman. A very old businessman.

Once he was ready for his journey he wove a magic spell which took him into Mortaland.

When he stopped spinning he found himself in the street of a town where he had once lived. There was a house here, with an inglenook fireplace. In the chimney of that fireplace he had left an object which contained his vulnerability. Every creature on earth, be he mortal or supernatural, has an Achilles heel. No being is totally invulnerable. Mallmoc's mortality was contained within the object he sought.

It was dangerous for him to carry the item around on his person – that was why he had hidden it, so that if it were found by accident it might not be connected to him. Yet if he were to travel back in time, which now seemed likely and necessary, he desired that the object go with him and a new place found. He felt safer when it was within easy reach.

Mallmoc made his way along a crowded street towards the house. When he reached it he saw that it was no longer a private dwelling, but had been turned into a shop. A sign above the window read 'Polkinghorne's Antiques'. Mallmoc entered. The shop-owner's assistant, noticing his expensive-looking attire, immediately came to him, even though there were other customers browsing amongst the antiques.

'Can I help you, sir?' she asked.

'Yes,' murmured Mallmoc, turning his hypnotic gaze upon the young lady's eyes. 'What is your name?'

'Jenny,' she replied. 'Jenny Pentworth.'

Mallmoc frowned. Where had he heard that name before? Surely from the lips of one of his slaves? But which one? There had been so many. That was the trouble with being ancient and brilliant. His mind was full of things that jostled against one another. He could not, even as a great warlock, be expected to remember *every-thing*. Mallmoc sighed and let the moment slip. Perhaps he would regret it, perhaps not. It was important to keep to the task in mind. He was here for a specific reason.

'I'm interested in that fireplace over there,' he said. 'It's very quaint. Those fire-irons in the grate, under that andiron. I'm – I'm a collector, my dear, of such ironwork. Could I inspect them?'

'Of course.' She was less interested now she realised he was not after something expensive, like the Queen Anne writing bureau or the painting attributed to Turner. 'Help yourself.'

Jenny Pentworth led Mallmoc through the old chairs and tables, the lamps and crockery, to the fireplace.

'Thank you,' he said.

He waited for her to go away. When she did not he grew impatient and stepped forward, reaching up under the mantelpiece, his hand finding the shelf which contained the flue. It was here he had left his property.

'What are you doing?' asked Jenny Pentworth. 'There's soot falling on the tiles . . .'

'Shut your mouth, girl,' snarled Mallmoc, his fingers scrabbling around like a spider on the hidden shelf. 'I'm looking for something.'

The two customers who had been wandering around the place were at that moment going out of the door, leaving Mallmoc and Jenny alone.

'I shall have to call the manager,' she said, 'if you don't stop that.'

'I said, shut up.' Mallmoc was panicking now. He couldn't find the bottle. It didn't seem to be there. 'Shut up! Shut up! Shut up!'

'Mr Polkinghorne,' Jenny Pentworth cried, shrilly, 'there's a strange man here poking around in the chimney.'

Mallmoc turned and gripped her by the head.

'You leave me be . . .'

She squirmed out of his grasp and ran for the back door of the shop. Her hand reached out to turn the knob. The digits that finally gripped the brass handle, however,

were hooked and hairy. They remained there, holding on
to the knob, but not trying to turn it. The owner of this
strange new hand, it seemed, had fallen asleep in the act
of leaving the room. Jenny Pentworth was now a giant
sloth. Someone tried to enter from the other side, but the
large slumbering beast blocked the doorway, preventing
entry by its sheer weight. It still gripped the twisting
knob with a hairy paw.

Mallmoc wasted no more time. He ducked underneath
the chimney and rummaged about, trying to find the
bottle which contained his names. All the names he had
ever used, would ever use, were in that bottle. If
someone had found it and removed the wax stopper, his
precious names would be scattered by draughts and
winds, and he would crumple to dust. He began cursing
in a tongue unintelligible to mortals. A man entered the
shop, heard the oaths, saw the sloth, and went white with
unknown fear. He left quickly, leaving the door wide
open and the chimes jingling every two seconds.

'Let me in!' cried a voice from behind the back door,
as someone hammered on the woodwork. 'I'm calling the
police!'

Clouds of soot billowed from the fireplace. When a
distraught and sooty Mallmoc finally emerged from the
inglenook, a film of black ash covered most of the objects
in the room. He looked about him wildly, hoping against
hope that his precious bottle was standing somewhere
amongst the antiques, waiting to be sold. He could not
see it anywhere. He wailed loud enough to awaken the
sloth who glared at him.

'If I still had a boyfriend you wouldn't get away with
this,' she muttered. 'Jack'd knock your lights out.'

Mallmoc stopped and stared at the beast.

'Jack?'

'Yeah,' said the sloth in a threatening tone. 'He's away at the moment, at engineering college. But when he comes back I'll tell him what you did to me and then you'd better watch out, you freak.'

'Engineering Jack!' cried Mallmoc. 'I might have guessed that youth was behind this.' His eyes lit up. 'That's right, the fairy Raminago'bris said he had been here. *He stole my bottle*!' A sudden thought caused his ancient heart to patter rapidly. 'He won't break it, will he?'

The sloth let out a hollow laugh. 'If he breaks bottles like he breaks hearts, you can bet your life he will.'

'My life?' groaned Mallmoc. 'You're right. It is my life.' He flared into anger again. 'Someone's head will come off for this! I'll turn them inside out and stamp on their heart! I'll burn their entrails in a copper bowl! Damn them. Damn their eyes. Get out of my way . . .'

The last few words were directed at a policeman, who was pushed roughly aside as Mallmoc fled the shop. Outside was a police car with a blue flashing light. Another policeman sat behind a wheel, writing something in a notebook. Mallmoc glared at him and remonstrated.

'What about my property? Stolen! And will you do anything about it? Not a chance in hell. You couldn't catch a burglar if he was tied to your shirt front, could you, you imbecile. Honest citizens like me – robbed in the street and you do nothing but scratch your warts. Dolts. Idiots.'

The policeman stared back at him, his mouth hanging open.

With that Mallmoc strode in fury down the road, into a back alley, and spun himself back into Faerieland.

Standing once more in the ruined chamber of his castle-ship, Mallmoc's thoughts cooled. He considered things in a rational state of mind. That boy, Jack, had his names. The youth held Mallmoc's life in his hands. Why hadn't Jack done anything about it? Why wasn't Mallmoc dust on the floor? Because Jack did not know the value of the bottle. He had done nothing with it. He had probably left it hidden it somewhere, that was the logical answer. Well Mallmoc did not care so long as it *stayed* hidden for the time being. Mallmoc could search for it later, when the world was his to wander at will.

The thing to do was to kill Jack before he retrieved the bottle.

But then, hadn't Mallmoc been trying to kill *all* of them, these past few Faerieland months? Especially Jack and that maiden, Rosamund. Yet there was a way he had not tried yet. What was it the sloth had said? *'My ex-boyfriend.'* That could be used. Jenny Pentworth could be used. And how? By arousing poison in the rose-maiden's breast, that's how. There was nothing so deadly or as poisonous as *jealousy*. Jealous men had killed. Jealous women had killed. Time to unleash a terrible blood-staining jealousy in the heart of the medieval maid.

FIVE

Jack took the antique writing case out of Kling's cart.
'What are you going to do with that?' asked Kling.
'Throw it away, I hope. Make Kling's cart lighter to pull?'

'No. I – I woke up this morning with a strange feeling. I felt I had to look at it. Maybe I dreamt that it had been stolen or something?'

Jack opened the lid of the writing case in which he had placed the bottle full of shadowy snakes. Yes, there it was, still snug in its nest of velvet. He stared at the embossed green glass, trying to see the nature of those snaky things swirling inside. They were surely not alive? The bottle was sealed tight with a wax stopper that had gone brick hard. Should he try to remove the plug? He had attempted that once and the bottle burned his hands, which is why he now kept it in the old writing case.

Kling stood on his hind legs and looked over Jack's shoulder at the object.

'Looks a bit dark-magicky to Kling. Kling would chuck the thing away if it was up to him.'

'I don't know,' said Jack, thoughtfully. 'I understand where you're coming from, Kling, but I have a feeling about this bottle.'

'What sort of feeling?'

Jack shrugged. 'A weird feeling. Every time I think about tossing it into a lake or a deep bog, I get a prickly feeling on the back of my neck.'

'Well, if it were Kling, he would chuck it.'

Jack looked at the water rat. 'Sure, you'd throw away anything that wasn't food.'

'There are many, many important things in life and they're all different kinds of things to eat.'

Jack closed the lid to the writing case just as Rosamund came up to the cart.

'What is it that you have there, Jack?'

'Oh, nothing really.' He put the case back into the cart. 'That bottle I showed you. How's the war going, Rosy?'

Jack could not help staring at his new girlfriend. To his eyes she was flawless. Her complexion was immaculate. She was trim-figured, with remarkable grey eyes borrowed from an eagle, her hands were slim and expressive and her feet were small and dainty. She was very, very pretty. Her smile contained the mild wickedness of an imp combined with the sweet innocence of a fledgling angel.

Jenny Pentworth, his ex, could not hold a candle to Rosamund, daughter of Baron Guillaume de Arundel.

And Rosy adored him.

Jack could see it in her eyes. Jack had *never* been adored in his life before. His mum loved him as mothers do. His father was very fond of him in the way that fathers are. Jenny Pentworth had swung between passionately possessive of him and completely indifferent to him. Now here was someone who actually thought the world of him in a boy-girl way. It was early days of course. He had his faults, he knew. He was probably quite unworthy. But for the moment here was a girl more lovely than a fairy princess and definitely better natured, who held his hand and looked into his eyes with love.

'Why do you stare at me so, dear Jack?' She wiped her mouth with the back of her hand. 'Have I the yolk of an egg about my face?'

He tried to be gallant. 'No, no – I was just thinking – you look like – you're – you're as beautiful as a summer's day,' he said, recalling a line from a Shakespeare sonnet, erroneously as it happened, 'but more cool.'

'Oh, Jack.' She blushed. 'How very fond.'

The fairy knights had gone out to do battle with the ulcugga. The kites were aloft. Spiggot, having been wounded once again, was back in camp organising the messenger service. There was not a lot for Jack and Rosamund, as non-combatants, to do. They decided to walk to a nearby hill, a relatively safe area, where they could look over the sea of thistles and gorse bushes to the meadow where Mallmoc's castle-ship was trapped.

The air was full of damselflies and butterflies. Parasol seeds drifted by on the breeze. The birds sang and the beasts snuffled in the brush as if the world was not in mortal danger and no war was in progress. Jack considered it a fine summer's day, lovely and temperate, with

fresh winds shaking the darling buds. This was not the
way Jack usually thought, but here he was in Faerieland
and such phrases often leapt into his mind. The two
young people sat on the kneb of the hill and stared out
over the faerie landscape.

Somewhere out there the goblins were still gathering
fruit to sell on their market stalls, the furniture-shaped
bogles were flying on the backs of nightjars and owls, the
pixies were busy mining their gems from Cornish caves,
the elves were marching up the airy mountain and down
the rushy glen in their green jackets and red caps with
white owl's feathers.

'Did you know,' said Jack, dreamily, 'that some of
them have frogs for their watch-dogs at night?'

'Who?'

'The faerie. And others eat pancakes of yellow tide-
foam?'

'No, I didn't, Jack.'

'It's true. And that an old, grey king crosses
Columbkill over a bridge of white mist?'

'How dost thou know these strange things, Jack?'

Jack came out of his reverie, shaking his head. 'I
dunno, Rosy, they just come to me.'

At that moment Jack noticed a familiar figure coming
up the hill, waving an arm. She looked lost and afraid.
Her body language was one of a damsel in distress. She
had seen Jack and rushed at him.

'Oh, Jack, Jack – what is this place? I went to sleep
last night, just the same as ever, and woke up here, on a
cold hillside.'

'Jenny?' cried Jack, astonished. 'What are you doing
here?'

Jenny Pentworth came to him and gripped his arm.

'That's what I'm asking *you*, you dope.' She flung an arm wildly, taking in the whole Faerieland scene. 'Where are we?' Then she seemed to notice the bewildered-looking Rosamund. 'And who's the slapper in the fancy dress?'

Jack glared at his former girlfriend. 'You watch your language, Jenny. This is Rosy – Rosamund. We're sort of going out together.'

'Pooh!' Jenny sneered. 'So this is her? I remember you said something in the high street the other day. She doesn't look much to me.'

'Fortunately,' replied Jack, 'that doesn't matter, because it's me who's going out with her.'

'Poor you.'

At that moment a wayward fairy arrow came from somewhere and buried its head in the turf of the hill. Jenny grabbed Jack in fright and clung to him like a baby monkey to its mother. Rosamund frowned and tried to peel the girl's arms away from her Jack. Jack was caught in the middle of the two young women and he struggled to rid himself of both of them. He felt put upon and suffocated. Finally, Rosamund stepped back, her eyes blazing green, and spoke with venom dripping from her tongue.

'Tell this witch to depart, Jack. I will not have her here.'

'Witch?' cried Jenny.

'Just a minute . . .' began Jack, overwhelmed.

'No, not just-a-minute. *Now*, Jack. If thou hast any feeling for thy Rosamund, thou wilt do as I ask. Send Jenny away. Banish her with harsh words and hard looks. Thee told me this Jenny was a witch. What can one do with witches but cast them off into oblivion?'

'You told her I was a witch?' cried Jenny. 'You bastard!'

'Figure of speech,' said Jack. 'You damn well are, in a way. Look, Rosy, we can't abandon her. She's like us when we first came here. She's lost in Faerieland. We have to look after her . . .'

'We? *I* do not.' Rosamund was full of fury now and her face was frightening for Jack to behold. 'I warn thee, Jack, if thou dost not dismiss this crone instantly from thy sight, I shall no longer be "thy Rosamund". I cannot be held responsible for what revenge I must take.'

'Be reasonable, Rosy – I can't.'

'Oh, Jack refuses my request.' Rosamund looked distraught now as well as enraged. 'He loves this enchantress. So be it. Blood shall answer. No man shall spurn the love of Rosamund Guillaume de Arundel and live to gloat. Am I a plaything, to be cast aside like a wooden doll? Am I thus forsaken for a witch? I ask thee, Jack, in the name of love.'

'I can't abandon her,' Jack said, miserably. 'If she was a lost cat I couldn't do it.'

Jenny, obviously seeing she could exploit the situation, kissed Jack on the cheek, inflaming things more.

'Oh, Jack – you used to call me your pussy-cat, didn't you?'

'I didn't mean that. I meant . . .'

But Rosamund was already striding off, back towards camp. Jack watched her go. What could he do? He couldn't leave Jenny Pentworth alone out here with a faerie war in progress. He had to ensure she was kept safe. That was the only manly thing to do. Rosamund would have to go into a stew. There was not much he could do about that at the moment. He would sort things out with her later, when she was being more reasonable. At the moment he had to find out what Jenny was doing here and find some way of getting her back to Mortaland without being harmed.

But on turning back to face Jenny, she was already becoming less substantial than before.

'What's happening to you?' he cried.

Jenny Pentword smiled. 'I'm fading away, like the morning mist.'

'You – you're a cipher,' cried Jack. 'One of Mallmoc's tricks!'

'Am I?' The smile was mocking. 'Am I really?'

Now he could see right through her. Mallmoc. Of course. He was trying to drive a wedge between Rosamund and Jack. Well, it wouldn't work. Rosy might be angry now but she would calm down once Jack explained what was going on. He'd always found Rosamund to be reasonable, once she had had time to cool off. Of course he'd never seen her quite so furious before. Jealousy was a terrible thing. Probably it would be better to let her alone for the rest of the day. He could go and help with the raising and lowering of the kites. Keep out of her way for a while. Once she had had time to reflect, he thought, she might be willing to listen.

'I'm going,' said the nebulous cloud of mist drifting down the hill. 'Goodbye, Jack. Have a nice death.'

'Good riddance,' Jack said. 'Don't come back.'

Rosamund was all spleen and bile. Jack had been wrong about giving her time to reflect. All that happened was that Rosamund's jealousy and anger simmered until it was a poisonous brew in her breast. The fury in her grew monstrous. She bit off the heads of all who spoke to her. When she tried to dismiss the fact of Jack's unfaithfulness (as she saw it) from her mind, she could not. Her thoughts always returned to his fickleness. How could it be borne? The daughter of a noble, dismissed with the wave of a brute boy's hand? No, it could not. The gentle maid in her had to be suppressed. Jack could not be allowed such cavalier ways. He had to pay for her shame.

Rosamund stole a small fairy dagger, a stiletto, and concealed it in her dress.

PART SEVEN

Jack be nimble, Jack be quick

ONE

Jack had been right about his friend. There was very little finesse to Spiggot's schemes, no matter that the boggart himself believed them to be intricate and cunning. Spiggot's *subtle* plan to rescue his beloved turned out to be a headlong charge on a borrowed horse, while brandishing a sword. Following him at a rattling pace was Kling, pulling an empty cart. Spiggot swept down towards Mallmoc's castle-ship, to where Fen dangled in her spider's cocoon, and with one slice of his trusty blade he cut through the cord that held her. Kling, whose timing was immaculate, caught her falling body in the cart. Then both Spiggot and Kling thundered out of the glade in magnificent manner worthy of such a bold, gallant rescue.

Once out of the possible clutches of the ulcugga, Spiggot cut the spider's webbing from Fen and allowed her to emerge. She immediately threw her little muscled arms around his neck.

'My hero,' she murmured, 'you can walk me through the dog daisies at any time.'

'Oh!' cried Spiggot, overcome. 'Oh, Fen.'

Spiggot and Fen went back to the camp. Here there was even better news. Prince Rincortle had sent a bogle messenger, asking for a truce and an end to hostilities. The ulcugga prince, on receiving assurances that his approaches were received positively, had followed up the message in person to negotiate. By the time Spiggot reached the glade kings, princes and chieftains were gathered in their armour. Prince Rincortle stood with some of his fairies on the far side of the glade. Spiggot and Fen entered to the applause of fairies from all over Britain and Eri-innis. He beamed. Twice a hero in one day. It was too much.

Out in the thistle forest and bush land, kites were reeled in. With relief, fairies stepped from their aircraft, glad to be on terra firma once more. Jack and these high-flying allies marched back to camp to receive another great welcome. The fairies grew hoarse with shouting Jack's name, and that of Spiggot, Rosamund and Fen. At one point Kling called for silence, then asked why the greenwood wasn't ringing with his name too. Just because he was a giant water rat? Hadn't he worked just as hard, pulling the cart, offering advice to his master's son on strategy and tactics?

'Kling was in the sewer rat wars of thirty-two and learned a great deal about pincer movements and heavy columns,' he said. 'All this valuable information was given freely and without reserve to the master's son. But

I don't expect gratitude. I don't even expect thanks. Something though – some little thing.'

'Like what?' cried a fairy from the Isle of Man.

'Oh, Kling doesn't know,' Kling said, offhandedly. 'A food basket, perhaps? A keg of treacle? A barrel of honey? A demi-john of jam? Just some little thing to show your appreciation of a job well done.'

King Cimberlin said he would do what he could about the honey.

King Fearghus from Eri-innis stood surety for the treacle.

Cragfeggian, chief of the seelie court clan, promised the jam.

Kling was happy and retired to the shadows.

'Well, then,' said Jack, confronting Prince Rincortle, 'are you ready to surrender?'

Somewhere beyond the fringes of the crowd the sinister-looking figure of a mortal shrank into the shade of an old oak.

The ulcugga prince looked Jack in the eye with utter disdain.

'Of course not. Boggart, tell him.'

Spiggot pulled Jack aside and whispered in his ear.

'Fairies *never* surrender,' explained Spiggot to his mortal friend. 'You shouldn't even suggest it. It is enough that everyone simply stops fighting.'

'But – but how do you know who's won?'

'We know, don't we,' Spiggot said. '*We* know, they know, everyone knows that the ulcugga has lost, so why rub their noses in it? It will only start up again if you do. Let them leave with dignity. Let them go back to their lands in mid-Liöfwende. Believe me, they will go with their tails between their legs, even though they look consumed with pride. They are crawling with shame inside. There's no need to crow over them.'

'Well, I wasn't thinking of *crowing* – just, well, letting them know they're a defeated clan.'

'No need. They already know. Everyone does.'

Jack accepted this. Nevertheless, he asked Rincortle, 'What about your master? Will he come in for a ceasefire too?'

An ominous shadow flitted through the trees as light as a zephyr through curtains of willow fronds.

Spiggot drew Jack aside again.

'Sorcerers don't have ceasefires, Jack. Rincortle would rather eat horse dung than come here to see us. Besides, Mallmoc is a renegade wizard. We cannot allow him to live. It would happen all over again.'

'Now, see here,' said Jack, folding his arms, 'you can't have one law for one species and another for another.'

'Why not?'

'Because – because it isn't fair.'

'No, but it's fair-y.' Spiggot beamed, pleased with himself. When he saw that Jack was not amused, he continued with, 'Seriously, Jack, we must get rid of Mallmoc. He's terribly dangerous. I know what you're thinking. You're wondering, what if it had been mortals versus faerie and the mortals had lost. Would we have let you go back to your homes in the same way we are allowing the ulcugga to go back to theirs?'

Jack admitted it was *exactly* what he was thinking.

'Well, put your mind at rest, Jack. We would have treated you in just the same way. Sorcerers, though, are different. They feel no shame, no remorse. They feel nothing but a terrible hatred and a desire for revenge. If we leave Mallmoc, he won't go and settle down somewhere and forget all this ever happened. He'll make new plans, new schemes, and won't stop until he gets his way. This isn't the first time Mallmoc has tried to become a dictator. The last time it was in the land of the Gauls.'

The dark shape, a female with a slim blade, moved slowly forward, to get closer to Jack, using the milling fairies as a shield.

'France? He tried to rule France?'

'It was in another century, but yes, it became France.'

'So, when are we going to get him?'

Spiggot replied, 'A contingent of fairies has been sent to capture him and bring him back here.'

Jack had to be happy with that.

'I see your subtle plan to save Fen worked,' said Jack.

'Like a dream,' murmured Spiggot, looking as though he had just swallowed a spoonful of sugar. 'Isn't she wonderful?'

Jack now saw that something had happened between his boggart friend and Fen. There was a new understanding between them. They kept looking at one another and smiling. They kept stealing little touches with their hands. They were, to put it bluntly, obviously in love. It was rather embarrassing, really. Jack had to look the other way once or twice when the smiles became sickeningly wide.

Suddenly Spiggot's expression changed to one of horror.

The shadow became a substantial mortal. She darted forward, the weapon raised.

'Look out, Jack!' he yelled.

Jack turned to see the glint of a knife about to plunge into his neck. Fortunately for him Prince Rincortle's hand flashed out and grasped the wrist of the assassin. There was a sharp twist, a cry of pain, and the weapon fell to the ground. The ulcugga had saved Jack's life. But it was his would-be killer that both astonished and dismayed Jack.

'Rosy?' he cried. 'What are you doing?'

'Trying to kill thee!' she hissed. 'And it will not be the last attempt. If I cannot have thy favours, nor can *she*.'

He stared at her grey eagle-eyes. They were hot with rage.

'Rosy,' he said again, having grasped what was the matter. 'That wasn't Jenny. It was a cipher. Sent by Mallmoc to make you jealous. In any case I couldn't love anyone but you. Not now that I've met you. You're the only girl for me – not just in the world but in the whole history of time – and if Jenny were twice as beautiful and ten times as nice, she couldn't hold a candle to *you*.'

'Is that true, dear Jack?' said Rosamund in a yearning voice. 'I wish I could believe thee, I really do.'

'Nothing could be truer,' interrupted Rincortle, 'and believe me, I am a most disinterested and dispassionate observer of this romance. The sorcerer did indeed send a cipher to pursue this mortal. I was there when this scheme was hatched.'

Jack turned to the ulcugga prince.

'Why *did* you save me? And defend me to Rosy? We are enemies.'

'*Were* enemies. The war is over. Nothing is the same anymore. Once it is all over, then any residue of the war must be stamped out. All must be as it was before the fight. Liöfwende must become itself again.'

Jack nodded, seeing the wisdom in this. He turned back to Rosamund again. 'I'm sorry about Jenny,' he said.

She melted him with one of her smiles.

'I forgive thee, Jack.'

'Jenny was too young for me, in any case – I prefer older women.'

Rosamund's smile turned to a frown.

'I am not older than thee, Jack.'

'Oh, but you are, Rosy. When were you born? In the twelfth century? That makes you almost a thousand years older than me. I'm afraid next to me you're a crone, Rosy. I don't mind, though. I like your wrinkles. I think your grey hair becomes you.'

Her smile returned but rather stiffly.

'Jack, wilt thou cut me a stick from yonder blackthorn bush, so that I might better hobble about in my dotage?'

He grinned. 'Not a chance, Rosy. You want to whack me with it.'

'So true, dear Jack. I wish to *whack* you very hard.'

At that moment, as the ulcugga were leaving for their midland home, a contingent of piskies entered the glade. They were carrying a jar. They called for Spiggot.

'Boggart,' one of them said, when Spiggot presented himself, 'where is the maid whose eyes we borrowed, for they are hereby returned?'

TWO

Thus Rosamund had her eyes returned to her. She said she was sorry to see the grey eagle-eyes go, for they had given her such sharp sight. But for his part Jack had to admit the blue ones were the best. They made her look stunning and he told her so.

The piskies also gave Rosamund some gems, to make up for the time they had borrowed her eyes. Rosamund thanked the piskies and casually put the little velvet bag of stones into her dress pocket. When you are a teenager in love you're not all that worried about wealth. It's feelings that matter at such times.

After Prince Rincortle and his ulcugga had departed, the allied army marched down to the castle-ship. In the hole in the ground created by the hard-working gnomes, they found the wreck. The iron plates had fallen away, revealing a foul interior. Now cold furnaces gaped, their mouths still full of coke and charcoal. Grey ash had spilled over hell's kitchen. Pots and pans, and all the other necessities of life, were scattered about the place. Mallmoc's chambers were empty. They walked through its vacant passageways, its hollow rooms, their footsteps echoing in a ghostly fashion wherever they went. To Jack it was like an old boiler room, fallen to disuse, not even a caretaker to give it some presence of life.

Mallmoc had fled. The contingent of fairies that had gone to arrest him had arrived to find him already gone. All his magic spell books and wizard paraphernalia had been taken: those objects that had not burned in the wrecking of the vessel. All that was left of the sorcerer were two halves of a forgotten torn parchment rammed behind a copper stove. On the parchment, in black ink, was the heading *The loving history of Mallmoc and Zobeide*. The rest of the parchment was blank. A glaring white testimony to unrequited love. The first sheet of what someone hoped would be a whole book. A parchment prepared to receive a tale worthy of Shakespeare's pen: a biography of two people who adored one another.

'Who was Zobeide?' asked Jack. 'His wife?'

'A lovely lady of Baghdad,' replied Fen. 'Some say she was even more beautiful than Helen of Troy. I have heard that a sorcerer loved her, but she forsook him for the Kalif Haroun-al-Raschid. That sorcerer must have been Mallmoc. It seems from this he never got over the rejection.'

'Destroyed by love,' said Rosamund. 'How tragic.'

'We must pursue him, of course,' said Prince Xixinia, 'to the ends of the Earth and time.'

Not only had Mallmoc gone but also the last of those servants and slaves he had kept captive and working for

him. They had vanished into the twilight, heading for
their homes. Any mortals remaining had joined with
faerie: friends they had made in adversity. Spiggot told
Jack they would be well looked after, as he had been by
his boggart companion. It was a time for healing spiritual, mental and physical wounds. Those poor creatures
who had lost several years of their lives to the terrible
sorcerer needed rest and security: the peacefulness of
home life. Faerieland was the place to obtain such tran-
quility. Here nature was soft and comforting. Here the
wildlife was not aggressive and minded its own business.
Here the butterflies were lovelier and the birds sang
more prettily and the trees were greener.

'We must do something about the thrum,' said
Spiggot. 'They must be driven back down to Gilscipe.'

'We need first to find the locking-stone to the magic
cairn,' Fen reminded him, 'otherwise they'll just come
pouring out again.'

It was true. The root-eating subterranean faerie would
not stay underground if there was a hole from which to
emerge. The locking-stone had to be found, and soon.
Spiggot had the quivvel which would hopefully lead
them to the missing stone.

Later, as they were going through the many corridors
and rooms of the castle-ship, Jack came across his
beloved motorbike.

'My bike!' he cried in delight. 'I wonder if it'll start.'

Without thinking of his companions, sensitive to loud
engines, he jumped on the motorcycle and turned the
key. After several kicks the engine roared into life,
thunderously noisy in the confines of the iron castle.

Excited, Jack sped up and down the narrow passageway, his eyes shining. Then he stopped and turned the accelerator several times, leaving the gears in neutral, listening to the engine. It was not tuned to his satisfaction any more. It would need a lot of work, once he got it back home again.

Realising the fumes were building up in the confined space and that it was *very* noisy, Jack switched off.

'Wow, Spiggot – what do you think of that, then?'

The boggart was standing white-faced and trembling by a doorway, clearly ready to bolt. He gulped hard but failed to speak. Fen was also pale, her eyes wide with horror. Rosamund had her hands over her ears and her eyes averted. When Jack tried to smile at her she stuck out her tongue at him.

'Oh,' said Jack, realising what he had done. 'Sorry.'

'Sorry indeed, Jack!' cried Spiggot. 'I think I'm deaf for ever. Also it stinks in here. It stinks of burning fossils, which is a horrible odour. I've never experienced anything like it in my whole faerie life. You must never, never do that again, Jack. Look outside.'

Jack looked through one of the portholes and saw that the fairies were gathered at the edge of the nearest woodland, weapons bristling from every hand. It was clear they were ready to attack this monster which had suddenly roared to life in the depths of Mallmoc's castle. Clearly, it seemed to them, the sorcerer had left behind a *demon* which would destroy them all. No doubt they believed that the boggarts and mortals were already dead – gone down the throat of this horrendous creature – and were now charred and blackened corpses travelling through the foul passageways of its innards.

Jack had to go outside and pacify them, tell them it
was nothing to be afraid of and that it would not happen
again. Then he wheeled his bike out of the castle and
parked it under a tree. The tree reacted violently, kicking
the bike over with one of its roots. Jack leaned it against
a rock. The rock ran away. Finally he just rested it on its
side on the turf. Daisies withered and grasses grew
brown, but there it remained for the time being. Then
everyone went to bed for a well-earned night's sleep.

It was decided in the morning that the gnomes would
simply fill in the great hole and bury Mallmoc's castle
where it lay. Some suggested the motorbike should join
the iron castle in this grave, but Jack would not hear of
it. Since it *was* his property, he was taken heed of. Of
course, nothing would grow in that field again, but this
would help to remind travellers that a foul sorcerer had
been defeated in this spot.

Before the shovelling took place, Spiggot went
through the castle with his quivvel to find the magic
cairn's locking-stone.

To his astonishment the quivvel did not vibrate.

'I don't understand, Jack. When we were here as prisoners, the quivvel was trembling like mad. I was *sure*
we'd find the locking-stone in the ruins of the castle.'

'Me, too,' said Jack. 'Well, what now?'

'I honestly don't know.'

They left the gnomes to fill in the hole. It would take
quite a while, of course, for a whole meadow had collapsed, but gnomes were good at digging. They had
strong backs and stout hearts. The fairies baulked at
such a task, but they had other qualities, such as their
skill at warfare. Boggarts might have helped, but

boggarts are always busy at their smithy work and have
little time left for unscheduled chores.

The four companions walked back to where the fairy
kings, princes and chieftains were waiting to take their
leave. As Spiggot passed Jack's motorcycle the quivvel
in his pocket began vibrating like mad. The boggart
stopped and waved the quivvel over the machine. It
almost jumped out of his hand.

'Is there a compartment or something on this infernal
device?' he asked Jack. 'If so, would you open it,
please?'

Jack shrugged, then lifted the saddle, under which
was a cavity where he used to keep his helmet when it
was not in use.

Nestling in the cavity was a chunky piece of granite,
the mica granules in it glinting in the sunlight.

'Jack,' murmured Spiggot, 'what is this?'

Jack picked up the rock and held it in his hand.

'Oh, I'd forgotten I'd got that thing. I found it – on my
way home from holiday in Scotland. Look how it glis-
tens, Spig. I've always been interested in minerals, being
an engineer and all that . . .'

Jack's voice trailed off as he realised he was under
intense scrutiny from his friends.

He looked at the piece of rock in his hand again.

'This is it, isn't it?'

'Yes, Jack,' said Spiggot. 'This is the locking-stone to
the magic cairn. Had you not said anything, I might have
believed it was placed there by Mallmoc. But you have
now made your own confession. It was you, all along,
who stole the locking-stone. It was you who released the
thrum and the skaggs from Gilscipe. They have caused

much damage to our precious forests, Jack, and the oaks
will never forgive you.'

'It was a mistake!' cried Jack. 'I had no idea what it
was. Besides, I was in Mortaland when I found it. I've
actually brought it back.'

Fen and Spiggot shook their heads, but Rosamund
came to Jack's rescue.

'Jack did not know of its magical properties,' she said.
'Who can blame him for what he does not know?'

Spiggot drew a deep breath.

'Well, I have to admit we might not have gone to war
against Mallmoc if it hadn't been for the thrum. Many of
those fairies up there wouldn't have joined our army if
their forests had not been threatened. So in a way Jack
unwittingly helped us get rid of a tyrant.' The boggart
made a sudden decision. 'We won't say we found it in
your machine. We'll simply tell the fairies it has come to
light, and hand it over to them.'

And that's what Spiggot did. He gave King Cimberlin
the locking-stone and told him, 'Here's what we found.'

The fairy king took the stone. 'Good, boggart. You
have done well. You may go home to your village in the
knowledge that we owe you a great debt. I shall inform
your father, Gnomon, of your great deeds.'

Spiggot shifted uncomfortably on the spot.

'Er, I don't think he'll be too pleased with me.'

'Oh, I know he expected you to behave as a boggart
behaves – to remain faithful to the boggart creed, which
disapproves of your kind putting themselves forward
and seeking fame. He believes you to have abandoned
your station in life and to have grown boastful and vain.
I know, too, he does not like boggarts who seek glory,

not many of your clan do. But in this instance I believe you will be forgiven. My proclamation will ensure it is so. The rat will look after you and confirm my feelings on the matter.'

'*Water* rat,' muttered Kling, never overawed, even by a fairy king, 'or vole, if you please.'

'Quite,' said the king. 'Now, as to Mallmoc. We have made enquiries of the birds and beasts and believe we know where he has gone. He has escaped to Mortaland. Someone will need to pursue him there and kill him. I suggest it be the mortals. They know the world and its ways.'

'Er, I'm not that good at killing people,' said Jack. 'It's not something I do well at all.'

'Mallmoc isn't *people*. He's a warlock, a sorcerer, a foul fiend in human form. You would be destroying a *thing* not a person. If he isn't dealt with all this will begin again.'

'Even so, it's not really my . . .'

'You will do it,' snapped the king. 'I have spoken.'

Jack shrugged in the face of the inevitable.

'Well, where's Mallmoc gone?' he asked, hoping it was somewhere like the moon, somewhere he couldn't possibly follow. 'I mean, is it a long way away?'

'More like *when*,' said King Fearghus. 'The twelfth century.'

'I can't go to the twelfth century,' gasped Jack. 'I don't know anything about it.'

'But *she* does.' The royal finger pointed at Rosamund. 'He has gone to Rosamund's time *and* place. He has gone to a *when* he knows and a *where* he is familiar with.'

Jack realised that if he said no to this mission they would send Rosamund on alone. He decided he could not let that happen. If Rosamund was going, he was going too.

'Well, if we have to chase after him, we will,' said Jack, sighing, 'but we may just track him down and ask some good knights to get rid of this meddlesome wizard. I'm sure there's a few around who enjoy butchering sorcerers in the name of the law, aren't there, Rosy?'

'Indeed there are, Jack. There are knights in my father's castle who enjoy butchering *anyone*, even illegally.'

'There you are, then.'

THREE

There was a good deal of wassailing once the evening came around. Fairies love more than anything to dance and dance they did. Great bonfires were built to light up the night. They pranced and leapt and somersaulted the whole night long. The Irish fairies did their fantastic jigs, the Scottish fairies their breathless reels, the Welsh mostly sang as they trod a light if not as stately measure, while the English stepped a lively cotillion. Yet they were all capable of joining in with each other and competing. Since amongst fairies there could be no such thing as impartial judges they tended to boast that their own steps were superior to those of all other fairies of any land or region. Jack was asked more than once for his opinion but he wisely declined to give it, knowing he could not help but upset *someone*.

The following day the fairies from Eri-innis and Thristlac said goodbye and made their way back to their

own lands. The rest of the fairies gathered at a nearby
well. Jack and Rosamund would be lowered down this
well which had its exit in the castle courtyard owned by
Rosamund's father. Other faerie were there – goblins,
elves, pixies, brownies, bogles, boggarts, gnomes – to
wish the two mortals good luck in their mission. During
their time in Liöfwende the pair had become more than
just celebrities: they were held in fond regard by many.
This is quite an achievement in Faerieland, where
mortals are normally treated with some contempt.

Jack had even received a present from the goblins. It
was a knapsack. Such generosity was unprecedented
amongst the most miserly folk in Liöfwende and Jack
was genuinely touched. He used the gift to carry the
green bottle and his crossbow, and still had room for
clothes, food and drink. It was one of those magical
knapsacks with infinite space inside. He could have
carried his motorcycle in there if he had so wanted.

Hollow Ben was also there to wish them bon voyage
on their journey down-and-out.

'I'd shake your hands,' said the amiable giant, 'if I had
not left my own somewhere I can't find them.'

'Have you looked in your pockets, dear Ben?' asked
Rosamund.

The giant did so and sure enough there were eight
fingers, two thumbs and two separate palms to hold them
all together.

'Thank you, Rosamund,' said Hollow Ben, 'I shall
miss you.'

Jack took Spiggot aside for a few private words.

In an Arnold Schwarzenegger accent he said, 'I'll be
back.'

This was, of course, lost on the boggart.

'I know you will, Jack.'

'So boggart,' said Jack, 'what's with you and the fair Fen?'

Spiggot shuffled his feet. 'She says I am to walk her through the dog daisies.'

'Ah, the fatal last mile.'

This too, went over Spiggot's head.

In the meantime Rosamund was talking with Fen.

'So,' said Fen, 'you will return home with Jack. What will your father say about him?'

'He'll slice Jack into gammon rashers,' replied Rosamund, 'if I can find no way of saving him. But of course I will.'

'I *hope* you will,' cried Fen, alarmed. 'I surely do.'

Rosamund sighed. 'We shall see.'

Jack and Rosamund were then ordered to stand in the large bucket. They did so looking like condemned prisoners. Then the bucket was lowered into the well by a baker's dozen gnomes, six on each side, the thirteenth being the anchor. Down they went, into the chilling, damp darkness of the narrow well, slowly, slowly, slowly. Suddenly the descent stopped, probably just before they reached the water. There was a long wait during which Jack could hear the steady echoing dripping of moisture from the surrounding stones. In the course of this the darkness seemed to change its texture.

A frog chirruped.

Then the rope went taut and they were hauled upwards again, slowly, slowly, slowly.

On reaching the lip of the well, Jack reached out and grabbed the handle, holding it fast, before it was released and they plunged back down again to the water below. There was a goat-boy in rags standing there. Sure enough on seeing the couple in the bucket he let out a yell and scampered away. Goats scattered in every direction, following the example of their minder. Jack did not blame the lad in the least. It was a frightening thing to raise a bucketful of people where you are expecting nothing but water.

Jack held on to the edge of the well while Rosamund climbed out, then he too scrambled from the bucket. When they were both safely on firm ground, Jack looked around him. The countryside was more like Faerieland than it was the scenery of his own time. There were great deal of trees for a start: forests of them. And the landscape was not marred by any sign of mining, modern buildings or metalled roads. There were tracks, of course, and wooden dwellings dotted about the green, but nothing taller than two storeys. Nothing that is, unless you counted the castle, which loomed over everything in the immediate neighbourhood. The castle dominated all except – far, far in the distance – a solid-looking cathedral with a sharp spire.

'Isn't it quiet here?' Jack murmured. 'Just the birds singing.'

'Is it not like this when you come from?' asked Rosamund.

'Nah. You can't hear yourself think in *my* world. This is like Faerieland, isn't it? Tranquil. Peaceful. A contented landscape. I'll bet everyone's happy here, aren't they?'

An elderly pedlar came up to the well for a drink. He was covered in pots and pans and looked hot and dusty,

weighed down as he was by his wares. His shoes were
ragged and worn and Jack could see the sores and cuts
on his feet through the holes. The pedlar moaned after
relieving himself of his pack. Then he sent the bucket
down and drew some water from the well. This he
drank with no obvious delight. It was simply a necessity.
Then the pack went back on again with much huffing
and puffing. Finally the old man set out again, hobbling
towards the distant castle.

'Well, not everyone,' admitted Jack. 'I suppose the
peasants are not dancing for joy.'

'Here's the kind of life peasants have,' answered
Rosamund. 'Most of them die of disease and starvation
before they become adults. Those that do manage to get
to seventeen or eighteen have to work all the hours in the
day tilling the fields, digging ditches, scouring pans,
building walls, or indeed any other hard demeaning
work. Then when a war comes along they have a spear
thrust into their hand and are told to fight and die for the
baron who has deprived them of land, food and shelter.
If they are crippled by the war they become beggars and
last perhaps one or two winters more. Some of the
women live to old age, when they are often cast from
their homes as being useless crones, out into the freezing
snow. Those that manage to stay alive by their wits are
usually burned at the stake as witches.'

'Not a lot to look forward too, eh?'

'While I, on the other hand, am owned by my father,
with no more status than one of his horses or cattle. At
some time he will hand me over to my future husband,
who will then assume ownership. I will be expected to
breed sons, weave tapestries, sit for ornamentation at any

banquets at which he requires my presence, and say as little as necessary. Yet I am a noblewoman. My dear Jack, it is only the bishops and prelates, the barons and earls, who have any kind of happiness in this world.'

'Well, we'll see about that,' muttered Jack. 'Let's get down to the castle and have a word with your dad.'

'I would not advise it, Jack.'

'You just leave this to me,' said Jack, feeling protective. 'I think it's time someone had a talk with your father.'

Jack marched purposefully to the drawbridge of the castle. It was down and people were using it to cross the moat, going into and out of the castle. A dirty-faced sentry in armour of sorts was asleep at the gate, propped up by his spear, which he had stuck into the ground, point first. In the castle bailey there was all sorts of activity. Goats and sheep wandered around; chickens roosted on steps and ran across flagstones; grubby ragged children scampered about, the slower ones carrying water jars; men in armour, some on horseback, yelled at one another. Everyone was up to their shins in mud and dung, including a bewildered elderly nun.

'Nice place,' said Jack. 'Home, eh Rosy?'

Suddenly Jack felt himself being lifted bodily off his feet by his collar. A bulky man had reached down from the back of a horse and grasped him. This same man, wearing a brass helmet and chain-mail shirt, roared into his face with all the force of a hurricane.

'What say you, humpback?'

'I'm not a humpback,' gasped Jack. 'I'm Rosamund's friend.'

'What will you with my Rosamund, you bent greasy cur? Shall you live past eventide? I think not. The moon shall glare on the gibbet that houses your crooked remains.'

He was not given time to answer but was hurled over the horse's head and into the mire. Some children gathered round him, pointing, laughing, and shrieking, 'Crookback!' and 'Humptyjake'. Jack realised he had his pack *under* his shirt and that was why they were yelling at him. They thought the shape the pack was making was his body.

When he managed to sit up a thick stocky man with a broad girth, the same man who had thrown him, was yelling at Rosamund, asking her what in the thunder she was doing in those confounded garments.

'Get thee to the tower, wench,' she was roughly ordered. 'Else thou feel the toe of my boot.'

'Kick me and I shall scratch out thy eyes,' said Rosamund with fire in her voice. 'Thou art an ill-humoured donkey, sir!'

The man laughed at this threat. Jack had at first thought the man was Rosamund's father but he was beginning to doubt this. Jack stood up again, to protest at the treatment they were receiving. He was knocked on the head immediately by the flat of a sword blade. Within a short space of time two soldiers were called forth to drag him and cast him into the deepest of the dungeons.

'Throw the hunchback into the cell next the garderobe.'

Jack knew that a garderobe was a deep-shafted toilet.

Within a short space of time he was tossed into a dim stinking cell, with damp straw that smelled of urine. He still had his pack on his back, which was some comfort to him. There was his crossbow wrapped in rags inside, which might come in handy later.

'Well, that's a nice welcome,' Jack said, when he had calmed down enough to draw a decent breath. 'I had expected a bit of an argument, but I thought I'd be given time to explain.'

'Explaaaiiin? Explaaaaaiiiin?' whined a thin voice from the back of the cell. There was the rattle of chains and Jack saw, through the gloom, a bedraggled skinny figure hanging from shackles. 'Explain what?'

Jack went to the figure and was driven back by the foul breath that issued from the creature's mouth. It was a man of sorts, but how old Jack could not tell, for his condition was appalling. He certainly had matted grey hair, was covered in sores and rat bites, and had but only one or two teeth in his head, but these were no indication of his years. Eyes stared at Jack from dark hollow pits. Fingers like claws gripped at the filthy chains and rattled them, presumably to get Jack's attention, already well-captured.

'Who are you?' asked Jack, shocked. 'Are you a murderer?'

'Me?' The voice was cracked and hoarse. 'I am Fitzwilliam, the older brother of the bastard who strides about this castle.'

'The baron?' cried Jack.

'The very same. I was asleep the night our father died. He being the younger would not have inherited. So he took what should have been mine and I woke up with these manacles on my wrists.'

Jack gulped hard. What sort of mercy could he expect from a man who imprisoned his own brother in order to inherit? None at all. Jack's life was actually worth less than that of a dog. A dog at least had some use.

'I have met the baron,' said Jack, and described how

he was treated. 'And that's how I came to be in here.'

A cackling laugh came from the throat of the prisoner.

'That wasn't the baron! That was Grandjean of Lavondiss, the latest suitor of Rosamund. The turnkeys told me she disappeared the night before he arrived. I blame the maiden not for vanishing. This villain has been through seven wives already. No one knows what happens to them, but I hear tell there is a stinking marsh not far from his castle gate which sucks down bodies into the bog and never do they surface again.'

'Her father would never allow her to marry such a man!' cried Jack. 'That would be monstrous.'

'Monstrous!' snorted the baron's brother. 'But Grandjean is a rich man with a large contingent of mercenaries. The baron needs fighting men, for he has turned against the king and is beleaguered. E'en now an army marches on this castle led by the king himself. All other barons have sided against my brother, for he has made many enemies in his time. Without Grandjean of Lavondiss, my brother is doomed. Rosamund is sold, youth.'

'Over my dead body,' cried Jack, then reflected a few moments after that yes, probably it would be. 'What can we do?' he asked Fitzwilliam. 'Shall I try to get those chains off you?'

'Oh, that's easily done,' said the other, and slipped his skinny wrists from the manacles. 'I only hang there when someone comes. If my brother knew he'd throw me into the wolf pit, which is likely where you'll end up, since they've not had a good supper in several days.'

Jack saw that the future had a definite gloomy look about it.

292   Garry Kilworth

'All we wanted was to find Mallmoc,' he said.

'Mal du Morc?' cried Fitzwilliam. 'Why, he too is here
to assist my beloved brother. They say he arrived yesterday on the back of a storm, a cockerel on one arm, a
basilisk on the other. That foul sorcerer is needed once
again, may God curse him in his cockroach soul. We
shall all end our time in hell if that fiend is let loose on
this fair land.'

FOUR

Jack showed Fitzwilliam the contents of his pack. The prisoner was most interested in Jack's crossbow.

'A weapon!' he said. 'This will assist our escape. At last I shall be free again, to wander the land of my birth.'

'Will you kill your brother?' asked Jack, nervously.

'Not I. God will deal with him. I do not even want this damned castle and the title to the lands. All I wish is to be free to walk over green hills and through valleys, to smell the clean air, to bathe in fresh water. You have no idea, stranger, how much I miss the sound of birds. Once we are beyond these walls I never wish to see them again.'

'Good for you,' said Jack. 'I approve.'

Sometime during the next several hours they heard a key grind in the lock. The door was opened and the turnkey entered with two trenchers of some slop that might have been mashed turnips. Jack was ready for him. He pointed his magical crossbow at the fellow.

'Drop the food and give me the key,' he said. 'Now!'

In the dim light the jailer laughed hysterically. Then he saw the other prisoner was loose. His expression changed. The trenchers fell to the floor and the key was handed over. Jack and Fitzwilliam left the cell, locking the turnkey inside. Once they were in the passageway the jailer yelled for help, but Fitzwilliam told Jack no one would come.

'They can't hear him.'

The pair sneaked through the castle, Fitzwilliam leading the way, it being familiar to him. At one point they crossed behind a balcony. From that vantage point Jack was looking down on a great hall. A noisy feast was in progress. He started when he saw Rosamund, looking very sulky, sitting next to an enormous man at the head table. She was dressed very prettily in a red velvet gown with a wimple about her face and head. On the other side of her sat that ugly knight Grandjean of Lavondiss, hot chicken fat glistening on his cheeks as he slobbered over a drumstick.

'Is that the baron?' whispered Jack to his companion, pointing at the big man next to Rosamund. 'Is that Guillaume de Arundel?'

Fitzwilliam ground his teeth and muttered, 'It is he.'

On the other side of the baron sat a young woman, but her face was hideously made up. It looked as if she had stained her cheeks with blackberry juice to give them colour. It had done that all right: they were bright purple. Her lips had been painted with something like beetroot juice and around her eyes blackened with charcoal. The rest of her face had white powder, probably flour, no doubt to give it an *attractive* pale complexion.

The result was a horrible mask which cracked and flaked with every movement, especially when the woman shrieked with laughter.

Then another figure attracted Jack's attention. There, behind the chair of Rosamund's father, stood the sorcerer Mallmoc. He was looking righteous and smug, reaching over and handing the baron various sweetmeats and pies, as he talked quietly in his ear. Around the room were knights, grabbing capons and partridges, stuffing their mouths with cakes and grapes, swilling wine from over-flowing goblets. There was much joshing and crashing of iron fists on thick oak tables. The talk was loud and bois-terous. Even the dogs under the tables were yapping.

The sight of his brother hogging food which had been denied him so long was obviously too much for the filthy, ragged and starved Fitzwilliam. A great rage seemed to overcome him and all thoughts of strolling through green and pleasant lands clearly evaporated. He snatched the crossbow from Jack and aimed it at his brother Guillaume, intending to kill him.

'Die, false brother!' he cried, releasing the bolt.

As ever, the bolt changed to a hawk in flight, heading straight for the heart of Guillaume. Someone yelled. Guillaume was halfway out of his seat, looking up at Fitzwilliam. Then just before the bird was to change back into a bolt and strike the baron, the hawk fell like a stone from the air, dropping dead at the feet of the terri-fied Guillaume. Mallmoc flashed an amused look at Jack. It was he who had saved the baron, with his dark magic, killing the hawk in flight by invisible means.

Confusion reigned in the hall. Tables were overturned as knights sprang to their feet and drew their swords.

Chairs went flying backwards. The great baron himself was entangled with Mallmoc as he tried to scramble past and reach a longbow hanging on the wall. In that confusion Rosamund ran from the hall, to join Jack and Fitzwilliam. Grandjean ran after her. He had his hand on her shoulder just as she entered the balcony. She turned her head and bit his fingers. Jack then rushed at him, butted him in the stomach with his head, and sent the knight tumbling over the edge of the balcony. Grandjean fell crashing on to an oak table, staring up in disbelief at Jack's triumphant face. The knight shook his gloved fist.

'Quickly, to the chapel,' said Rosamund. 'I know a secret way out of the castle. Let us take it and get back to the well, Jack.'

'What about Mallmoc?'

'Thee saw what he did. We cannot kill him, Jack. He is invincible. The magician must be destroyed by someone else. Let us hope the king is able to do it, once he defeats my father.' She paused for a moment, looking rather sad. 'I am unhappy for my father,' she continued, 'but he must reap what he has sown. Mayhappen the king will be satisfied with confiscating his castle and lands, and let him live in exile. Now we must get back to Liöfwende and our faerie friends.'

Fitzwilliam asked, 'Where is Liöfwende?'

'Somewhere you'll probably like,' explained Jack. 'Rosy, this is your uncle. He's been in the dungeons since the death of your grandfather.'

'Greetings, Uncle Fitzwilliam. I thought thee dead.'

'Alive but not too well at the moment, niece – but I hope to be better, child, once we are beyond these walls.'

The three escapees raced through the passageways of

the castle, led by the intrepid Rosamund. She knew her
route exactly. There were few soldiers around, since
most were on the battlements, watching for the invading
army of the king. Those they passed were guarding door-
ways and simply looked bemused. Shouts and cries
were echoing throughout the castle, but these were confused and confusing. Finally Rosamund reached a chapel
wherein a monk was kneeling, intoning his prayers.

She rushed past the holy man and twisted the head of
a stone statue of Mary in the corner of the room. There
was a grinding sound and the rear wall opened up.
Fitzwilliam grabbed a flaming torch out of its holder and
the two friends followed him into the hole.

'Vespers!' came the indignant friar's voice from behind
them. 'Holy vespers!'

They heard him ringing the vesper-bell, presumably in
protest at their rude interruption of his orisons.

The chase was on, over the dark fields. Bleating sheep
scattered before the runners. Cattle bellowed and stam-
peded over grassy knolls. Dogs, pigs and chickens in
smallholdings took up the cry, adding their voices to
those others out in the night.

Jack fell over badly once, his foot catching in a hole.

'You blasted Normans,' he grumbled, as he rubbed his
ankle, 'why did you have to bring rabbits with you?'

The other two apologised.

Another sound came out of the darkness, that of the
drawbridge being lowered. Hooves clattered on the
woodwork of the bridge. Knights on horseback and soldiers on foot were now abroad, searching for the missing
trio. A loud halloo was going out over the land. Serfs,
vassals and villeins were roused from their beds. Some

had lit torches from their all-night fires and were wandering out of their hovels. Others were stumbling blindly through the darkness, banging into ploughs and water butts. Most, Jack imagined, would believe the king's army had arrived. It served the purpose of the escapees that there were few lights to be had and that even the knights on their fast mounts were caught up in blind chaos.

'This way, this way,' cried Rosamund.

'Are you sure?' questioned a breathless Jack. 'I thought the well was that way. Fitzwilliam?'

'I have no idea. I have been locked in a darkened dungeon these past few years. From what I recall there are wells everywhere.'

'All right, Rosy — but you'd better be right about this, otherwise we're goners. Heck, this pack is getting heavy. I'm going to ditch it.'

Jack took off the knapsack and threw it on the grass. He was fed up with having to leave the crossbow, but it was hampering his escape. At the last moment the moon came out from behind a cloud. Jack saw his dark green bottle roll out of the pack on to the grass. The old glass glinted under yellow lunar beams, presenting a mysteriously antique appearance. There was something about this strange bottle and its obscure symbols which made Jack loath to leave it behind. He had been close enough to magic and magical beings now to have a feeling for a significant object.

Instinctively then, Jack picked the bottle up, still unsure of its importance with regard to the dread sorcerer who plagued their lives. Instantly it grew hot beneath his naked fingers. He then snatched up a rag which had protected the crossbow and wrapped it around the neck of the bottle. Thus he was able to carry the object without getting burned.

They found a hill which seemed faintly familiar to Jack and he knew Rosamund was on the right track.

'Good lass, Rosy,' he grunted. 'There's the well!'

As they approached their escape hatch to Liöfwende, however, a horrible figure appeared in front of the well. It was Mallmoc with a leash in each hand. On the end of the leads were two savage hell-hounds. Snarling viciously, the curs strained to get at the three escapees. Their slavering teeth and jaws seemed intent on ripping flesh from bone. Mallmoc's wicked sneer was visible in the moonlight and Jack's heart sank.

'So, there you are, wizard,' said Jack. 'You think you've won.'

'Of course, boy. Did you think you could outwit an accomplished sorcerer with over two thousand years of magic behind him? You never stood a chance. Now, I think I will release the dogs and watch you be devoured. There has been talk enough to last a millennium.'

Jack raised the green bottle above his head, intending use it to club the nearest hell-hound. Mallmoc saw the object just as he let go of the leashes. He stepped forward, arms outstretched, at the same time letting out a hollow cry of dismay.

The savage hounds bounded forward, snarling and snapping.

Jack, now terrified, threw the bottle at the beasts bearing down upon him, Rosamund and her uncle. It missed both targets, flying between the loping creatures. Mallmoc tried to catch it. Alas for him his cricket skills were only equal to his ancient body. The bottle went between his clawlike hands, through his legs, and struck the side of the stone well.

The green glass shattered.

The dogs vanished, instantly.

Streams and strings of letters climbed snaking into the night air, to be taken aloft by the gusting winds. They were like ribbons of language, caught on the back of eddies. Some were clutched for a moment by the black fingers of the trees, but were soon snatched back by the wind. Most of them drifted aloft like smoke, into the far reaches of the ether. It seemed that before long they would all, every one, be lost to celestial regions.

Mallmoc ran about, trying to snatch the last of them from above his head, without success. Cries of 'My names! My precious names!' escaped his lips as he began crumbling before the eyes of the amazed watchers. Bit by bit he fell apart in small lumps of dust. His face disintegrated before their eyes, the mouth still gasping, pleading. In less than a minute he was nothing but a pile of soot upon the grass. This too, was soon removed by the wind, as if nature wanted no trace of such a fiend left upon her good earth.

FIVE

With the baron's troops hot on their trail, Jack decided it was time to depart. The sounds of horns and drums were all around them now. The hunt was near and the quarry trapped.

'In the bucket, Rosy. I'll lower you.'

'But what about thee?' she said. 'Who's to lower thee?'

'I'll jump down.'

'No, no – it's too dangerous.'

Just then, from somewhere out in the night, came a different noise. It was the sound of marching men. Trumpets were heard: a far more determined sound than the horns of the baron's hunting party. Drums were rolling in their hundreds. *Thump, thump, thump* came the reverberating beat of boots on the hard ground. Then a chanting could be discerned, drifting over the downs: the marching songs of thousands of infantry.

A vast army was coming and would be upon them very soon.

'The king's men,' whispered Fitzwilliam, in an awed voice. 'My brother has met his match at last.'

'But,' Rosamund said, 'what of the mercenaries? Won't they defeat the king's army?'

'No,' replied her uncle, 'for Guillaume is without his magician. Without Mal du Morc he is lost. The king's army is too large, too well trained to resist. There will be a siege, the castle will fall, and thy father will be punished. Listen, I must stay and plead my brother's cause. He has wronged me greatly, but I cannot stand by and see him beheaded. He must be chastised of course, for what he did to me as well as whatever he has done to the king. But not death. Not if I can help to avert it. He is, after all, my younger brother.' Fitzwilliam made a decision. 'Get thee both into the bucket. *I* will lower thee. Godspeed, niece. And, young man, look to her, keep her safe, I charge thee with her well-being.'

'Listen Fitz, you don't know your own family very well, do you? She's more likely to watch over me, rather than the other way around. She's one tough cookie, is Rosy.'

'I understand thee not, boy, but I will hold in mind the words you have used this day.'

With that, the pair climbed into the bucket and were lowered down into the depths of the deep damp well.

Once at the bottom they yelled to be raised again.

The bucket was winched up. The light of day fell on them. The beaming faces of Spiggot and Fen were there to greet them. They were back in their now beloved

Liöfwende. King Cimberlin and Prince Xinixia were also in attendance.

'Well?' asked the king. 'Is it done?'

'Mallmoc is no more,' confirmed Rosy.

A solemn cheer went up from all those who were listening: gnomes, elves, fairies, goblins, boggarts and the like. Spiggot clapped Jack on the back and Fen hugged Rosamund. The charismatic Puck was present and this famous faerie pronounced judgement.

'You are two truly great mortals,' said Puck. 'It is a pity King Oberon is not here to crown you both with tiaras of mayblossom.'

With that all the faerie departed.

All, that is, except Spiggot and Fen.

The boggarts invited Jack and Rosamund back to their village. Jack was suddenly filled with foreboding, wondering what was going to happen between himself and Rosamund now. He had learned much in Faerieland, but not how to control the future. It was with great dismay that he considered that he and Rosamund were actually not suited to remain together. They were different from each other. Over a thousand years of difference. Even supposing they stayed together in the short term, they might grow apart over the coming years. They were a couple from two distinctly separate cultures: neither totally understood the other. And their ordinary everyday ways were quite alien to each other.

Now that all the excitement was over the future actually looked quite bleak for them as a pair. Oh yes, her eyes were shining with fondness for him at the moment. And his heartbeat quickened every time she looked at him from under her curls. But he was at least aware enough to know these feelings would not remain at the same high pitch. They could not. Every mountain has slopes on all sides. The view is quite heady from the top, but eventually one has to take a track down to the valley and to more mundane surroundings.

Such feelings raced ahead of themselves at present, but eventually would slow to a crawl and then more practical considerations would loom. Where were they to live? Would they indeed stay together long enough to become a real couple? What were they to do in the way of work? At the moment Jack was experiencing the joy of infatuation alongside the misery of knowing that joy had a limited timespan. What could be done to preserve it long enough for it to be able to crystallise into real love?

There, his medieval maiden might say, was the rub.

Kling sidled over to him.

'You don't understand her, do you?'

Jack started. 'How did you know what I was thinking?'

'You're staring at her. It's written all over your face.'

'We're from two different worlds,' admitted Jack, miserably. 'A millennium apart.'

'Never mind the gap, sunshine. Youths like you have *never* understood the female of the species. Did you understand Jenny Pentworth, your erstwhile girlfriend and soulmate?'

Jack reflected. 'No,' he admitted, 'not a great deal.'

'There you are, then.'

'But what are we going to do? I can't stay here. My parents will be going frantic. Oh, I know time has sort of stopped in Mortaland, as far as I'm concerned. But I don't want to become like Colm Brody and pretend I'm faerie when I'm not. That's sort of like dropping out and going to a desert island. I have to go back. If I take Rosamund, she'll go crazy. The twenty-first century would drive her mad. Yet if I leave her here . . .?'

Spiggot was now by his side, also concerned.

'Perhaps she ought to go back to her time and you to yours, Jack?'

'But we won't be together and she'll be forced to marry some thick-headed knight with knuckles for brains.'

'Why don't *you* marry her, Jack?'

Jack shook his head. 'No, no, we're not old enough.'

'Well, then, come back to the boggart village and have a holiday. Stay there for a while so that you can see each other. Rosamund can live with Fen's parents and you can live with mine. Oh, don't worry about my dad and mum, they're all right really. Now that I'm ready to settle down with Fen, they'll be as good as gold, you'll see. What do you say? You can make your mind up about the distant future after you've had a long vacation. Perhaps you can go to this engineering college you speak about and come here when you can to see Rosamund. We will see her happy enough, if she wants to stay with us.'

'I do, dear Spiggot,' said Rosamund, 'for there are nothing but unsuitable suitors waiting for me at my father's castle. There must be plenty to do here, to keep from being idle? I can make things with my hands! Perhaps thee can teach me the art of the smithy, Fen?'

'Indeed I can,' answered that able boggart. 'I shall have you making bronze statues fit for the gardens of fairy queens.'

'All right,' said Jack, thumping his right fist into his left palm, 'we'll do that. A holiday first though. What do you say to a holiday, Rosy?' he called to her.

Rosamund nodded her head enthusiastically.

'Good – I think we all deserve one.'

'I think we do too, Jack,' replied the boggart, his eyes twinkling. 'Now, what shall we have for supper tonight, before we set out on our journey home. Any ideas, Kling? You are allowed to think as broadly and deeply on the subject as you like. King Cimberlin's gift.'

The excellent water rat was suddenly trembling with excitement. His whiskers quivered and his tail rippled. When he spoke it was with great gravity in his tone.

'Kling never thought he would hear that question in a million years, master's son.'

Fen asked, 'So what's the answer, water rat?'

Kling cleared his throat, took a deep breath, and delivered the evening's preferred menu.

'For starters, Mediterranean breads with tapenade, harissa and pesto. For main course, smoked salmon, wasabi spiked crème fraiche and pink grapefruit followed by pavé of beef on neeps and tatties, haggis fritter and horseradish jus. For afters, poppyseed bombé with charred pears and maple syrup. All washed down with a nice bottle of elderberry wine.'

'That's it?' said Spiggot. 'Just those? King Cimberlin left us with enough magic to produce whatever we desired. I think lashings of vanilla ice cream and strawberry fruits would not go amiss either.'

Kling quivered from head to foot with reverence for the fairy king.

'Oh, master's son, I am in water rat heaven at last.'

In the far distance, on the skyline, the headless figure of Hollow Ben was kicking a round object through a field of buttercups.

Garry Kilworth was born in York in 1941, and has travelled widely around the globe ever since. He has written a number of acclaimed novels for both children and adults, including the Carnegie commended Bronte Sisters and the much-loved Welkin Weasels series. You can find out more about him at www.garrykilworth.com and at the Atom website www.atombooks.co.uk.

Have you read . . .

WAYWALKERS

by Catherine Webb

Sam Linnfer works part-time at a London university. He's a quiet chap with a real skill for tricksy ancient languages, and an affinity for cats. He's also immortal and the Son of Time. You might know him better as Lucifer. And with all the Gods in Heaven about to go to war over ownership of Earth, you're going to be extremely glad he's not *exactly* the person history portrays him to be.

In Catherine Webb's stunning new book you'll come face to face with Jehovah on a cold Moscow night, walk the Ways between Earth and Heaven with Buddha, take a hair-raising cab ride with Adam (yes, *the* Adam – only he's into denim now, rather than fig-leaves!) and find yourself trusting the one person you never dreamed you could . . .

Because when the gods go to war and Earth is their battleground, only the devil can save your soul.

www.atombooks.co.uk

If you like great fantasy, you'll love . . .

FROM THE TWO RIVERS

Part One of The Eye of the World

by Robert Jordan

The Wheel turns and the greatest fantasy adventure of all time begins . . .

Life in Emond's Field has been pretty boring for Rand Al'Thor and his friends until a strange young woman arrives in their village. Moraine is an Aes Sedai, a magician with the ability to wield the One Power, and she brings warnings of a terrible evil awakening in the world. That very night, the village is attacked by blood-thirsty Trollocs – a fearsome tribe of beast-men thought to be no more than myth. As Emond's Field burns, Moraine and her warrior-guardian help Rand and his companions to escape. But it is only the beginning of their troubles. For Moraine believes Rand Al'Thor is the Dragon Reborn, and that he is fated to unite the world against the rising darkness and lead the fight against a being so powerful and evil it is known simply as *the Dark One*.

www.atombooks.co.uk